Best wishes

Sally Beacon

# The Clearwater Diamond

Sally Breach

authorHOUSE®

*AuthorHouse™ UK Ltd.*
*500 Avebury Boulevard*
*Central Milton Keynes, MK9 2BE*
*www.authorhouse.co.uk*
*Phone: 08001974150*

*© 2010 Sally Breach. All rights reserved.*

*No part of this book may be reproduced, stored in a retrieval system, or transmitted by any means without the written permission of the author.*

*First published by AuthorHouse 1/7/2010*

*ISBN: 978-1-4490-6286-6 (sc)*

*This book is printed on acid-free paper.*

# Acknowledgements

I think I might be eligible for some sort of prize for the length of time it took me to write this book because I started it in the year of our Lord 1977 when I was a student at Newbury College of Further Education doing English Language at 'O' Level. One of the homework assignments I was given was to write the opening page of a story, the page that would say 'pick me up and buy me' to the person that was reading it in the bookshop, and having first been given the opening line, which was *'She had no idea how long she had been sitting there…'* I completed my work I handed it in, and when it came back to me, my tutor (whose name I forget in the mists of time unfortunately) asked to see me after the class, told me she'd loved it and suggested to me that I really should give writing a go. For many reasons my life took a different direction, but from time to time I wrote articles and things that seemed well enough received, and always in the back of mind I had this nagging thought that I was missing an opportunity to take that advice. Now, after 30 years of beating about the bush, and having met a wonderful writer who nags, I am mightily proud to say I've finally done it, because this is, in reality, my completed homework assignment.

So if by any chance you happen to be reading this, my English Language tutor at Newbury College in 1977, this is for you, and I'm sorry it took me so long!

I want to thank my lovely husband Nick for putting up with eighteen months of house dust and no shirts due to a perpetually full ironing basket while I grappled with this.

I have to mention BK Mitchell, Betty, my autoimmune buddy, excellent writer and e-friend who nagged, encouraged and cheered me on though the tricky bits that became tantamount to juggling fridges at times. If I hadn't been ill with the same thing as you my friend and met you on the internet I probably would never have done this, and if it kills me I'll afford the health insurance sufficient to please the USA and we SHALL meet one day...!

Big posthumous thanks to Thomas Hardy, my literary hero, for making me hungry to write, even an eensy bit, like him.

Also thanks to:

My good friend the Reverend Buff for giving me the seeds of inspiration for Dizzy by having twins at 40...

To Lesley and Gill for your help and encouragement, and Heather for lending me the swimming pool changing rooms story. And thanks for being my bestest friends too x

Thanks to Caroline and everyone at Authorhouse for sticking with me through the publishing process and supporting me for so long.

And thank you to Gillian... one of the most loyal, genuine and funniest people I've ever met; for never even suggesting her mum was wasting her time, I love you.

Last but definitely not least. Huge, Huge thanks to Amy Foster-Gillies and Michael Bublé, because the words of your beautiful song were the inspiration for the rest of this story.

*STB*

*It is difficult for a woman to express her feelings
in language which is chiefly invented by men
to express theirs…*

**Thomas Hardy. Far from the Madding Crowd**

# Chapter one

She had no idea how long she'd been sitting there, perched on that window seat, arms wrapped around her legs and her head resting on her knees: her eyes entranced by the lake and the slow breaking dawn.

She'd certainly watched the sun come up. She'd watched as it made its way gradually skywards from the horizon; leaving a golden trail of reflection on the surface of the water towards the shore as it rose.

She had watched the swifts swooping to take their early morning drink, and as each one skimmed the surface of the water the sun's reflection exploded into a confusion of tumbling golden diamonds. They should have been long gone by now, but it had been unusually mild for the time of year.

Climate change, she supposed.

The wood pigeon that lived in the beech tree outside the window was up now too, making its plaintive and annoyingly repetitive call and sounding for all the world as if it were a small child grizzling '*I waaant one mummy...*' over and over again. She looked across the room to the bedside table to the clock that stood there. It was approaching six thirty now, so there was absolutely no point in going back to bed. She rose and walked over to the bed, pulled up the duvet and straightened it, and replaced Dodgy, Jemmies ragged old dog toy that she'd named that because she couldn't say 'doggy' when she was that little, to the top of the pillow.

She stretched a bit, careful not to hurt her back anymore than it hurt already these days and then, returning to their room she pulled her joggers over her pyjamas and added Paul's blue hooded fleece. That was a joke. He'd said she had made it stretch in all the wrong places now; and possession was nine tenths of the law; or so they said.

She tugged open the bottom drawer in the big oak chest that stood between the door and the window, and took out the grey sparkly hat, scarf and gloves that her grandmother had knitted her for Christmas when she was fifteen years old, and smiled slightly as she remembered that long gone Christmas day when she'd unwrapped them and watched grandma's face light up with pleasure as she'd laughed gleefully at the sparkly strands in such a conservative coloured wool. She'd said it fitted her personality perfectly: outwardly a home girl, but with a sparkle in her soul.

She was spot on there. Now of course they were old and thin, and the gloves much mended, but she still loved them, and had spurned all the others she had gained on, oh so many Christmases, and birthdays ever since.

She crept quietly down the stairs but wasn't sure why: there wasn't anyone around to wake up.

In the kitchen, Barney, the fat black Labrador, opened one eye balefully towards her from his basket under the table; resentful at being woken so early and blinking at the sudden harsh light.

'Don't worry,' she said, 'it's my walkies not yours.'

At that time of the morning he was totally immune to the word that would normally have him dancing around the room in anticipation, and so he positioned his nose back under his tail, and heaved a deeply aggrieved sigh.

She pulled on her dry but still caked in mud boots and unlocked the back door. The first hit of October dawn air brought her sharply awake and, venturing outside into the awakening day, the heels of her boots crunched deliciously on the deep wet gravel as she made her way out and down the garden path, sounding just like Jemmie's old grey pony 'Sparkler' eating an apple.

The swifts had quenched their thirst and gone, and the sun's reflection was now unbroken, though nearly gone as the sun was almost up. She looked up into the sky and prophesised that it was going to be a lovely day. Thomas Hardy had said that this kind of a day had, *'A summer face with a winter constitution,'* and he was absolutely right; Hector would be very proud of her for remembering that.

Hector Hardy-Mitchell, Incumbent Rector of St Mary's parish church, Frincham, was the dear husband of her closest friend, Dizzy. A proud descendant of Hardy's and one of his most devoted and biggest fans, he could come up with a quote for any occasion, and so did, frequently.

Her eyes scanned the lake again, her mind back in the moment. The jumble of assorted trees and bushes around the lake were every shade of red and gold, and the swifts would very soon be swooping onto another lake somewhere much warmer than here.

She loved this time of year. She'd never been much of a one for too much heat, and much preferred thick sweaters, and hot drinking chocolate with marshmallows, because thick sweaters covered a multitude of dinner party *'Oh go on thens'*.

Paul had always loved the sun, and so they always had a villa in the South of France or Spain when it was absolutely boiling and the children would complain at being forced to wear hats and then being coated in inches of sticky sun cream. And of course she'd spend weeks eating celery and cottage cheese beforehand. She pulled a face with the recollection, and looked down to the water, and into the eyes of her own reflection. She'd be able to use those bags in Waitrose soon.

And suddenly she wasn't seeing her own green eyes anymore, but Paul's deep brown ones. He had that little crease between his eyebrows that he got when he was worried or stressed about something.

'I'm so sorry Jules. I never meant for this to happen.'

Maybe that's what he would have said, if he'd said it himself.

Which of course he hadn't.

It was still so recent and raw, but yet he was so very much a part of her; half of her. Even though he'd gone in the physical sense, he remained. Still in their home in every sock or sweater cast off and left. Still there before every aching breath she took, and lurking before every thought she made; and every step she took, because after thirty years he was indelibly cast, inside the very depths of her soul. Without him she was imperfect.

In those dark mornings since, and in that *Neverland* moment between asleep and awake: before she was aware of the year, the day, the time, she would lay with her eyes still closed, and fancy she could still hear him. In sleep, he had a snore that would have given his position away to enemy forces and awake, the shower would actually click off, the towel rail would really rattle as his towel was pulled from it; only to be left in a damp heap on the floor that in unconscious moments she was still surprised not to find later. She would hear him humming something. She would hear him vigorously brushing his teeth.

The sounds of every passing day that he'd probably never even been aware of himself, had now become the ghostly echoes of her early mornings.

They'd been at the same school in the early 1970's and he'd been quite the school heart throb in the year above her. He was a bit of a glam rocker, when it was the right thing to be one, and Marc Bolan had been his hero.

He'd grown his black hair as long as he dared before being sent home with a note, and his mum had done him a secret home perm at the kitchen sink, to help him emanate his hero.

He had actually gone into mourning when Bolan died too, and was black and moody for weeks afterwards, which made him even more appealing to the 'in crowd' of girls, who all wanted to be the one to make him feel better.

He'd never noticed her though: had no idea she even breathed on the same earth as he.

They met up properly in 1978 when she was eighteen and he was nineteen. She'd been working in her aunt's hairdressing salon as an apprentice and was going out with one of his friends, called Colin Freemantle. He was dating a girl called Trudy Cleverley, who worked as a waitress in a tea shop to pay her way through university. She'd made a life plan one, presumably wet, Saturday afternoon when your mind made you think of things like that. She'd actually written it all down, cleverly, and marked it all out and with bits of it underlined in red felt tip pen. She was going to be a Solicitor, marry Paul, live in a large detached house; with a view, obviously, and have two children and a pedigree dog; breed non specific. She'd had it all mapped out.

Except that Jules had had most of that package and not Trudy.

She'd known something was up when Paul would ring her most evenings and talk for hours about how his parents, the intimidating George and Penelope Taylor, had got his life all mapped out for him also; in the family business. They owned a large chain of shoe shops, specialising in beautifully crafted shoes from the continent for the classier feet of England.

They'd made up so many shoe related jokes on that.

Her parents were quite the opposite, and deeply loved. Her mother was a meat and two veg cook, and of a generation that never knew pasta. Her Sunday roasts were legendary though; her Yorkshire puddings practically hit the top of the oven in uniform shape and colour and desire to please. The meat was basted in lard and seemingly cooked for days, but if she closed her eyes she could still taste it.

Her vegetables were quite another matter. Boiled to oblivion and into a soggy pile of indeterminate lineage, she once told Paul that it hadn't been until she'd had Sunday lunch at his house that she'd realised that sprouts were supposed to be round....


Paul could create a likeness with a pencil or a piece of charcoal to remarkably uncanny perfection, and paint like a dream, so he wanted to be a professional artist; but of course his parents wouldn't have it. They had acknowledged that he was talented but said that *'It Wouldn't put Bread on the Table'*, in the way that parents do.

Trudy was making him feel trapped too with all her plans, and had made him feel inadequate just because he didn't have his whole life mapped out for himself like she did. Jules remembered telling him that it sounded to her like he did have his life mapped out but that his parents had drawn it, and so obviously it just didn't match his own idea of what his map should be.

She'd said that you should be in charge of your own map for goodness sake. She'd said that there was no way he was cut out for the shoe trade, and that he was metaphorically trying to get through his life in the two left shoes his parent's insisted he wore. And you can't set out on a journey in two left shoes.

He'd asked her if she would be his right shoe that night, and she'd said she would, and then he'd kissed her and made her toes curl up and her insides do somersaults. He was a superb kisser.

And so they'd met frequently and in secret to start with. Their mutual attraction and need for each other had been a bit startling to both of them after that first kiss, but even so it was quickly apparent that they were bound irrevocably together for ever.

Paul of course hated confrontations and avoided Colin like the plague.

He tended to stick his head in the sand rather than face up to things; but then he'd always been like that.

He had an uncanny knack of hiding behind his own face somehow.

But it had all come out eventually, that night the Michaelmas funfair came to town and Paul and Jules were coming out of the Tunnel of Love, wrapped around each other, just as Trudy and Colin were going in, wrapped around each other.

It was all plain sailing after that really.

They'd married in 1980 on her twentieth birthday, in an effort to keep the significant dates he'd have to remember on his own to a bare minimum.

This was helped the following year when Marcus had been born on their first wedding anniversary and her parents told everyone that she had received the ultimate in twenty first birthday presents.

She had taken to the role of mother a little shakily at first, and remembered with a little smile the night she'd gone to bed early with a migraine. Markie was only about two weeks old then, and Paul had woken her up at 10.30 to feed the purple, angry faced and screaming child. She remembered reminding him resentfully that she had a migraine; but he'd looked at her helplessly and apologised that he didn't have the right plumbing.

That was the defining moment.

It was precisely at that moment that the significance of this Life Changing Event everyone talked about, hit home, and the penny dropped that she was, for the rest of her days, going to take second place to this, and any subsequent child's every need, and that anything that her own life threw at her, from headaches to open heart surgery, would become insignificant trifles up against that responsibility of Being a Mother.

Surprisingly, this fact became a distant memory very quickly as the days and months passed and she got used to her new role.

It always does, as any mother will tell you.


Jemima was born on Christmas Day two years later, and Jules congratulated herself on her continuing efforts to make Paul's life simpler when remembering special occasions. Paul hadn't liked the name at first and said she'd be called 'Jemima Puddleduck' at school. He'd wanted to call her Carol or Noelle, but Jules thought that was far too corny. So she'd quickly become known as 'Jems' or 'Jemmie', and to Marcus, until she was about three and figured it out, 'Jemmiedidit.'

There's was a content and squashy armchair sort of comfortable marriage, as most marriages are. Not the stuff of the romantic novels and love songs Jules loved to indulge in secretly, or those endless romantic films she watched on TV when he wasn't around. She adored the sound of big bands and romantic smooth Jazz too, and whatever the musical fashion of the time, would always prefer to listen to something jazzy, which in latter years had meant endless Michael Bublé, on the huge radio cassette player that stood on the crooked kitchen shelf, acting as a bookend and stopping everything else from falling over.

They'd moved from the one bedroom flat over the family shoe shop in Cheltenham that they'd lived in when they first got married, after Jemmie was born. Paul had won the career argument with his father and was working in a gallery in Cheltenham for an eccentrically gay art dealer called Victor Allen-Frobisher, who always wore a cravat and a pocket watch on a long chain across his harlequin patterned waistcoat, and by then he was painting enthusiastically in his spare time too.

His father, on the other hand, had lost a lot of his former vigour after Penelope died of cancer just before Jemmie was born. She was diagnosed and died within six weeks. Good in one way; that she was diagnosed far too late, so didn't have to go through all the chemo and radiotherapy treatments and lose the hair she swore she never dyed, but an awful bomb shell for George, who acted like he'd been pole axed. She'd done absolutely everything for him for nearly thirty years and so consequently he could barely fill a saucepan never mind put something in one.

Paul of course had gone for the 'stiff upper lip' option over the death of his mother, and martyred himself admirably. He just did lots of dog walking, and redecorated his father's entire house, including all the bathrooms, the shed in which you could have hangared a small aeroplane, and the garden fence, that was so long it must have had an impact on the destruction of the rainforest on its own.

He'd had moderate success with his career as an artist; largely due to Victor's efforts on his behalf, and wall space at the gallery, though he still harboured a dream of creating vast canvasses with the kind of 'three stripes and a blob' paintings of the style that went right over Jules's head. He had found a temporary and fairly lucrative niche in portrait painting though; and he was really very good. So for a while he concentrated on painting humans, dogs, cats: and horses if it never meant getting too near one.

He had quickly gained Victor's total confidence; as well as, albeit secretly, his heart, and had the run of the gallery whenever he'd flown off to his Spanish villa to top up his rather orange tan. He could soon run it better than Victor could, and gained a lot of kudos within the artistic community, that liked his well educated and intelligent persona as well as his talent with a paintbrush.

But even so he longed for a studio of his own to concentrate on his true artistic passions, away from the children and the general chaos that was home.

The next move was into a three bedroom terraced house in Swindon with a postage stamp sized back garden and neighbours on one side that played very loud music at all hours and on the other a dog that barked all day and all night. It didn't matter how loud she turned up the radio cassette player in competition and there was no painting of any genre done for some time.

They'd been helped out of this situation very conveniently following the death of George prematurely at the age of 67, from a heart attack. As an only child Paul inherited all of the family money, and the much hated shoe shops. Uttering the last of his terrible shoe related puns, he declared that selling the shoe shops for an absolute fortune was a 'step in the right direction.'

So they'd bought Clearwater House, and had lived there ever since.

Nestled in the leafy Berkshire countryside near Newbury, it sat comfortably adjacent to the calm and peaceful but for a few fishermen, Clearwater Lake. The house itself came with almost five acres of land, incorporating two stables, a paddock and a ménage, a reasonably sized field and a huge walled, and used to be the kitchen garden. It had six bedrooms; three ensuite bath and three ensuite shower; cloakrooms everywhere so you could never find the right magazine, and bumper packs of toilet rolls disappeared in one round of deliveries.

It also had a boot room for the assortment of England's best weather proofing gear, and a sleeping place for wet dogs in one corner.

The kitchen was big enough to play the part of post office or hospital down one end while Jules cooked fish fingers and spaghetti hoops down the other.

Best of all, for Paul: among the assortment of out buildings there was a huge garage with a workshop and an observation pit (or wine cellar) and a self contained room above it the length of the building with a superb lakeside view through a huge picture window, which quickly became his dream studio.

He'd decided that they were 'financially stable' for a few years at least, so he'd given up his job at the gallery, avoiding Victor's tearful farewell tactfully, and decided to concentrate on his painting full time.

She'd given up her job as a teaching assistant in a local junior school when they'd moved too.

Very often, she wouldn't see him all day and, as the years moved swiftly on, he often worked into the wee small hours and so slept on the huge squashy sofa that was covered in paint stains in the studio pretty often as well.

Meanwhile Jules became a superbly efficient Domestic Engineer.

Looking back on it, she'd realised that this was when things really started to change for them.

Paul began to make a name for himself in the art world with his 'stripes and blobs'. Largely thanks to Victor's continued efforts people started to already know who he was at parties when he told them his name, but feign surprise all the same. They would seek him out and try to start conversations with him.

And Jules recalled that she became quite proficient at talking to fat relatives on sofas at those parties.

There were increasing numbers of exhibitions of his paintings at galleries up and down the country; all the paintings so quickly adorned with those little red stickers that meant 'Sold'.

He got noticed by the press, and became the Golden Boy of the Art World. Everyone who was anyone was talking about him, everyone who was anyone had a Paul Taylor in pride of place somewhere, and by then he was an awfully long way from Marc Bolan lip gloss and shoe puns.

He took on an agent: a loud and vivaciously camp character called Hugo Dinsmore, who had carried a 'mobile phone' the size of a brief case and wore a sharp suit and a silly little pony tail. He carried a black filofax as thick as a yellow pages phonebook, Markie and Jems instantly thought he was an absolute hoot, and Paul suddenly became excellent at remembering where he was supposed to be, and when.

Efficient as he most definitely was, he was far from perfect. The air around the mobile phone was permanently a vivid shade of blue because he would constantly swear like a squaddie. As much as Paul tried to break him of this habit, especially near the children, it came to a head one day when Marcus, then aged five, fell off his bicycle in the garden and inserted a perfectly placed 'Gobshite!' to his reaction. Paul, Hugo and Jules were having coffee on the terrace at the time, and heard it. Paul and Jules both turned to Hugo, who'd had the decency to accept the blame without either of them saying a word, and sucked in his lower lip and bit it in a silent expression of '*oops* '.

After that he really did try. Paul suggested he try replacing his swear words with other, less offensive ones, and so he had experimented with a few and finally settled on varieties of breads; foreign ones. Hugo could be heard daily spitting out substitutes like 'Oh Baguettes!' and 'Peshwari Naans!' and if the situation demanded a real expletive he used 'Focaccia-ing hell!'

This proved very successful, mostly, so was adopted by Paul as well, though he favoured staple foodstuffs and used things like 'oh Gravy!' and 'oh Cheese!'

Even Jules would, to this day, utter the occasional 'oh Custard!' when she reached the bottom of the stairs without the thing she'd gone up there for in the first place.

The years passed by, the mobile phones got much smaller, and Hugo's pony tail got swept away at the hairdressers one day, and he came back spiky and bleached blonde. His sharp suits lost their American footballer shoulder pads, and the filofax became a Blackberry.

He was quite scarily efficient despite his vocabulary, and planned all Paul's trips to far flung places down to the last tick on the electronic list. And Jules found herself asking Hugo when Paul might be available to discuss school reports, Jemmie's pony club gymkhana dates, sports days, and school concerts.

As his career became more and more successful, it got less and less easy for Paul to act normally. There had been such a buzz in the room on the one occasion that he had actually attended a school sports day, and there had been more eyes on him than on the children, so he never went again.

## Chapter two

Jules was plucked stoutly from her reverie by the arrival of an overexcited young Springer Spaniel that had plunged into the lake after a duck. The duck had sensibly taken off at this point and flown much farther out, but the dog was in hot pursuit. It took off once again and this time disappeared into the distance, quacking with derision, until the dog realised that it was very cold, he was a very long way from the shore and not as good a swimmer as he had thought. Jules jumped up and looked around but the lakeside was deserted, and she couldn't see or hear the dog's owner anywhere. By this time it was yapping and splashing and floundering in distress, so Jules ran to the water's edge and started calling it as best she could without knowing its name. She hit on an idea and grabbed a short but quite substantial stick. She threw it towards the dog to attract its attention and hopefully to remind it of its fetch and return instincts, if it had any.

Thankfully, the dog grabbed the stick.

Jules started smacking her hands hard against her thighs and calling the dog to her. 'Come on! Come on!'

It was looking straight at her and seemed to understand, and responded.

It tried to swim towards her but by now it was very tired. When it had made it to within a couple of yards of the shore and looked as though it wasn't going to make it any further, she jumped into the water up to her knees, her breath catching sharply at the temperature, grabbed its collar and helped it to the bank, where it promptly shook freezing cold water all over her in gratitude. She looked around once more: still nobody. The dog was shaking in fear but his little stump of a tail was wagging furiously and he was whining with relief. Jules pulled his collar round and looked at his name tag. 'Dipstick' she read, and a mobile telephone number. 'That fits you anyway!' she said, bending down and ruffling the dog's ears. Not wanting him to run off again, she took hold of his collar and threaded her scarf through it to make a lead. She then set off back towards the house, with the dog trotting happily beside her, to call the owner on her phone. Which would be somewhere in the kitchen, probably. She'd gone only a few steps when she heard someone calling her from somewhere behind.

'Hello! Stop!' he shouted. 'Dipstick! That's my dog!' Jules looked around to see a man hobbling, obviously painfully, towards her, wearing knee length khaki shorts and a rather tatty and faded red sweatshirt. He was carrying a broken flip flop in one hand, and had a trickle of blood heading southwards from a cut, on what looked from this distance like a very bruised right knee.

'I assume the dog is a dipstick and you are not insulting me for rescuing him from a near drowning?' she said, but she was smiling, and told him what had just happened. The dog was deliriously happy to see him and jumped against his injured knee. He yelped and sat down quickly on a very large rock that was worn smooth with the passage of time and many bottoms, blowing on his knee fitfully like Markie used to do when he was little and had taken a tumble. He looked up as Jules sat beside him and, once on the same level, he noticed her wet boots and joggers. 'I'm sorry,' he said, 'and thanks so much for doing that. Fashion statement?' he remarked, just as she noticed the hem of her baby blue pyjamas hanging down from one leg of her sagging trousers.

She shook her head slightly. 'It was a bit of a spur of the moment decision to walk this morning.'

She looked at his knee more closely, and asked him what had happened, and he nodded towards his dog. 'He did. That dog is a complete idiot. You wouldn't think so, seeing as I bought him from the police. He was failed drugs detection dog.' He adjusted his sitting position to face her. 'Trouble is he's brilliant at scenting things but forgets he's supposed to look where he's going at the same time and barges around like a bull in a china shop. He gets into all kinds of mischief! He sent me flying this morning when he trod on the back of my flip flop at full gallop in the woods back there. When I fell over I shouted at him, so he took off... and then I lost him.'

Jules looked sideways at him as he continued to blow gently on his knee. His age was not easy to guess, but he was in his early to mid thirties, she supposed, and with fair, tight, curly hair. Not handsome in the obvious way, with a slight scar on his left cheek just below his eye, and a wide, possibly a little too wide, mouth. Nice teeth though, and a dimple in his chin. He needed a shave, she thought absently, and she wondered how he'd got that scar.

'Where are you from?' she said, to break the silence, 'I haven't seen you around here before.'

'That's because I've not been here very long,' he replied between blows on his knee. 'We've, sorry I've, recently moved into Hill Cottage...just up the lane there.' He turned and pointed up the hill to a white cottage that was just visible through the trees and, she already knew, from her house.

She took in his correction and wondered what to say next, assuming he had recently divorced or something.

'Oh, you mean old Mrs Bennett's cottage, oh that's good. I don't like to see places empty for too long.'

'I bought it at auction a few months back. They said the owner had died.... Sorry, I should have introduced myself. I'm Martin,' he said.

'Yes, Mrs Bennett died about a year ago. She must have been well into her nineties.' She continued, 'I'm Julie Taylor, Jules usually.' She put out her right hand and he shook it briefly.

'So Jules, do you live close by or...'

'Just here,' she said, and indicated with her head. 'Clearwater House: that's my garden gate there. Can I give you a hand and get you cleaned up before you tackle that hill with your bad knee?'

'Oh, I don't want to be any trouble,' he said, and stood up, very gingerly. She stood beside him and he put his arm around her shoulder for support as he realised that his leg was stiffening up by the second. Jules took Dipstick in his new grey lead and they made their way slowly back to the Clearwater House kitchen.

Barney heaved himself off of his bed as they entered, but his tail and hackles shot up at the appearance of Dipstick. They did the doggy version of introductions by sniffing each other's rear ends and circling for a few seconds, then dipstick adopted the play position with his front elbows on the floor, his backside in the air and his stumpy tail wagging furiously, delighted at the prospect of a new friend. Barney got back on his bed, circled, and feigned indifference as he lay back down again. Jules smiled and showed dipstick to a giant earthenware water bowl on the floor in the utility room, which was adjacent to the kitchen. Dipstick drank noisily, and then took another look at Barney hopefully, then flopped resignedly onto the threadbare rug by the Aga. He panted for a few seconds, before resting his chin on his front paws but was watching Martin closely.

Jules opened the cupboard above the kettle and took out the first aid kit, busying herself finding antiseptic, cotton wool and plasters, while Martin's eyes scanned and absorbed the kitchen. 'Homely' that was the word. A huge table with a bowl of fruit in the centre that were all well and truly past it, stripped pine fittings; its work surfaces held a riot of jumble and unopened post, and over by the kettle stood a battered old cassette radio covered in the kind of little round stickers awarded to small children at school at some point for things like correct spellings and for 'being kind and helpful'. Children's pictures adorned every little piece of spare wall space, most of them yellowed with age and a bit fly spotted but obviously just as precious as the day they'd been put up there. There were brightly painted hand and foot prints, and there was a block of modelling clay on the wall with the footprints recorded for ever of what he surmised to be of her two small children. There was a sunflower made with pasta shapes, painted somewhat enthusiastically but without much accuracy in a very cheerful yellow, and with an orange smiley face in its centre. There were even height marks, with names and dates on them, cut into the back door frame.

Every surface he could see sported a 'bad hair day' pot plant, and the spider plant on top of the huge welsh dresser by the back door was obviously vying to take possession of the whole room.

This kitchen stuffed full of happy memories was obviously not happy now, and all was not well, he could see. Rotting fruit in the fruit bowl, the sink full of dirty dishes and the drainer full of clean ones, and the dishwasher was winking its little red finished light too.

'So, Jules' he said, trying not to wince as she cleaned up his knee and attached a plaster, 'You live here with your family?'

'Would you like some coffee?' she said, absently. He nodded, and there was another little silence.

'The kid's are grown up and gone and I'm... on my own... at the moment.'

He said nothing.

She turned to place the first aid kit on the dresser and then sat down. 'My husband is away,' then, adding, 'he's away a lot.'

Close enough.

She stood and walked across the kitchen, extracted two clean mugs from the dishwasher, tipped the kettle into them and placed them on the table in front of him.

Two mugs of hot water.

'Sugar?' she said, absently.

'No, thanks; just some coffee in mine please,' he smiled.

She reached across and grabbed a jar from the dresser. 'Sorry' she said, 'I'm a bit rattled at the moment: not sleeping too well.'

Not sleeping at all, truth be told, she thought.

He stood up and replaced the instant gravy granules and took down the instant coffee. Both had red lids; easy mistake. She didn't even notice.

'Tell me about your family,' he said, to change the subject.

She told him about Markie and Jemmie. Markie, who hated being called that now and used his proper name, was 28 and living with his girlfriend in London. He was a dentist and she was his nurse and they were far too busy with that to get married and have grandchildren for her. Jemmie was 26 and had just qualified as a doctor, lived alone at the hospital, worked 24 hours a day and never phoned.

'You?' she asked. He shook his head but said nothing.

The room was full of unasked and unanswered questions, she holding back and he reluctant to share, but the atmosphere was broken suddenly by the muffled ringing of her telephone.

Found it! She thought, pulling it out from under a three day old newspaper. So there it was hiding itself....

She answered it, and was distracted for a few minutes while Martin had a good long look at her. 'Forties' he thought. 'Attractive, but she had tired eyes, and a head that was a tangle of long and unkempt dark brown curls that could have swallowed a comb in there somewhere. And was that a piece of straw stuck in there? Neither pencil thin nor hugely fat, but somewhere cuddly in between, she had a nice face. All the best people had dimples in their chins. What were her eyes? Do you call those green or hazel? Green; definitely green,' he decided.

'Sorry about that,' she turned to face him again. 'My daughter,' she said, holding up the phone. 'Talk of the devil. She was after her dad.'

Then she got that hunted look again.

Plucking up the courage, he said, 'Jules,' then, reaching for her hand and going on a little nervously, 'tell me... what's going on here?'

She took a sip of her coffee and looked at him.

Here was a complete and total stranger, but he had a nice face, and his eyes showed compassion: she felt comfortable with him.

'How did you get that scar below your eye?' she said.

'I got mugged when I was seventeen... guy came at me with a knife so I fought him off but he almost took my eye out...'

'Really?' she asked, amazed.

'No. I was playing Cowboys and Indians with my best friend when I was seven and tripped over my own feet, almost taking my eye out with the sucker end of the arrow...'

She smiled a little.

'You can trust me...' he said quietly.

She drew a very deep breath.

'My husband has left me,' she found herself blurt.

There, it was said. Taking another sip of coffee, she carefully placed the mug back on its little coaster. 'You know...usual cliché; middle aged man meets a 26 year old blonde who looks just like all the other 26 year old blondes these days; well... admittedly I've never actually seen her in the flesh... but in the Hello magazine I saw at the hairdressers she looked like a clone in heels with ironed hair. Anyway she comes along to make him think he's still Got It, flutters her impossibly long eye lashes at him, thrusts out her boobs that probably came in a packet, lies back and gives it up to him and then he thinks he's in love with her and dumps me. Somewhat publicly... unfortunately, and now I've been...replaced. I am the weakest link... goodbye!'

She gulped again at the hot coffee and tears sprang to her eyes as it burned down her throat, and she gasped for cool air as she felt it go all the way down towards her stomach. In fact it was such a gulp that he heard it going all the way down too. She took another deep and cooling breath and looked at her hands, shaking uncontrollably against her mug.

'When was this?' he said.

'Oh, a couple of months ago...' She grabbed a crumpled and somewhat fluffy tissue from her sleeve and wiped her eyes. 'I wondered why he hadn't come home from a trip when he said he would be and his... well when I rang his agent he... told me.'

Martin looked at her in disbelief.

'His *Agent* told you your husband had left you?'

'Paul leaves all his awkward situations to his agent,' she said, with no apparent irony, and as if this made it alright.

Martin handed her a fresh tissue from the box behind him and she blew her nose noisily. 'They're living together in his apartment in London now...so I hear, and he hasn't been near here since.... It's like he died, except it feels more like I have... and now another woman is living my life with him instead of me.'

His gaze wandered as he tried to think of something else to say, and was attracted by a large abstract painting on the wall of the dining room, visible just through an archway leading from the kitchen. And then his eyes opened themselves involuntarily right up to his eyebrows and he knew.

'Your husband,' he said, '... Is Paul Taylor, the artist Paul Taylor?'

She nodded.

'Oh.'

He knew of him only too well. Everyone had, he supposed. Not one of his favourite people either. A real jet setter and often seen in the aforementioned Hello magazine mixing with the rich and famous. He pulled a face and looked around the room again, and then his gaze returned to Jules, who was sipping at her coffee but was a million miles away.

Paul Taylor was married to… this?

Being a kind hearted soul and knowing a damsel in distress when he saw one, and this was definitely a damsel in distress, he took a deep breath and made a quick decision. Placing the palms of his hands flat down on the table in front of him as he stood up, he looked at her. 'You know what you need?' he said.

'A drink?' she replied with a crooked half-smile. 'It must be five o'clock somewhere…' and she attempted a weak laugh.

'No' he said. 'You look exhausted, you need a bath; a long, hot, relaxing bath.'

He put out his right hand to take hers.

She took it and stood up.

Turning away and pulling her along, he asked her; 'where is your bathroom?'

Overtaking him and leading the way through the dining room she said; 'take your pick. Corner, sunken or roll top?'

※

Jules lay in the steaming water of Paul's absolutely huge sunken bath, with the spa on, and bubbling gently. She luxuriated in the mass of musk scented masculine bubbles that were increasing by the minute with the aggravated water. He must have put the whole bottle in here.

So what!

Downstairs, she could hear him clattering about in the kitchen. She had an obscure thought that he'd got her out of the way so that he could ransack and steal everything in the house.

And frankly didn't care one jot if he did.

Stepping out sometime later, with her skin as wrinkly as a walnut, she wrapped herself in Paul's big white bathrobe, and twisted her hair up into a fluffy blue towel, feeling much better. The smell of bacon wafted up the stairs and reached her nostrils, and her stomach gave a significant grumble.

Had she eaten anything yesterday?

Realising she was starving and rubbing her hair vigorously she untwisted the towel and let it fall to the floor, then wiped at the steamed up mirror with the back of one hand. Grabbing a comb from the glass shelf, she began to tug at her unruly head of hair, and the piece of trapped straw was finally freed from her tangles and fell unnoticed to the floor, landing as gently as a feather on the fluffy blue towel.

Downstairs Martin had made himself busy. He wiped down the draining board, folded the cloth over the edge of the washing up bowl and looked around himself with satisfaction.

Jules appeared at the archway with her hair in a low twist over pony tail tied with a black scrunchie, and wearing a long faded denim skirt with brown leather boots and thick green polo necked sweater.

'Better?' she said,

'Much better...' he replied.

Jules looked around the kitchen and her mouth fell open.

'Wow!' she said, as she flopped into a chair at the table. Martin pushed the plate of bacon sandwiches towards her and offered the bottles of brown sauce and ketchup like a wine waiter, draping a very faded 'Rules of Cricket' tea towel across one arm. She took the brown sauce. 'Excellent choice,' he said, and sat down opposite her.

She lifted one slice of bread from her sandwich, added a generous squirt and, then replacing it, took a bite and began to chew.

'Mmm, heavenly. Thanks Martin!'

'Bacon sandwiches... the perfect comfort food,' he mumbled, with his mouth full.

'Tell me more about you,' she said, still chewing, and sinking the plunger on the coffee pot he'd also made up, and pouring out two mugs. 'How come you're on your own?'

She pushed one of the mugs towards him, and he nodded his thanks.

'Not much to say really.' He swallowed, taking the mug. 'Failed relationship; *another* failed relationship.'

Then he sighed deeply through his nose before he continued. 'She left me so I moved here and decided to enjoy my own company for a while.' He took another bite of his sandwich and continued talking with his mouth full. 'Managed about a month and discovered I'm not really that exciting, and got Dipstick,' looking at his dog, 'who is.' He put down his sandwich and bent down to ruffle his ears.

Dipstick was up on his feet in seconds, sniffing Martin's hands for titbits.

'Any children?' She took another bite, and wiped away a stray drip of sauce from the side of her mouth with one thumb, and then sucking it away greedily.

He smiled but looked down at the table. 'No; as I said before, there's just me.'

'Well aren't we a fine pair of rejects...' she smiled, a little wanly.

Knowing it was more of a statement than a question, he decided it didn't require and answer.

The days passed slowly, and she became so lonely at night she could almost taste it. It felt like she'd been sacked as a homemaker as well as his wife too: no one to cook for, no time schedule to plan to... no washing or ironing; well, not enough to do daily anyway.

She'd left the telephone on answering machine after the day she'd grasped it with such joy at the thought it might be him, calling to say the whole thing had been a big misunderstanding and he was coming home, only to get some snooping reporter asking her for her comments on her husband's defection. She was almost a prisoner in her own home. Press vultures were lurking to pick over the carcass of her marriage at the bottom of the drive, and so scared was she of the knowing glances from people in the village, or in the shops and supermarkets if she tried a little farther afield, that she couldn't bear the thought. She'd cancelled her daily paper for fear of seeing their marriage splashed all over it day after day, but then in the absence of any other communication, missed the chance to keep up with what he was doing.

The clocks changed, and soon it was dark by 5 o'clock. The long uneventful days stretched in to long uneventful evenings in an endless monotony of waiting for it to be an ok time to have a drink.

The one highlight in her endless days was that Martin and Dipstick took to appearing at the back door about 7pm most evenings. The first time it happened, she'd been her pyjamas all day and had eaten her way though a whole packet of chocolate hobnobs. By the second bottle of wine she'd suggested watching a film and he'd made popcorn, somewhat drunkenly, in the microwave. Burnt popcorn has a smell all of its own and she'd spent the whole of the following morning shivering with the back door open in order to clear the smell, so they decided not to repeat that experiment.

But knowing he was coming each evening did give her motivation to get herself up and dressed in the mornings now. So that was a plus. In fact their evenings had turned into a bit of a routine as well. He loved to watch anything, because he fell asleep anyway, and she loved romantic comedies with predictable happy endings that required no real concentration.

Sometimes she would cook him dinner too, once she'd decided he was far too thin for his height, and it was nice to cook for a man again. Especially such a grateful one who had discovered the only things he could cook were bacon sandwiches and fry ups.

Paul on the other hand had always been totally at home in the kitchen, and followed Delia Smith recipes with military precision, even if he did use every utensil in the kitchen during his culinary sprees, and the aftermath always resembled one of his paintings and took hours to clear up. There wasn't much he'd ever failed at really,

Except me... she thought.

It wasn't that he hadn't been in touch since he'd left her; just that he'd email rather than phone her, so she then had to pluck up the courage to open it and see what he had to say. He was, in his defence, full of apology, but still avoiding direct confrontation. He used clichés like, '*I need to find out who I am...* ' and '*She makes me feel so alive.'* It was like he'd swallowed a Mills and Boon romance novel and it made her feel quite sick.

Every day when the post came she looked anxiously for a solicitor's letter, and lived few years longer that day when there wasn't one.

One evening Jules decided to try and make Paul jealous by making a play for Martin. She'd just finished reading *'The Man Who Made Husbands Jealous,'* by Jilly Cooper from the mobile library. An outrageous but brilliantly silly story about a young stud hired at dizzying expense by betrayed wives to pretend he was their new love interest, in order to bring their errant husbands scurrying back into line, she thought it was worth a try. So she made a special dinner and invited him over. She'd managed to get herself and him spectacularly drunk, and after some shameful and really not very good flirting she'd launched herself at him. They'd gone to bed clumsily and had a drunken and entirely unsuccessful coupling, about which she remembered little, apart from the fact that he'd slunk out in the morning before she was awake and she'd ended up feeling a million times worse than before.

To fuel and increase her low self esteem even further, he hadn't come over for several days after that. Jules sent him a text eventually, one wet and depressing Sunday afternoon, to say sorry and to please come over. She missed his company, and Barney was, grudgingly of course, missing Dipstick. Within half an hour Martin had arrived with Dipstick and a huge bag of marshmallows and a pot of drinking chocolate. They hugged each other in a way that acknowledged a true friendship, without any sex, ever again.

There's was such an easy and genuine friendship that there was no awkwardness at all as he sat down at the table, but he still took a very deep breath as he looked into her eyes. 'I haven't been entirely truthful with you,' he said, handing the two packages across to her. Jules put them on the dresser and went to the fridge for the milk. While she was busy making the drinks he continued. 'You're very lovely Jules. It's not that, honestly.'

He took another deep breath and let it out slowly, and she turned to face him.

'What is it?' she asked quietly.

They looked at each other, and his voice broke as he said; 'I need to admit that I went to bed with you to hurt Paul as much as you did… It's Paul's blonde clone, you see.

She was my blonde clone.'

# Chapter three

Martin was an electrical engineer, specialising in lighting galleries for prestigious exhibitions, and when that wasn't happening, he worked on theatre productions. He had long ago decided that he was not very good at relationships, after a series of both blind and eyes wide open dates, arranged by friends, had all turned out to be non starters, and expensive.

He'd met Catherine Dempsey; never Cat, Cathy or Kate, at a dinner party when she'd been with someone else and so had he. They'd sat opposite each other and he'd become completely mesmerised by her mouth. She was blonde and tall and elegant. She did that thing that girls with long hair do, and tossed it back over her shoulder by swinging her whole upper body around to move it. But it had been her mouth that did it. His mother would have called it a rose bud mouth, and he'd quickly decided that it looked extremely kissable after watching it smile, frown, eat, drink, laugh and, at one point, yawn discreetly, all evening.

She had a BA in art history and was now an Art Critic, and people learned quickly not to challenge her opinions on anything she said, once they had tried it. With a reputation for being a bit of an ice maiden, she worked for the Sunday Times. She was confident, intelligent, and was very well respected.

She also had legs right the way up to there.

She'd focussed her big blue eyes on Martin during one particular discussion and he was dazzled; hooked lined and sinkered.

The day after the dinner party he called his friend Tim, who had hosted it, and asked him how he could get in touch with her. Given her number he counted to ten and rang to ask her out.

She'd said no.

Several months passed and their paths crossed at galleries and theatres on a few more occasions. Then one morning they met in Starbucks in Marble Arch, in the queue, and he'd asked her out again. This time she agreed. He took her out to dinner in a restaurant he'd never been to but had read a Michael Winner review of the previous week, and she'd ordered Lobster and a hugely expensive white wine. He knew that they were chalk and cheese, and that she was way out of his league and most definitely out of his bank balance, but it couldn't be helped. He'd wooed her with his sense of humour really, and she told people he made her laugh.

After six months they'd moved in together, to her penthouse flat in Lavender Grove. He'd let his much more modest accommodation to a fellow engineer called Sid, but known in the trade as Hissing Sid because he kept snakes in a great big glass tank and didn't get out much. He wore a faded t shirt that proclaimed '*Hissing Sid is innocent*,' that you had to be of a certain age, like he was, to understand the significance of.

Martin was deliriously happy and took her home to meet his parents, but that visit had not been a success.

It wasn't that they hadn't tried; maybe they just tried too hard. Dad stood in his Lord of the Manor way with his legs astride, his back to the electric fire and his hands on his hips. Chin thrust up, he looked like he was about to burst into a song from Seven Brides for Seven Brothers.

Mum had made one of her infamous fruit cakes that sat in your stomach for a week, and egg sandwiches made with salad cream on pre sliced spongy white bread. Catherine had sat politely on the sofa with one arm resting on a crocheted antimacassar, and her legs elegantly crossed and angled to one side. She sipped her black tea from Mum's best china, and professed to be still full up from the green salad with no dressing she'd eaten at lunchtime.

But Martin loved her.

The first time he'd come across Paul Taylor was at a gallery in London when he was lighting one of his exhibitions. He'd swept in wearing an astrakhan coat and was joined at the hip to one of those camp flunkies, tapping away on a Blackberry, with a Bluetooth thing attached to his ear that flashed its little blue light incessantly. Paul was obviously important because everyone else in the room dropped what they were doing and leapt to attention. He radiated importance and was moodily handsome. Martin looked down at him from his stepladder and thought he looked like a character from an extravagant American soap, and found himself looking behind him for Joan Collins and her Dynasty shoulder pads.

Martin had gone along with Catherine to the launch party at the gallery that evening. She'd talked about Paul Taylor non stop for at least three days beforehand, and had taken two hours getting ready. Even that was after taking the afternoon off to get her hair and nails done, but he hadn't known that.

She looked a million dollars.

He hadn't passed muster.

Appearing in a crumpled grey suit she'd sent him back to their room to think again, and then once she'd approved him, she'd promptly abandoned him at the party as soon as they walked in the door.

Paul Taylor took one look at her as she walked in the door wearing a shimmering gold designer gown, totally off one shoulder and slashed almost to indecency up to one thigh, and he was visibly smitten that night. Catherine visibly failed at feigning indifference, but simpered and giggled in his presence like a fourteen year old who had been asked to dance with the sixth from heart throb at the school prom after sneaking in without a ticket in the first place.

It had started right there and then, and Martin had found himself watching it from behind a pillar with a glass of white wine in his hand and an air of doomed inevitability. He'd had no idea at that point that Paul Taylor was married. He wore no wedding ring, never acted like it for a second; often to be seen with a bit of eye candy in tow from some model agency in a rented frock.

As the weeks passed he had looked on helplessly as their relationship was not only noticed by everyone around them, but condoned, and Catherine became less and less content with Martin and found fault with everything he did. He'd confided in the pub one night to his good friend Tim, who hadn't been in the least surprised and had said that he'd known her since they were at school together. Catherine was ambitious even back then, and had always been a self confessed and unrepentant gold digger. He described her as being like a Praying Mantis, who treated men like stepping stones to where she really wanted to be: reeling in the new one and then eating up and spitting out the remains of the one before. He said she'd even told his wife that Martin would do until she had a better offer. Martin threw a punch that sent Tim reeling backwards across the bar, and then he walked out.

They say love is blind, and Martin needed a white stick. He burned with the recollection of the total humiliation he'd felt the night he'd sat in a restaurant waiting for her until way past eleven, when the head waiter's discreet cough had reached asthmatic proportions and he'd gone home alone. She'd arrived home after midnight that night with guilt written all over her face, and the foot of one of her stockings hanging out of her bag. They'd had an almighty row, when she had turned everything around and made it sound like his fault somehow, and had demanded that he move out right then. Worst of all was that his bag was already packed for him, and ready and waiting for the closing act of this tragic play, under the bed.

Martin had got very, very drunk that night and had slept on the sofa next to the snake tank at Hissing Sid's.

After several weeks of that he decided that he needed to pull himself together and the first step towards that was a change of scenery. Sid's lease was up and he wanted to move back up north and be fed and clean clothed by his mother, so Martin sold the flat. He'd gone to an auction on a whim and bought a cottage *'in a much sought after location'* that was *'in need of some updating,*' in the village of Frincham, in Berkshire. Local attractions included Clearwater Lake with its stunning scenery and open woodland, two pubs, (one with no less than two Michelin stars for its restaurant chef), a General stores and Post office, and a butcher's shop that had been in the same family for almost two hundred years and famed for its sausages and pies. Perfect.

His work didn't matter because he was mobile anyway so could live where he wanted, and if he didn't get away from London and all its Catherine look-alikes, he would suffocate.

Martin signed the papers and moved in within five weeks.

'In need of some updating,' had really meant 'complete renovation.' The old lady that had owned it for fifty years had died having not really done anything to it in all that time. It had no central heating or mains drainage either, and the garden was a wilderness of indeterminate proportions. And judging by the lush green of the jungle down the bottom, he took an educated guess that the septic tank needed replacing too. Mrs Bennett had married an airman in the war who'd died in the Battle of Britain before any issue, and the distant nephew she'd left her cottage to had cut and run pretty sharply, so Martin spent most of the profit from selling his London flat in local DIY shops. After a couple of months though, he had made significant improvements and discovered a decent sized garden and, thanks to the leak in the old septic tank, very fertile soil.

He also discovered he hated his own company.

When he tried planting vegetables he thought about Catherine and her green salad with no dressing. When he sat down to watch TV with a beer, he thought about Catherine. When he went to bed he thought about Catherine. Essentially he thought about Catherine - and Paul Taylor.

He hadn't met anyone locally other than the postman and a couple of people in the less fancy of the two pubs, The White Hart, and his nearest neighbour was half a mile away in a great barn of a place down by the lake. He'd heard that house belonged to some celebrity, and so was probably miles outside of his social group anyway.

Watching TV one night and already on the second six pack of beer since yesterday, he saw one of those pet adoption programmes and knew that what he needed was some canine company that would get him some fresh air and exercise and stop him dwelling on his disastrous love life perfectly. He bought a local paper at the post office the next morning, saw the ad about re homing failed drug detection dogs from the police training centre in Reading, and called the number. A couple of weeks later, having passed his home check once he'd mended a fence or two, he picked Dipstick up in his Land Rover and took him home.

He'd settled in at the cottage quickly and they'd become good friends. He even loved the Land Rover and if Martin ever left the door open while he either loaded or unloaded his lighting equipment, he always new where to find him; fast asleep on the front seat. But their friendship had very nearly ended after one particular morning, when Martin had had a very rude awakening. Dipstick had taken a joyful leap onto his bed just after dawn and almost ruined his marriage prospects for ever, obviously desperate to go out. Martin had dressed quickly and, without much regard for the weather outside, set off for the woods. Dipstick, once he'd relieved himself against a tree, had almost immediately caught the scent of something nocturnal and disappeared off into the undergrowth, so Martin continued walking down towards the lake. Soon afterwards Dipstick had come thundering down the footpath at full pelt from somewhere behind him and with his nose to the ground. Totally scent focussed he trod on the back of Martin's flip flop and sent him flying, landing heavily on his knee and onto a sharp flint that was sticking out of the ground. His loud exclamations and blasphemies had scared Dipstick and sent him fleeing into the distance with his stumpy tail as close to between his legs as he could manage.

Martin had picked himself up, dusted himself off, and inspected the damage to his knee. Cursing, not very quietly, he set off with a painful hobble and one bare foot to find his dog. Reaching a fork in the path he heard barking coming from the lake direction, so he headed off that way. In the distance he saw a woman putting a woolly scarf through a very wet Dipstick's collar and starting to lead him away.

And that was how he met Jules.

# Chapter four

'I don't really know what to say,' said Jules. 'Other than that you can't have a very high opinion of me.'

'It's your husband I don't have a very high opinion of,' he replied. 'Anyway if anyone should be cheesed off it should be you with me. I took advantage of you and you've so much more to lose. You two are married, we're not.'

'Married nearly 30 years...' she said, quietly. 'He was the only real boyfriend I ever had that lasted longer than a few weeks. My father would normally give anyone I dared bring home the Spanish Inquisition, but the first time Paul came to call for me, my dad was trying to heave a flat pack wardrobe up the stairs with just my poor mum to help him because I was all of a dither getting ready to go out. It weighed an absolute ton, and Paul quickly grabbed the bottom end from her and helped him. When they finally got it to top my dad thanked him, and then asked him who he was... and then that was that, he was part of the family.' A single fat tear escaped her lower eyelid and crept down her left cheek, waiting patiently on the edge of her jaw for another one to join it, and give it the weight it needed, to drop.

'Has he even spoken to you properly about all this yet?' he asked, 'or have you tried calling him?'

'I tried...' she said, 'but his phone goes straight to voicemail, and I just can't... and when I tried the land line number at the flat, Catherine answered and asked me if I wanted her to give him a message.... She said if I did, she'd do her best to remember to give it to him.... It was so humiliating...' she swallowed and coughed. The tears were coming thick and fast now and Martin pulled the last tissue from the box on the table in front of her. He fumbled in his pocket and brought forth a rather grimy looking white hankie, and thinking better of that idea, quickly shoved it back again.

'What about your children... Jemmie and Marcus?' he said, slipping his arm around her shoulders.

Jules let her head fall onto her folded arms, and her shoulders began to heave.

'They don't know!' she wailed, 'I just thought if I didn't say anything it might all blow over. That he'd realise he'd made a terrible mistake and he'd come... home. This is like some awful dream and I keep thinking I'll wake up!'

After a minute or two of sobbing as he rubbed her back gently and made soothing noises, she lifted her head, blew her nose very hard, and breathed deeply for a few times. 'Enough!' she said. 'Let's get drunk!' She heaved herself up from the table with an indignant screech of chair versus quarry tiled floor and led the way through to the sitting room.

Later, once Jules had sunk into a deep and mostly drink induced sleep on the sofa, Martin went over to the telephone table by the big bay window. The telephone address book was easy to locate, and he looked up Jemmie's number, which wasn't. He spent some time trying to figure out Jules' entry system, and eventually found her under H for hospital.

He left the room so as not to wake her and crept out of the back door as his mobile started to connect the call.

She took some time to answer, and when she did, she sounded sleepy and yawned as she answered.

'Dr Taylor...'

'Hi,' he said. 'I'm sorry to bother you. You don't know me. My name is Martin Ryan. I'm a friend of your mother's...'

✯

Jemmie was a junior house doctor in the accident and emergency department at the Royal Berkshire Hospital, having qualified the year before with flying colours at Brighton and Sussex University. She fulfilled every stereotypical idea of a junior doctor, in that she looked half asleep, generally because she was half asleep, though mentally alert, if running on autopilot. She had been on duty in the accident and emergency department for twenty two hours straight, and when Martin called she had been asleep in an armchair with no fabric on one of its arms in the doctor's rest room, with a plastic fork in one hand, and a clear plastic tub of Caesar salad perched on her lap. Its lid had been quivering in unison with her breathing, for the last twenty minutes.

Her Doctor's training, and practice, had her instantly awake at the first ring to talk to him and, after she hung up she began mainlining treacle thick black coffee from the machine to wake herself up.

An hour or so later, having called her boss to announce a family crisis and request a few days immediate compassionate leave, she'd driven the 20 miles from the hospital to Frincham on automatic pilot, climbed out of her car still shivering from the blast of air conditioning she'd aimed at her face to stay awake on the journey, and from an adrenaline boosting can of Red Bull, and let herself in the kitchen door at Clearwater House with her key. Martin heard the door and went out to greet her. He watched her as she bent down to greet an ecstatic Barney by rubbing his tummy as he rolled fatly over in his basket, bearing his wiry grey belly for her and whimpering happily, his tail thumping rhythmically against the wall.

'Hello Barneyboy!' she said, greeting him by his old pet name.

She looked just like her mother, he decided. Her hair was the same mass of tight chestnut brown curls that tumbled unashamedly and unrestrained around her shoulders. She had the dimple in her chin, and she was about the same height. She was pencil thin though, and she looked very pale. In fact he thought she looked like someone who needed a good holiday: either that or a few puddings. Nice mouth; he thought, with lips that were dressed with nothing more than the cherry flavoured chap stick she'd placed on the table with her car keys.

He introduced himself properly, shaking her hand, and then went across the kitchen to make her even more coffee. Jemmie went into the sitting room and was visibly shocked to see her mother, fast asleep in a totally uncharacteristic but definitely drunken stupor on the sofa, with a line of dribble oozing from one side of her mouth most unbecomingly.

Martin appeared from behind her with two mugs and placed them on the coffee table. Looking back towards Jemmie he said; 'I wonder if you'd mind giving me a hand to get her up to bed? I'll carry her up and then you can get her undressed and…so forth.'

As he picked Jules up from the sofa she instinctively put her arms around his neck and murmured something unintelligible. He was very strong thanks to years of lugging around lighting equipment, and carried her effortlessly up the stairs to her room, where Jemmie had gone before him and taken a nightshirt from the wooden chest and laid it on the bed. 'I can manage now, thank you…Martin,' she said, turning to him as he made for the door, and smiling slightly. 'Leave the door open, we'll need to hear her if she's sick or she might choke….'

※

Jules woke up the following morning in the marital king-size and wearing her pink nightshirt that was patterned with strawberries. The sun was poring through the window painfully through a gap in the curtains and when she tried to attempt being vertical she felt like she should be the other way up. Going into her bathroom she looked at her tongue in the mirror, and it had at least an inch of fur on it. Her eyes, on closer inspection in the same mirror, looked like a tree full of owls. She wondered how she'd got to bed, and especially into that one.

She shuddered.

She pulled on her dressing gown in complete slow motion and padded gingerly and barefoot down the stairs.

Unaware of her arrival at the archway, Martin was sitting in the kitchen, chewing on a pencil and attempting a very hard Sudoku puzzle in her own book of them, with some coffee in a mug on the table in front of him. Barney and Dipstick were curled up nose to nose, a little muddy and therefore presumably post walk, along the Aga. She was about to speak to him when she caught her breath in surprise. Jemmie was there too, and came in to view from the sink end of the kitchen carrying a steaming mug, and joined him, smiling, at the table. She rested her chin happily on one upturned hand and began looking at the puzzle, which he had pushed slightly towards her.

It was 11am according to the clock on the wall.

They both looked up when they heard her clear her throat slightly and come in the room.

'Mum...' said Jemmie. She jumped up and ran tearfully into her mother's arms. 'What's going on? Why didn't you tell me?'

Jules looked across at Martin.

'Thank you,' she mouthed, and Martin acknowledged her with the slightest nod of his head.

✯

When they had walked and talked the whole sorry mess out into the open whilst feeding the ducks with some stale bread Jemmie had found lurking in the bread bin, Jemmie opened the back door and stood aside to let Jules and the dogs go inside first. Martin was laying three plates on the table and the smell of bacon greeted them.

The room echoed with very loud lapping as the dogs eased their thirst companionably at the enormous water bowl that Paul had thought was a bird bath when she'd brought it home from the pet shop.

Jules sat down with a thud and eased off her boots. 'Martin's life saving bacon sandwiches,' she said.

'Mum's told me everything...' said Jemmie, looking at Martin and sitting herself down.

'Everything?' Martin looked at Jules nervously.

'Nearly everything...' said Jules, looking across at her. 'Jems, darling there's one more thing. Martin isn't just my neighbour. This...mess... affects him too...'

# Chapter five

Paul Taylor turned over in the bed and looked at Catherine lying beside him, blonde hair fanned out on the pillow around her sleeping face, and once more it occurred to him that couldn't believe his luck. He was on a roll. His career was everything he'd ever dreamed of, and more. Every time he flicked his paintbrush near a blank canvas these days it seemed the results would be worth thousands; and to crown it all, this blonde... goddess, was finally his... so all the lies could stop now.

He continued to lie there, watching her sleep. Now and then she would move a little and sigh; then slowly, she opened her eyes as if she knew he was watching her, and smiled. She reached over with one of her long bronzed legs; finding his, and rubbed her knee against the inside of his thigh suggestively. He leaned across and kissed her, again.

An hour or so later, Paul stood under the shower and let the fierce jets work their healing powers on his skin.

Exciting as all this was, he ached in places he didn't know he still had. Catherine was 26 and had the sexual appetites to match. He, on the other hand, was nearly 50...

He banished the niggling thought from his mind, again, and reached for the shampoo.

It was only because they were in a new and exciting relationship, obviously. One day they would get married and then things would become more normal. Normal...

It had been very different when he'd married Jules. They hadn't slept together beforehand. She was a Christian and the no sex before marriage thing had been important to her, he recalled, and it had been different back then, anyway. Once they'd married, though, they couldn't keep their hands off each other, and consequently she'd fallen pregnant very quickly, and Marcus had been born a year to the day after the wedding.

He felt his first nagging little stab of what anyone else would have acknowledged as guilt, of the day.

Marcus: his son and heir.

And Jemmie; his darling Jems.

And Jules... the family: his family. What were they doing right now?

Banishing the thought again he put his face under the still gushing showerhead and shook his head vigorously.

✫

Across the other side of town and in a block of trendy apartments just by Battersea Bridge on the River Thames, Marcus, the aforementioned son and heir, was also in the shower, so didn't hear his phone ringing. 6 feet 2 inches tall with black hair and brown eyes like his father, he was lean and fit thanks to swimming downstairs in the private pool every morning, and an hour of cardio vascular exercise three times a week in the local gym. He lived with Sam Mason, his partner of almost ten years. They'd met at university. She too, swam every morning and trained three times a week at the local gym.

Now specialising in cosmetic dentistry he had a small but lucrative practice in central London, and she was both his nurse and the practice manager. Some people were surprised that they could work together as well as be a couple, but he liked it that way, and so did she.

He prided himself on being in a well oiled machine of a relationship, and saw no reason at all to complicate things by getting married or having children.

They neatly fitted the criteria of what had been known in the 1980's as 'Dinkeys', (double income no kids), and lived very well in a large and balconied apartment overlooking the busy end of the River Thames, so if they wanted to they could wave at the tourists on the boats while they ate their breakfast, or lunch, or dinner.

Wrapped in a not quite adequate white towel he wandered into the bedroom still attempting to get swimming pool water out of his ear with one corner of it, when he saw his phone flashing its little blue 'missed call' light, and picked it up.

Seven missed calls.

He scrolled the menu to see what the calls were: all Jemmie.

She must just be tired and stressed out again.

He sighed, and preparing himself to be the reassuring big brother, adjusted his towel, sat on the edge of the bed and pressed 'yes' to 'return call.'

✯

The last piece of information in the saga had all been too much for Jemmie, and she had run out of the house in floods of tears, and was now sitting on an old wooden bench beside the lake, at least half a mile from Clearwater House, which was as far as she could run on shingle, and in Wellington boots, without stopping.

The bench had a little plaque on it that declared forever in brass;

*In loving memory of Arthur and Enid Williams, devoted to each other in marriage for sixty two years.'*

Wow.

Her phone was still in her hand and she picked up Marcus' call on the first ring.

'Hey Jems...' he said brightly, 'for what do I owe the honour of seven missed calls?'

'Oh Markie...' she said, and burst into tears again.

'Oh come on Jems... what's up?' he said. 'You're just tired I expect. Aren't they letting you get *any* sleep in that hospital?'

'I'm not at the hospital; I'm at Mum's,' she sobbed, 'Listen to me. Dad's gone... he's left her...'

'He's what? Marcus leapt off the bed as if he'd sat on a nail and his towel fell abruptly to the floor. 'You're joking!' Realising he was on full view of the tour boats on the river he grabbed at the towel with his other hand and attempted to put it back around his waist.

'Do I sound like I'm joking?' she sniffed, trying unsuccessfully to find a tissue in her jacket pockets.

Marcus was shocked and struggled to think what to say to her. 'What...why? Did she say why?'

Jemmie took a deep breath. 'Oh Marcus, it's all so hard to believe.... She said... he's been having an affair... she even knew about it! She said he's been with her... here. And now he's left her... and run off with this... Markie, she's the same bloody age as me!

And… and her boyfriend is even down here too… he's in the house… here… with Mum.'

Marcus was pacing the room now and running his free hand through his hair, but at that he stopped abruptly. 'What? You mean him and… Mum too? What is this…Celebrity wife swap?'

'No! No… of course not! Don't be daft! He's moved into Mrs Bennett's cottage!' she said impatiently. 'They met walking their dogs… they didn't know at first, and then he saw Dad's painting in the dining room, that hideous red one Mum hates… and then… he just put two and two together… and came clean.'

'So who is this girl then?' and, not waiting for an answer, continued, 'Jemmie, I'll come down.' He looked at the clock on the wall and made some rapid calculations. His mind was already on finding the car keys.

'No don't come down Marcus…. Not yet anyway,' she said, thinking fast. 'Can you go over and see him first? Go and see Dad? And try to find out what's going on?'

'Go where Jems? Where is he?'

'He's in Eaton Square,' she said flatly, 'in his bachelor pad. With her.'

✷

Alone now, Paul dressed, and then put all the clothes littering the floor; mostly hers, into the laundry basket. He then made his way down an elegant wrought iron spiral staircase to the kitchen. Catherine had gone to work, late thanks to the sexual lie in, and the remnants of her breakfast still lay on the breakfast bar. Paul picked up her plate, glass, and coffee cup and put them in the dishwasher. He returned the orange juice and the milk to the fridge and wiped the counter with a dual personality face cloth. He reassembled the morning paper into its intended shape and page order, and then finally, shut the door on the microwave.

Hungry himself, he looked in the fridge once again. Assessing its frugal contents without much hope he took out a lonely fat free yoghurt carton. Looking at the date on its lid, he pulled a face, tossed it into the bin, and gave up.

Returning from the bakery at the end of the road a few minutes later with his croissants in a bag in one hand, and balancing a grande cappuccino with a dodgy lid in the other, he walked out of the lift in happy anticipation, only to find an unexpected visitor waiting there for him, slumped on the floor outside his front door.

Marcus' head was disconsolately resting on its side on his bent up knees, and he was playing with a sweet wrapper on the plush red carpet with one hand, while the other lay miserably on the floor at his side. One look from Marcus into his father's eyes when he'd heard the lift doors ping open, told him the game was well and truly up, and the bubble went pop: that bubble of bathroom window frosted innocence that he'd been shielding himself with for almost two months; and the reality of what he'd done hit him squarely between the eyes.

# Chapter six

Jules said goodbye to Martin with a hug and watched him make his way down the garden path, with his delinquent dog bouncing along in front of him. She wondered if being betrayed in your own home, and then abandoned, was easier if you weren't married. She looked at Martin's slumped shoulders and heavy dragging footsteps and supposed not. No partnership commitment was worth anything if one half of you didn't mean it.

She went up the stairs and into their bedroom; her bedroom now she supposed, and looked at the bed.

It had been the previous June 23$^{rd}$ at 10.30am: the day and the time that she'd gone from being deaf, dumb and blind to his faults, to being neither deaf nor blind, but just dumb, with shock. The day and the exact time that she'd realised she was married to another man altogether to the one she thought she knew down to his very soul. Based on that day, if she met him in the street now she'd have walked right past.

She'd arrived home from a shopping trip to Paris with Jemmie, only to find that Paul had stripped their bed and put the sheets in the washing machine. When she'd remarked that she'd only changed the bedding two days previously, he'd said he had spilled his morning tea: so plausible.

Later that day, as she began to put the clean sheets back on the bed her eye caught something, glinting in the sunlight from the window, on the carpet by her feet. It was half on the carpet and half attached to her slipper, and so she bent down and picked it up in her fingers. It was a long, long strand of hair; blonde hair. Dropping it in the waste paper basket with a dismissive shake of her head and continuing her bed making task, she found another one attached to the headboard, on her own side of the bed. And there were more of them, she discovered, in the drain of the shower when she cleaned it, and even in her own hair brush on the dressing table.

'You're quiet?' he said at dinner later, and shockingly, he looked perfectly normal; he hadn't grown horns, or a tail.

'Headache' she replied.


Her senses spinning out of control with suspicion by now, she started to do odd things. She dialled 1471 when he came off the phone to find out who he'd been calling. And she checked the call log and messages on his mobile phone whenever he left it on the table.

She went online to check their bank and credit card statements.

She checked his pockets when he took his jacket off and left it hanging across the back of a chair.

She started timing his dog walks.

If he told her he would stay in the Kensington flat during this or that exhibition, she would ring the gallery concerned, pretending to be a member of the public, to find out how long the exhibition actually lasted.

She had spent a weekend in London in the July, meeting up with an old school friend. During the day they shopped till they dropped and then spent the evening going to the theatre. They'd gone to see Mamma Mia. Then they had both stayed that Saturday night in Paul's apartment rather than stay in a hotel. The following morning Jules took a tube of Lancôme mascara from the bathroom and tried to give it back to her. But she said it wasn't hers.

Things just didn't add up.

Or did add up, depending on which way you looked at it.

But back at home she never challenged him, and he never said anything.

And then there were the letters, or the lack of them: specifically the ones with windows. Now it seemed he had his post intercepted by Hugo and she never got to see any of them- unless she looked online of course, so she did.

She could go online and look at the joint credit card bills, and it was all there as bold as brass. The florists, the restaurant bills, the hotel suites, theatre tickets and even, on one occasion, £2,000 spent in a jewellers in Hatton Garden that she never saw the fruits of, even though the date of the purchase had been on her own birthday back in June.

Since she'd found the hairs she'd been unable to sleep in that bed.

Come to think of it she didn't really sleep much anywhere; or use that shower.

Or that hair brush.

Paul meanwhile was blissfully unaware of any of this, because he'd either been away for weeks somewhere anyway, or sleeping in his studio after working late into the night.

She was stuck in the lie of a happy marriage in the family home, surrounded by everything that was her and Paul, and now he was in clover in his love nest in swanky Eaton Square in Kensington with his trophy blonde; Martin's trophy blonde.

✯

Martin was lost in thought and walking along the shore, back towards his cottage, when he heard Jemmie sobbing hysterically down her phone, and looked up to see her sitting on the bench. She hung up just as he approached, and looked towards him, her eyes sparkling with defiance at the interruption and shocked to see him standing there.

'Go away...' she said, still sniffing noisily as she continued to search her pockets for a tissue.

'Here,' he said, handing her a now clean one from his own pocket.

She snatched it away from him, and wiped her eyes.

He sat down on the bench next to her just as it began to rain again, and he pulled up the collar on his fleece.

Neither of them said anything but it was plain to see that she was seething with anger, and her breathing was short and shallow, as if she'd been running. She hadn't even noticed that she was beginning to get wet; the raindrops settling and glistening on the tight ringlets in her hair like little gem stones.

The rain got harder and he pulled a face as he looked up at the sky.

'Fancy a cup of tea? We can talk,' he said, turning sideways to face her and leaning across to pull up the hood on her jacket. 'Come on.' He took hold of her hand and called Dipstick to drop the stone he'd been playing with, and follow them. She stood, but pulled her hand away angrily, saying, 'I can manage perfectly well thank you!'

Dipstick dropped his stone as commanded and followed them up Clearwater Lane, and the steep hill towards his cottage.

Quite why she was going with him, she had no idea, except that she could not face any more of her mother's despair just now.

✶

While he busied himself in his tiny kitchen making tea, Jemmie was having a look around, trying to find fault.

'You've changed it,' she said. 'I remember this when Mrs Bennett lived here. That sideboard was over there,' she pointed, 'and there was an aspidistra on a stand... just here,' she stood by the kitchen door as he came back into the room, carrying two mugs.

He handed her a thick black mug with a big yellow smiley face on it. She looked at it and pulled a face that was quite the opposite, but took it from him.

'Yes. Well the flowery wallpaper wasn't really my thing either.' He attempted a weak smile and tried to laugh a bit, but she was hard work, and proud of it.

They sat down awkwardly in two shabby armchairs, both covered in a layer of dog hair.

'Did *she* live here with you?' she said haughtily.

'No *she* didn't. And her name is Catherine. I moved here after we broke up.'

Her eyes fixed on him. 'Did you know that *Catherine* was moving in to steal my dad, break my mother's heart and wreck my family?'

He looked back at her, flat lined his lips and then licked them, making a slight sucking noise, and decided to be completely honest with her. 'I knew she was after him… anyone could have seen that, but I didn't know he was your dad. I didn't know he was anyone's dad… or anyone's husband for that matter either.'

'She's the same age as me!' she retorted, 'that makes him old enough to be *her* dad! It's disgusting!' She glared at him with those sparkling green eyes, so like her mother's, and even in this charged atmosphere, he stifled a smile as he imagined that she had probably been pulling that face all her life.

'There was nothing I could do,' he continued seriously. 'I didn't know anything about him. I didn't know he was married…'

He looked down into his lap.

Looking back up at her slowly he said, very quietly, 'It wasn't my fault you know.'

She thought about that for a minute.

Martin said nothing; wanting her to speak next, and she said nothing, wanting him to.

Eventually, she crossed one denim leg over the other and took a sip of her tea, sat farther back in her armchair and seemed to thaw, just a fraction.

'So how did you come to meet my mother then?' it was still a little feisty, but she was definitely warming up a bit.

Dipstick, sensing the atmosphere, went over to her tentatively, and placed a rubber dumb bell toy that was glistening with dribble in her lap, by way of a peace offering. She smiled, ever so slightly, and took hold of his face between her two hands and bent her head down to meet his nose affectionately.

Catherine wouldn't have done that in a million years.

Dogs were so very good at that, he thought, as he sat back and relaxed a little. He proceeded to tell her the story of Dipstick's dice with death in the lake, while Dipstick retrieved his toy from her lap and circled with it in his mouth, before lying down contentedly at her feet.

# Chapter seven

Paul poured half of his coffee into another cup and offered it to Marcus. Then he took the croissants out of the bag and hunted for some clean plates.

This apartment needs more crockery; he thought impatiently. It needed to be more like a home and less of a stay over place in general really. It needed things, it needed some character…it needed…

'Don't think much of her housekeeping skills, Dad,' said Marcus, interrupting his thoughts as he looked around. There were heaps of her dirty washing piled up on the floor beside the machine, which was also full, and a pot of something that might once have been basil on the windowsill that had given up the ghost and died a slow and thirsty death.

The cooker, obviously not overworked, was in pristine condition, but the bin was overflowing with gourmet takeaway cartons.

He should have seen it before I cleared up; thought Paul, but he decided to lead off with a somewhat pathetic; 'you don't understand.'

'Try me...' said Marcus, taking the croissant in the piece of kitchen roll his father offered him as a plate.

'Did your mother ring you?'

'No, Jemmie did. She's staying at the house with her, to take care of her and watch her as she falls apart. Make sure she doesn't do anything desperate... you know.' Seeing that there was no butter or marmalade on offer, Marcus took a large bite. His mobile phone made them both jump with its loud and incessant incoming text alert. Picking it up, Marcus looked at the screen. 'It's Sam,' he said, licking his fingers. 'Damn. I forgot she was doing the food shop after her gym class this morning. She's just got in from the supermarket and I'm supposed to be at home helping her unload the car and get it all up in the lift.'

Paul pulled a face that looked distinctly impatient, wanting to get back to their talk.

Marcus began typing a text reply quickly. 'I told her this wouldn't take long. Unlike you I care about my partner and worry about letting her down, however mundane getting the shopping in might seem to you.' He wolfed down the last off his croissant and looked right into his father's eyes. 'I hope you're proud of yourself for what you've just done to Mum, Dad.'

※

It hadn't gone very well, Paul decided, when Marcus had gone. Everything he'd tried to say had come out sounding so very lame; feeble, even. Then Marcus had been very rude and Paul had reminded him that he was his father and demanded he be treated with some respect. Marcus had given him a look of such hatred at that point that Paul knew he would never forget it, and said it was his mother who deserved all the respect. Then he'd called him a middle-aged prat and walked out.

Paul now sat in the study and switched on his computer. Ignoring the '97 unread emails' message, he double checked his diary page for that day. Picking up his mobile to ring Hugo, he looked at his watch and made a decision.

※

Back at Clearwater House, and just around lunchtime on that same day, Jules was sitting in the kitchen trying to get her mind off worrying about Jemmie, and concentrate on looking through the local paper while listening to her cherished old radio. She heard the DJ announce one of her favourite singers, and reached over to turn it up a little. Michael Bublé began to sing, and the words she hadn't really taken in before filled the room. He was singing 'Home'.

Now HE really knew how to put it, she thought, and found that she had tears coursing their way down both cheeks, without even realising it.

*'It's like I just stepped outside, when everything was going right.'*

She had just made herself a cup of tea and opened a tin of chocolate chip biscuits left over from last Christmas. Grabbing a thick and crumbly one and munching it loudly, she heard the back door open. Barney heaved himself up with his tail banging against the Aga, just as Jules turned and saw Marcus and Sam coming though the door. Sam looked tearful, and he looked just like he did when he was little and thought he might be in trouble.

Jemmie must have been so upset she'd been on the jungle drums to call in reinforcements.

Getting up, she moved towards them, and Marcus moved forward and took her in his arms.

'I made some tea,' she mumbled, into his chest.

'Got anything stronger?' he said.

'If you want comfort have some of these they work wonders,' and she turned and pulled the biscuit tin towards him.

'I'll pour the tea,' said Sam. 'You look like you need to sit back down.'

✯

Jemmie and Martin appeared just after them, smiling at something Dipstick had just done as they came in the back door, and carrying a huge bag of fish and chips, so Jemmie must have known they were coming. After the introductions and reassurances Marcus and Sam had been continuing to try and cheer Jules up a bit and were telling her about one of his patients.

'You can't be serious Marcus... you must be pulling my leg!' Jules' hand was over her mouth in horror, but at least she was smiling.

'No he isn't,' Sam laughed, 'She honestly did. She thought her upper denture was a bridge and hadn't taken it out to clean it or anything in over twenty years!'

'And there really was!' Marcus laughed.

Picking up on the conversation Jemmie pulled a face. 'That's disgusting!' she said. 'Really was what though?' and putting down the chip shop bag, she began to hand around the paper parcels.

'You really don't want to know... and anyway...food! End of subject please! Let's have some table discipline here!' said Jules, but she was still laughing.

'Was what?' said Martin, closing the fridge and putting the ketchup onto the table. Marcus looked across at him, and hid his mouth from Jules with the side of one hand. 'There was a tomato pip germinating in her palate!' he whispered.

'That is *GROSS*...' Martin shrieked. Looking at the ketchup on the table, he picked it up and put it solemnly back in the fridge. 'Got any vinegar Jules?' he said quietly, holding his stomach as if in fear of throwing up.

The kitchen was blissfully full of laughter and chattering after what seemed to Jules like years of shock and horror, as she went over to the cupboard and took out some plates.

Marcus and Jemmie looked at each other and then back at Jules.

'What?' she said.

'It's supposed to be comfort food Jules,' said Martin. 'Let's slum it and eat them out of the paper....' Then, as she still looked unsure, 'I won't tell anyone if you use your fingers.'

Jules looked to Marcus.

'Oh come on Mum,' he said. 'We promise not to drop any on the floor or feed Barney from the table... anyway he's far too fat already!'

Barney looked from Marcus to Jules, blinked resignedly, and got back in his basket obediently.

✯

It was dark by 5pm and Jules had lit the fire in the sitting room. They were all warming their hands and feet after a long trek around the lake to walk off the fish and chips and Jules was feeling much brighter. It was so lovely to have all the children home, and Martin got on so well with them all.

She watched Marcus and Sam's ease in each other's company; Sam pulling her legs up under her on the sofa while she was talking to Jemmie, and Marcus' arm automatically going up for her to slip under it for a cuddle. They never said a word and weren't even looking at each other. It was completely normal behaviour for them.

She thought back to the last time she and Paul had ever been like that together, but her mind was a blank because she didn't think they ever had been. He had his chair she had her chair and never the twain shall cuddle; Paul thought that sort of thing was for in bed with the lights out.

Well with her anyway.

She found herself wondering if they swung from the chandeliers or anything…

She shuddered a little to get herself out of that train of thought and then found herself watching Martin and Jemmie, and thought how lovely that would be. Their movements towards each other were very different. Tentative; shy almost. He looked at her when he thought she wasn't watching, and she looked at him when she thought he wasn't watching. But Jules was and any fool could see there was definite chemistry between them, even if they had only met yesterday. They were talking about Martin's cottage and Jemmie was telling Marcus about the garden.

'Martin has taken up deforestation and cleared the Secret Garden,' she laughed, letting her hand rest on his arm. 'He's even found our gate at the bottom that leads to Narnia!'

'And did it?' said Marcus, smiling.

Martin pushed Jemmie's hand playfully away. 'No, sadly. It just leads down to the shed and the dustbins.'

'But where's your imagination?' Marcus laughed, 'didn't you find sickly cousin Colin too?'

'I didn't, no... but Dipstick dug up some interesting bones so you never know!'

Jules went across to a cupboard at the base of a solidly built dark wood wall unit and took out the family photo album, to groans of protest from Jemmie and Marcus. Sam sat up to make room for Jules to sit down; keen to see the familiar but always entertaining pictures of Marcus as a little boy. Jules settled herself between her and Martin and leafed through the pages, looking for the picture she was after. And about a third of the way in, there it was: the two of them playing in the Secret Garden, and both of them absolutely filthy. Marcus was holding Jemmie's hand and smiling up into the camera, and Jemmie's head was tilted over to one side. She was wearing her little white sun hat with Peter Rabbit eating a carrot on it, and was squinting into the sun with one eye closed, poking out her little pink tongue. Marcus was showing off a very large and misshapen cooking apple.

Sam was in hysterics.

Jules remembered taking that photo, and it had been such a beautiful day. Marcus was about seven years old, and Jemmie six. Paul was there too, in the background, standing on his paint spattered step ladder passing cooking apples down to Mrs Bennett, who was putting them into a washing up bowl. She was wearing her habitual faded floral wrap over apron and slippers, and she had rollers in her hair, covered with a headscarf and tied in a knot at the back.

Jules became lost in the moment, and deaf to the giggles and teasing around her as she looked at the picture more closely, and specifically at Paul's face: a happy, smiling profile. He was younger, certainly, but happy in his task, and obviously sharing a joke with Mrs Bennett.

Not the serious and stern Paul of later years.

He had the most fabulous smile. She wondered why she hadn't it noticed before; she'd looked at that photo album often enough.

He was wearing those awful khaki shorts he loved, a green bush hat, and his ancient Marc Bolan tour T shirt had a rip in one shoulder.

She smiled slightly at the memory of Paul at school: back when she'd first noticed that dazzling smile: the glam rocker Paul of the early 1970's. There were no photos of that kind to laugh at in any album anywhere because he'd tracked them all down from his mother's and shredded them so they wouldn't be used against him.

Breaking the spell, Martin looked over Jemmie's shoulder at the photograph.

'Jemmie look at you!' he said. 'You look just like yourself!'

They all turned to look at him; eight furrowed brows in silent amusement.

'What?' he said, and then smiled. 'Sorry: I have an Irish grandmother. It means you haven't changed a bit!' he laughed.

Jemmie pulled a face and stuck her tongue out at him.

'See?' he said, still laughing, and ruffling her hair.

She punched his arm playfully.

Any excuse to touch each other, thought Jules, and wondered if they were as conscious of it as she was.

Jules' eyes were drawn back to looking at the album; this typical album of random photographs that truthfully told only a fragment of the story of the life of this family. The real story lay in the photographs that were never taken and framed, or carefully catalogued just like this, and kept. But here they were anyway, the fragments. The beaches, the sandcastles, the sticky faces; stately homes with grand gardens, cub camps brownie camps and endless gymkhana photos, with the young Jemmie grinning from ear to ear and showing off her coloured rosettes, and hugging Sparkler's velvety nose.

'Your dad must have taken most of these,' said Martin, turning to Jemmie. 'He's not in very many of them, is he?'

It was true. There were hardly any photos of him, glam rock or otherwise.

'That's because he was hardly ever there,' she said quietly.

'We had to look in the daily paper or Hello magazine if we wanted to see our dad...' said Marcus, fun now over and closing the album, placing it back on the coffee table.

Paul was standing in the kitchen. He had entered quietly, unsure of the reception he would receive, and Barney was caught napping and snoring loudly in his basket. Dipstick was curled up in front of the sitting room fire, and also fast asleep.

He had been taken completely by surprise when he heard their laughter as they looked through the photograph album, though he couldn't be sure what they were actually looking at, and he had wondered who the other man's voice was; so at home with his family. Worst of all, he had heard what Marcus had just said, and the truth had certainly hurt. He felt awkward and unready for another run in with Marcus that day.

He'd waited to see if there would be any defence from Jules on what Marcus had said, but there wasn't.

Of course he'd been around, he thought indignantly.

Well, some of the time.

He heard Jules say something about making some more coffee but then heard the sofa creak as Jemmie said she'd do it and obviously stood up. She came into the kitchen slowly and stopped dead in her tracks when she saw her father standing by the back door.

'What are *you* doing here?' she snapped.

Her exclamation brought Martin out into the kitchen after her, and Paul thought he looked vaguely familiar, and frowned slightly as he tried to think why.

Marcus followed them in next, and finally Sam, and Jules.

Both dogs woke up at that point and there was a superbly tactless chaos of welcome from both of them for a few minutes, Dipstick's raised hackles having retreated instantly at Barney's obvious joy at seeing his master after such a long time, before they were both banished into the utility room and the door banged shut on them.

Jules still looked flushed and as if she'd been laughing when she came in the kitchen, which was not what he had expected at all, and he found himself feeling slightly foolish. Faced with this tableau of solidarity, he blinked back what felt suspiciously like tears and became defensive, remarking the cosiness of the scene, and he asked Martin who he might be. Marcus smirked with some satisfaction and a great deal of deliberation as he introduced him.

'You remember Martin, Dad; Caroline's boyfriend? - ex boyfriend now I suppose, thanks to you.'

'Her name is Catherine,' said Paul, quietly.

'Well excuse me,' said Marcus.

Paul turned to Jules. 'What's he doing here Jules?'

The resentment, even hatred, in that kitchen was palpable, and he both felt it and saw it on all their faces; even hers. She didn't answer him, and Martin put his arm protectively around her shoulders.

Truthfully he hadn't been quite sure what to expect in the car driving down here, but he had kind of expected Jules to be at least a bit tearful or something. What he'd got though, looked decidedly like the gathering of the troops, and nobody was on his side of the battlefield either.

He pulled out a chair and sat heavily down at the table, and Jules looked around in silent request that they be left alone.

Marcus looked mutinous and his nostrils were flaring, but Jules nodded slowly, and gave him a not very confident but hopefully encouraging smile. She was well practised lately that a brave smile is remarkably good camouflage, and Sam gently took his arm and pulled him back towards the door.

Outwardly Paul's face showed complete control, but she knew that face as well as she knew her own, and every twitch and flicker that rippled across it. He was upset by this. Very upset indeed.

She went across to the sink and filled the kettle for something to do.

Paul continued to sit at the table and not say anything, but he drummed his fingers, ever so slightly.

In the sitting room Jemmie and Martin went over to the sofa. Martin patted the cushion next to him for her to sit beside him and, without even thinking about it, his arm slid around her shoulders at she sat down. Without even thinking about it she let her head rest against him and placed her hand on his chest. Three of her fingers slipped unconsciously between two of the buttons on his shirt, and she could feel thick and wiry chest hair beneath it.

She could feel his heart beating, and he could feel hers.

He bent his head slightly and kissed the top of her head very gently, and her fingers moved, just a little.

Marcus was standing with one arm on the mantel and staring into the fire, kicking absently at the logs with one foot to move them farther back, and Sam sat on the corner of one armchair facing the door, and biting her thumbnail nervously.

Nobody said a word: they were all listening.

# Chapter eight

'So...Jules. Please say something,' Paul said.

Jules, making a large pot of coffee and arranging cups on a battered old wicker edged tray with heavy horses pulling a plough on it that Marcus had won at a fete somewhere, was fighting for words but outwardly her rigid back and stony silence was making him even more uncomfortable.

She placed two cups and saucers on the kitchen table with a clatter, and then carried the tray into the sitting room. Returning with the half empty coffee pot, she poured the last two. Placing the empty pot on the table and exhausted of anything else to put it off, she sat down.

Damn it. She'd left the sugar behind. Well he'd just have to do without it, like she did.

'Well?' he said.

'Well what...' It wasn't a question. Then before he could reply, she lifted her head and thrust her chin towards him. 'You were asking what Martin is doing here?' Only her shirt collar was betraying the heavy beating of her heart as it quivered slightly.

'I was,' he said, 'I wasn't sure... at first. But then I saw he's fond of... Jemmie; it may be a bit awkward but...'

'Oh... it's *me* who's had sex with him...!' she blurted, to gain the upper hand. 'After all, you know what they say... what's good for the goose is good for the gander...'

His mouth fell open and his chin dropped. 'You've *what?*'

Her voice pitched higher and became shrill. 'We had sex, Paul...and what's more we had a marvellous time!'

From the sitting room Jules heard a cup and saucer rattle and then crash onto what she assumed was the coffee table. Then there were sounds of movement, she heard Martin's voice say 'No! Wait, please!' and she heard the sound of someone running up the stairs.

Jemmie.

There was some shouting that she could not distinguish, and then a bedroom door slammed.

She closed her eyes in horror, and covering her mouth with one hand, she began to shake her head, slowly.

Paul's head suddenly went back like someone had thrown a punch at him.

'What is this Jules? What on *earth* is going on here?' he demanded.

'Paul, please, just go. Get out of here and leave us alone...' she said.

'I most certainly will not! Not until you explain what this is all about!'

That took her by surprise, and she snapped. He'd betrayed and humiliated her, all over the newspapers, he'd left her; he'd gone. What had just happened was her crisis, and here he was, still demanding to be the centre of attention.

She stood up, placed the palms of her hands decisively on the table in front of her and looked directly into his angry eyes; that blinked first. Her whole shirt was shaking now: what gave him the right to swan in here and.... She took a very deep breath and thumped down on the table with a clenched fist that clattered the cups and saucers noisily and helped to clarify every point she made.

'*This...* is the crap hitting the fan Paul.

*This* is what happens to your family when you run off to play the stud with some clone that's the same bloody age as your daughter!

*This* is what happens when you betray and abandon the woman you professed to... how did it go? To... love and honour for the rest of your life forsaking *all* others... 'Till death us do part... that you seem to have conveniently forgotten.'

*This*, Paul, is your wife; yes...your WIFE.... Remember me? and your FAMILY in freefall: It's what happens in the real world while you're pretending there are no repercussions to your selfish actions... hiding your head in the bloody sand...' adding, as he stood up, his mouth gaping like a goldfish gasping for breath, 'as per usual.'

'You never swear!' he said, bizarrely, but he looked sufficiently shocked.

She closed her eyes briefly and then opened them again. 'I'm doing lots of things I never do, Paul. I never committed adultery before; I thought it would be liberating but as you can no doubt see it just made everything a whole lot worse. That's what adultery does Paul. Every time. It's *never* worth it.... And what's more I'm turning into a lush and am generally drunk by eight o'clock.' She sank back into her chair and sighed deeply, willing herself to calm down.

'You moved the goal posts Paul, and everything is different now.'

The awkward silence was broken when Martin barged through the kitchen at some speed and out of the back door without looking at either of them.

Jules closed her eyes again and began to cry softly. 'Please Paul, just go away and stay away. You're ultimately responsible for the madness that is reigning in this house now. Just leave us alone,' she repeated.

※

Jemmie lay on her bed and sobbed into Dodgy, her threadbare old dog toy. Until that moment she hadn't realised just how much she wanted Martin, and it had shocked her. She'd had her fair share of boyfriends and had even thought herself to be in love once; but she had never felt anything remotely like as strong as this before, and after so short a time too. If she closed her eyes she saw his face, his smile. She'd felt his skin beneath his shirt with her hand; felt his touch and the heat of his breath as he had kissed the top of her head just a few moments ago. She'd had to physically force her lips from reaching up to meet his, as if they were magnetised or had a mind of their own, impatient for the right moment. But now it would never be the right moment; could never be the right moment, and she was spinning, reeling, from the truth. She felt physically sick and the bile rose in her throat when she thought of it: her own mother…and him… she shuddered. She couldn't even think about it.

He'd run up the stairs after her of course; pleading with her, trying to grasp her arm, but she had slammed her bedroom door shut on him and locked it, only narrowly missing his fingers, and now he'd gone. She'd heard the back door slam behind him and the sound of his boots on the gravel path, retreating rapidly down to the gate that had been flung open and hit the stay post with a such a crash; she thought he might even have been running. He hadn't even collected his dog, still imprisoned and whining in the utility room with Barney.

Her room was directly above the kitchen, and she turned onto her back and listened, but all was quiet downstairs now. On a sudden and overwhelming impulse to get away she realised she couldn't stay there in that house of horrors a minute longer. Pulling herself up from the bed hurriedly she tugged her bag out from the bottom of the wardrobe with such force that the whole thing wobbled precariously and a huge sombrero, a keepsake from a long forgotten holiday in Spain, fell and rolled in a spiral like a coin to the end of the bed. Kicking it out of the way angrily she grabbed wildly for the few clothes she'd brought with her on this fateful trip, and with hangers flying in all directions she stuffed her clothes into the bag and made for the door. She could not wait to leave this house and get back to some kind of reality, even if it was her reality; work and sleep, work and sleep.

She passed Marcus on the stairs without saying a single word to him, despite his efforts at trying to calm her down, and let herself out of the front door: grappling with the thick iron bolts and the chain on the enormous oak door that never got used, so that she wouldn't have to cross the kitchen and see or hear either of them try to talk to her. Once outside she fumbled in her bag for her car keys in the pitch dark, and she had an obscure thought to blame her father for not being around as he should have been, to fix the broken porch light.

From the kitchen Jules heard Jemmie's car start and ran outside into the rain, calling her. Jemmie almost ran her over, and sped off, narrowly missing both her and the gate post, and up Clearwater Lane towards the main road; music blaring over the sounds of her mother's tearful shouts, and deep puddles leaping in shock up the grassy banks in the lane as she plunged through them.

It was raining very hard now, and her wipers beat in rhythm with the anonymous but very loud thumping music from the car radio.

She flew past Martin's cottage with a howl of rage and distress, but as she approached the top of the lane, her lights caught something in the way, just ahead. She slowed down and leaned forward, wiping frantically at the steamed up windscreen with the back of one hand in an effort to see what it was.

It was a vehicle; a dark green 4x4, virtually invisible in the dark and the rain, and worse still because it was parked across the road, at right angles, and there was no way she could get past it in the narrow lane that had four feet of rabbit hole polka dots puncturing the grassy banks on either side.

Only idiots drive dark green cars in the country, she thought angrily. You just can't see them.

Stopping her car, but leaving the engine running, she got out.

Her headlights on main beam in the dark, the gusty wind and the incessant rain made it impossible to see any obvious reason why it could have been left there. She looked ahead of it for signs of a fallen tree or something, but there was nothing. It didn't seem to be damaged and there were no lumps of bank in the road so it was unlikely it had skidded…. Moving back towards it she walked around to the passenger door and cupped her hands to blinker her eyes from her own car's headlights as she tried to look through the window.

Suddenly the back door flung open and someone reached out, grabbed her from behind and pulled her inside.

✯

Back at the house, Marcus and Sam were trying to comfort Jules at the kitchen table. Paul had gone at practically the same moment as Martin, likewise in disgust and without even looking at her. Her darling Jemmie had fled into the dark, far too distressed to be driving anywhere, and her mobile phone rang forlornly from the coffee table in the sitting room when Sam had tried ringing her as well.

Marcus went to the drinks cabinet in the sitting room and came back carrying a bottle of his father's very good brandy, and a brandy glass. Pouring out a generous, even for a double, measure, he passed it to Jules.

'Medicinal,' he said.

Jules took it meekly, and then gulped at it. She spluttered as the burning liquid seared down her already raw from crying throat and drew in a sharp breath before wheezing; 'thanks....'

Meanwhile, making good time in the light traffic of the late evening, and currently negotiating joining the M4 at Reading , Paul was very rattled. His house was in total chaos and his wife had shocked him by totally flipping out.

Jules never flipped out.

And as for that Martin... specimen; what was his game? Destroying the women in his life just to get back at him for stealing his girlfriend? It was like a plot in one of those silly films Jules liked to watch and didn't think he knew about.

Catherine hadn't mentioned anything about Martin being malicious. She'd said he'd been a pussycat about the whole thing.

He hadn't acted up, she'd said.

He'd been a walkover, she'd said.

And what's more he hadn't even been in touch with her since they broke up, or caused any embarrassing scenes at galleries, sent any texts or got in the way... or been even the slightest awkward.

'No, it was because he was sadistically setting about wrecking my family for me in revenge instead,' he thought.

Listening to Classic FM as a calming influence he was going much faster than the national speed limit, but once his brain had started to recognise the emotional opening bars of Barber's Adagio for Strings, he pressed the radio's 'seek' button to find something less gut wrenching to listen to. Finding a different station the car suddenly exploded with a loud and hideous drum and bass booming noise and, pulling a very impatient expression he quickly pressed the seek button again.

It found Jazz Fm; that was much better, and better still, they were playing a live Michael Bublé performance.

Michael Bublé. He thought about him for a moment as he sailed along in the outside lane, and smiled slightly.

They'd met on a flight to New York a couple of years ago, and had sat together on the plane. He remembered him saying that his wife was a big fan and had a few of his paintings and some sketches. They'd got talking then, and Michael told him that he'd missed being with his wife for her birthday the day before due to some TV appearance mess up, and felt really bad about it.

A little while later he had fallen asleep, and Paul had been left to his own thoughts. He could never sleep on flights himself, and had taken out his sketch pad and had absently begun to draw Michael as he'd slept. He had been thrilled to bits with it when he woke up and saw it there, on the table in front of him, and intended giving it to his wife as a gift for missing her birthday. He'd been really excited about it, and said she would love it, Paul remembered, and it had made him feel good.

As the sound of his voice filled the speeding car, he was totally engrossed in the concert and his memories and wondered if Jules knew it was on. He was even about to ring and tell her, but corrected himself as he'd reached for the phone, clenching his fist away from it and shaking his head to stop his mind from wandering.

He was just about to leave the motorway at the Hammersmith Flyover when Michael began to sing 'Home'.

He hadn't heard that one before, and the contemporary style took him by surprise a little.

*'I feel just like I'm living someone else's life...'* and then it went on, *'and I'm surrounded by a million people- I still feel all alone...'*

The words of the song made the whole mess of his disastrous journey hit him at that moment. He pulled over into a derelict garage forecourt as his vision began to blur and, gripping the steering wheel tightly, he'd never felt so desolate in his life. He sat there with his head on the steering wheel until the song finished, and then turned off the radio, but within seconds jumped horribly, his heart pounding, when his mobile rang and broke the spell. He wiped his eyes with the back of his hand, taking a few deep breaths before he answered it.

'Where are you?' she said.

'I'm just on my way back...' he replied.

'I was getting worried...'

'I'm almost there,' he said, and hung up quickly before she could hear the crack in his voice.

# Chapter nine

Catherine put down the telephone and smiled to herself as she went into the kitchen to check the oven; ten minutes to eight; perfect timing.

Lifting the lid on the bin, she extracted the bag and tied its yellow neck strings together. She went into the hallway; pulled open the waste disposal hatch, placed the bag inside, and pushed the yellow button. Then she returned to the kitchen and washed her perfectly manicured and acrylic French-tipped-that-afternoon hands.

Evidence successfully destroyed; she thought smugly, whilst peeping once more into the oven at the highly professional looking rack of lamb, Paul's favourite, warming inside.

She opened the ready cooked and glazed baby vegetables and put the dish into the oven to warm up, then lifted up the equally professional looking roasted in goose fat potatoes and put those in too.

She checked the frozen lemon roulade, also Paul's favourite, to make sure it was suitably semi defrosted, and then she checked the table.

Satisfied, she dimmed the light switches, lit the candles on the table and walked across to the CD player.

Michael Bublé; she thought, extracting the CD from its box: definitely time for a little smooth and sexy Michael Bublé.

When Paul walked through the door he looked absolutely shattered. His hair was a mess and looked as though he had been tearing his hands through it, and his coat was undone, with the belt wet and dragging muddily on the floor. From the look of it, it had been shut in the car door and been dragging the road surface all the way there.

She finished pouring the wine as he entered, and took a glass over to him as he just stood by the door. She helped him remove his wet coat and pushed him gently backwards towards a huge leather armchair whilst sexily removing a tendril of hair from his forehead, out of his eyes. Once he was seated she unlaced his shoes. Removing each one very gently, she massaged his feet; letting her hands caress them seductively. Kneeling up, she ran her hands along the length of his thighs, and lifted her face up to kiss him.

Meanwhile the song that had so upset him in the car was coming back in for another attack from the CD player.

*'...my words were cold and flat, and you deserved more than that...'*

His arms shot around her as he leaned in to kiss her back, so passionately that she almost lost her balance and fluffed the single movement that was intended to take her from kneeling on the floor to sitting across his lap.

His breathing was ragged and his heart was pounding.

'Down boy!' she said seductively, thrilled with the way should make him want her with no effort at all and pulling away from him, 'I've cooked you something special,' adding, 'I've been slaving away all afternoon.'

Pulling himself together and taking a mammoth gulp of his wine he straightened his tie and stood up.

'I thought something smelled tasty,' he said, with forced enthusiasm. 'I'm famished.' Then, heading for the CD player he pressed the stop button to halt the attack and said; 'let's listen to something else; I've been listening to him all the way ho...here.' He changed the CD for a Simply Red one that was on the top of the pile on the floor, and put the Michael Bublé one back in its case, trying to ignore the knowing smile that looked up at him from the cover photograph.

Turning, he watched as she brought the food through from the kitchen with total and completely plausible innocence, and placed his meal in front of him. Realising that he was in fact famished, he demolished the whole plateful in record time, but apart from the occasional 'mmm', he was very quiet and she could see he was most definitely preoccupied with something.

'Am I the perfect cook?' she said, gathering up his plate.

'You are,' he said, visibly snapping out of whatever it was that he was preoccupied with, and patting his full stomach.

'Better than Jules...?'

He really wasn't in the mood for her games, not after the day he'd just had. His shoulders slumped, and he snapped at her. 'Don't fish for compliments against Jules, Catherine. It doesn't do you any favours with me.'

She looked hurt and gave him the benefit of her ultra long eyelashes in an exaggerated blink as if she were going to cry so he apologised instantly, and crossed to take her in his arms. 'I'm sorry, I've had quite a day,' he said, closing his eyes tightly as he held her there, willing the picture of Jules' stricken face out of his head.

After recovering himself to enjoy the perfectly semi defrosted lemon roulade, Paul folded his napkin slowly and was surprised when Catherine came back out of the kitchen carrying a bottle of very expensive champagne in an ice bucket, and some fresh strawberries in a little glass dish.

Collecting the only two crystal champagne flutes in what was an otherwise empty glass cabinet, she turned to face him.

'What are we celebrating?' he asked, looking up at her.

She smiled, silkily, 'Just us my darling, just us.'

She knew perfectly well he'd been to see Jules in Frincham. She'd phoned Hugo looking for him before she'd phoned him in the car, and he'd been so evasive about Paul's whereabouts she'd guessed, and her mind had been working overtime ever since. She hadn't worked this hard to get him only to see him go back to that worthless plump frump of a woman with the mad hair wife of his.

Alone in the bedroom momentarily because she'd encouraged Paul to take a shower and relax, she sat down on the bed, opened her handbag, and removed a small sheet of paper.

There were three steps in her plan to keep her prize.

Step one: The best way to a man's heart is through his stomach. He might not have fallen for her attempt to get him to prefer her cooking to Jules', but it was obvious he'd loved every mouthful.

Step two: Was to just about to happen: she smiled to herself; that would be easy. Sex with her against sex with the frump was no contest at all, and her eyes glanced at the lingerie shop carrier bag lying, almost smouldering, by the side of the bed.

Then step three, she smiled again, should seal the deal.

She looked at the prescription she'd received for her contraceptive pills just that afternoon, and tore it slowly in half, and then in half again, dropping the pieces like confetti, into the waste paper basket.

# Chapter ten

'What the hell do you think you're doing?' she yelled, arms flailing, legs kicking, and trying everything she could to get away from him.

'I'm not letting you go until you've given me a chance to explain,' he said, trying to keep a hold of her, and protect himself from her flying fingernails at the same time.

He let go momentarily and leaned over to push the child lock button in the driver's seat door to prevent her from escaping.

'Let me out!' she yelled. 'Martin! Open this bloody door.... Right NOW!'

'Stop it!' he said, tugging her hand off the door handle to stop her pulling it off, and then, slightly more calmly, 'Jemmie stop it. I just want to talk to you.'

'Drop dead!' she yelled, but had at least given up the fight with the door handle. She folded her arms mutinously, and stared down into her lap rather than look at him. He watched her as her chin jutted forward with her own variety of pout again and she looked about six.

There was silence for a moment, apart from her very heavy breathing and the sound of the rain and the wind against the windows.

'Have you quite finished?' he said. 'May I speak now please?'

She didn't answer him, but her heart was pounding and he could see it bouncing away under her sweater. Still trying the get her to talk to him he said; 'you're steaming up the windows...what will people think?' and he tried to smile.

'They'll probably think you're in here with my mother!' she said, fixing her eyes on his briefly, and glaring at him.

Martin took a sharp intake of breath and let it out as a huge and frustrated sigh, and shook his head slightly.

'It wasn't like that!' he said, 'please Jemmie, trust me, it wasn't like that at all.'

'Oh do tell me,' she snapped, 'then I'll have something to say when we go on Jerry bloody Springer!'

He waited for her to stop hissing before he started to explain.

'We were both... we were both so... reeling, I suppose, reeling from losing the partners we'd loved and trusted Jems... and it was ten times worse for her... she's given him thirty years Jemmie... thirty years!'

'I'm well aware how long she's given him Martin...'

'Yes but Catherine and I were only together for eighteen months... but I still loved her with all my heart... or believed I did. We needed to know we were still, I don't know... desirable, I think. It sends you sideways; a bit deranged, when you get dumped for someone else like that, believe me. You don't know which way is up, even... you can't eat... you can't sleep....'

He adjusted his sitting position to face her and continued, 'We'd got into the habit of spending our evenings together and we were drinking... a lot. We didn't know what we were doing that night. I don't even know if we actually did... it.' He looked at her, giving up on that tack; he knew full well what they had done as well as Jemmie did, but only he knew why, and he was too ashamed to say.

'It was just that one time Jemmie.'

She snorted and turned away from him, watching the raindrops trying to beat the blustery wind and trickle down the window.

'It was Jems, honestly. And it wasn't her fault, it was mine. I lost my head that night. We both realised it was a mistake right then and I left before she even woke up. It was awful. We didn't speak for days. She knew it was a terrible mistake as well as I did. Eventually it was her that broke the tension and sent me a text, so I went over. I... I can't get right round the lake without passing the house and Dipstick kept vaulting the gate to get to see her and kept whining for Barney... and we're really good friends and I missed talking to her... we had this... mess, in common you see... and no one else understands like she does. Anyway we talked it through and we agreed never to discuss... never to discuss it. Ever....'

'Until she threw it in my dad's face tonight.'

'She was just trying to hurt him back, that's all. I realise that now.'

'It worked. He took off up that lane doing about 60 miles an hour. I'm surprised he didn't hit you, parked like this.'

'No... I saw him take off when I was still running back home along the water's edge. Once I got there I got into my car and was going off... I don't know where. Then I turned round at the top and found myself heading back towards the lake. I was on my way back to you, Jems. I could hear your mum shouting and you screeching away over the top of the engine.... So I just stopped here and blocked the road, to stop you. I had to stop you.

I don't want you to go Jems, not like this, not before I'd had the chance to explain properly.' He took her hand and kissed it, and she didn't take it away. 'Jems, if I could change it I would and it never would have happened.' He wound his fingers through hers. 'Trust me... please, I'm not in love with, and I'm not having an affair with, your mum.'

She looked at him, and pulled her hand away. 'You can't *seriously* still be in love with Catherine the Clone that has wrecked everything?'

'No I'm not,' he said, taking it back again. 'I'm falling in love with you... and I never felt anything *like* this about her Jemmie. I never felt anything like this with anyone before!'

He lifted her hand with his to wipe away an angry tear, and then carried the tear on her hand to his mouth, and kissed it away.

※

Back in the kitchen at home, Marcus put down the telephone. Jules was still sitting at the table and looked absolutely terrible; her eyes puffy and her nose red from crying. Her hands were cupped around the mug of hot chocolate with a drop of brandy in it that Sam had made her, and she was distractedly chaineating marshmallows. She was warm from sitting alongside the Aga, but still shivering from the shock of the last couple of hours, and the dogs had been freed from their prison and were curled up in a comforting heap in Barney's enormous basket, watchful and attentive and with their ears down dejectedly at the atmosphere in the room.

Marcus sat down next to his mother, put his arm around her shoulders, and moved the huge bag of marshmallows farther away from her.

'That was Martin,' he said quietly. She shuddered and cast her eyes downwards, and closed them.

'It's ok Mum, he's found her, and she's fine. He's taken her back to his cottage, and… he says he wants to take care of her.'

She laid her head on his shoulder.

'He said he loves her, Mum.'

'Of course he does,' said Sam, 'anyone can see that, Jules. They'll be ok… and once she wakes up and sees she loves him too she'll be ok too… honestly. This is the blessing that's come out of all this Jules.…'

She started to cry again; great heaving sobs this time and Marcus sat and gently rubbed her shoulder, knowing that at this point, this was all better out than in, and Sam went to find a fresh box of tissues.

✶

At about 3am the following morning, Martin was still awake and staring at the ceiling, trying to comprehend and believe everything that had happened during the last few hours. His bedroom curtains hadn't been drawn together and the rain was still falling in all directions, tapping at the window in the blustery wind as though somebody was throwing millions of tiny little stones up at it, trying to gain his attention.

The moon was full but its beam was intermittent between the storm clouds that were rapidly scudding across the sky. When freed to shine though, it cast a brilliant golden shadow across the bed, and a smaller moon shone out like a glowing eye in the darkness, reflected in the mirror on the wardrobe door.

…And Jemmie was there, curled up next to him and breathing the long slow breaths of contented sleep; her head resting on his shoulder and her hair tickling his neck just has it had earlier that evening. He turned his head and looked at her lying there, with her skin glistening like a marble statue in the reflected moonlight. His heart was almost bursting with what felt like he'd just drunk at least thirty cups of very strong black coffee, and when he kissed the top of her head, she murmured his name sleepily.

He smiled; a great beam of a smile, in the certain knowledge that she was all his, and that although it was quite true: most people would say it had all happened far too quickly, he knew he'd argue. He'd known it before tonight. He'd known it from the first moment he'd set eyes on her in Jules' kitchen, when she'd looked so tired and small, with her hair all over the place and her face devoid of all cosmetic adornment save for a cherry flavoured chapstick. From the moment she'd walked in the back door he could see the rest of his life ahead of him, and she was in it, and he wanted it no other way.

✦

Jules went to bed, Jemmie's bed, with an awful headache. The kind of headache she always got when she was upset or stressed out: across the back of her neck and right up into her skull, and the kind of headache that no tablet would help.

She'd found the little bottle of Paul's sleeping pills, or elephant pills, as he called them, in his bathroom cabinet, taken a couple and gone out like a light.

She woke up around ten o'clock the next morning to the enticing smell of bacon again, and she managed a small but nonetheless definite smile. What was it about the smell of bacon anyway?

Creeping out from under the duvet she put her hand to her head and groaned slightly, reinforcing the certain knowledge that you should never go to bed with a headache because you are sure to wake up with it too. She pulled on Jemmie's dressing gown and, trying to ignore the insult to injury induced sleeping pill hangover, looked over the banisters.

She could hear the soft mumble of voices in the kitchen, and the sound of the radio.

Heading down the stairs and into the kitchen she found Martin, Jemmie and Sam companionably making breakfast. Jemmie's arms were wrapped around Martin's waist and she was nibbling at his left ear as he tried to turn the bacon over in the pan with a fork, and he was both protesting and laughing at the same time.

They turned around when they heard her come in, but looked very far from the angry and upset people they'd been last night. In fact there was a distinct sparkle in two of those eyes, she realised: and her cheeks were flushed too. The overworked automaton casualty doctor look of the last few days was well and truly gone, and she looked... amazing.

Head slightly tipped to one side, and her eyebrows slightly raised, Jules looked at her daughter in silent query. Jemmie came forward and hugged her tightly.

'I'm so sorry about last night Mum. That was the last thing you needed.' She looked back at Martin, and then she smiled a huge beaming smile. 'Oh, and I've nicked your toy boy...' she laughed. Jules was speechless but before she could make a reply Marcus came in the back door at that moment carrying a loaf of bread, still warm from the bakery, and a container of milk.

'Mum, you need to do some shopping!' he said, and kissed the top of her head. 'Sam and I almost resorted to dog biscuits as our breakfast cereal this morning but we didn't even have any milk to put on them. These two lovebirds arrived in the nick of time and brought the bacon over.' He pulled a face and pretended to put a finger down his own throat and Sam slapped his arm playfully as she took the bread and milk from him.

Buoyed up by the atmosphere in the room and blissfully happy to be forgiven by Jemmie and Martin, Jules sat down at the table.

'I'll have shower and go to Waitrose this morning,' she said tentatively.

'I'll take you,' said Marcus, 'I was starving after you went to bed last night and resorted to eating all your marshmallows... and I know how ugly you get if we haven't got any!'

✯

A couple of hours later Marcus and Jules were wandering the aisles of the nearest Waitrose, scanning the shelves for bargains but inevitably talking about Paul.

'He can't be serious about her!' said Marcus.

'I think he must be,' she replied, her eyes scanning the bread shelves for a loaf that would feed five people for lunch and resorting to two long baguettes.

'But his reaction last night when you said about Martin...'

'He was just taken by surprise that's all. That was just his male pride.' The bread went into the trolley and they headed for the meat aisles.

'*He* was taken by surprise? You should have seen Jemmie's face!'

'Don't!' she said, putting a hand across her eyes, but was able to afford a smile.

'No, seriously Mum, his reaction just proves he still has feelings for you, I'm sure of it.'

'Don't get your hopes up darling, I have to believe it's really all over and so should you all. He's made his bed...' she pulled a face at him and decided not to finish the quote. 'We've just grown apart over the years, it's nothing new. It happens in marriages when you spend so much time apart. He's spent years fulfilling his dreams and I've just been... here.'

'Bringing us up...' he said.

'I wouldn't have had it any other way.' She kissed him on the shoulder because he was too tall for now for the more familiar motherly kiss on the top of his head.

'Well I'm not going to make that mistake with Sam,' he said. 'Where we go, we go together.'

'Anyone can see that,' she replied, smiling at him.

Stopping suddenly as she made an instant decision she said; 'Marcus I've been thinking,' as if she had, and he stopped pushing the trolley. 'I need to do something with my life...Half my problem is I have too much time on my hands. I need something to do. Not to mention if your father has really gone... for good... I need to provide for myself...so... I've been thinking of going back to work.'

# Chapter eleven

'If I intend staying in this house I'll need to earn some money,' she continued, back in the kitchen and taking the packets and tins from Marcus as she stacked them neatly on the shelves in the pantry.

'Don't you think something smaller would be more manageable? said Sam, 'I mean this is a huge place for just you...'

'I'm staying here,' she said, with conviction. 'This is the family home and it's where all my... memories are. I can't leave here...I just can't.'

Marcus looked at her. 'Well if you really want to stay here then Dad can help you out, he owes it to you. There's no mortgage or anything to pay on it and it's not as if he can't afford to let you stay here. It's the least he can do...' he said, heaving a large bag of potatoes to the corner of the pantry so his mother wouldn't have to.

She closed the pantry door and went back into the kitchen with Marcus following behind.

'I don't want him to support me,' she said defiantly.

'Call it compensation then! And then you'd get a decent settlement if it does come to a divorce…you're entitled to that you know.' He flopped down on a chair at the table and took the mug of tea that Sam held out for him.

Jules looked uncomfortable, 'Yes, well, in the meantime, I want to support myself,' she said brusquely, sitting down opposite him and taking a mug of coffee from Sam. 'There are the stables and the paddock too, I can rent those out, and I could advertise the walled garden as allotments. There's a real shortage of allotments you know and people want to grow their own things these days, with all those pesticides. There must be a few plots worth over there… and it's sheltered and south facing… I'm sure it will get snapped up.'

'You have been giving this a lot of thought,' Marcus said.

'I have,' Jules replied, convincingly; all the way back in the car.

'I'm far too old to be a trendy hairdresser these days, but there'll be a job in a school or something I could do. I liked that too. I'm sure I can do some kind of a refresher course or something…'

'I'll get online for you,' Marcus said.

'I'll get the computer switched on then,' said Sam, getting up and heading for the study.

※

Three days later Jemmie was saying a long and passionate goodbye to Martin outside his cottage, having already said a long and passionate goodbye to Martin inside his cottage, and a considerably less emotional one, but still heartfelt, to her mother an hour and a half before that. She was hugely encouraged by her plan to get a job, and by her new money raising schemes.

She sounded so much more positive now. Marcus had found a Teaching Assistant's course in Woodley, not very far away, and he'd also found a number she could call to talk to someone about setting up allotments in the walled garden. There was light in her eyes now, like she had a purpose again, and Jemmie knew it was time for her to go, and get back to her own life; how ever hard the pull to stay.

'I have to GO!' she said, pulling away from him and opening her car door.

'Stay forever,' he said.

'I'll lose my job and then what will I live off of?' she laughed.

'Me' he replied.

Sam having already gone home on the train, and having dutifully made his mother a great long list of things to do and people to call about her new projects Marcus finished packing his bag and headed downstairs to the kitchen. Jules was unpacking the dishwasher and tunelessly humming to a song on the radio.

'Are you sure you're ok if I go?' he said.

'I'll be fine,' she smiled. 'I've got loads to do, and I start college in two weeks and then I'll go and find a school.'

He walked over and hugged her tightly. 'I know I don't say this often enough but, I'm dead proud of you Mum,' he said.

'Get back to London then and help Sam sort out your appointments or you'll get struck off!' she smiled.

She walked out to the car with him, wiping her hands on a tea towel, and reached up to kiss him goodbye.

'When did you get so tall?' she said, pulling at his shirt so she could reach his face. He smiled, giving her a great bear hug, and climbed into the car. Starting the engine, he began to pull away slowly, and then leaning slightly out of the window he looked back at her, still smiling; 'I love you Mum. Keep your dimple up!' she drew in a sharp breath and was caught out momentarily: he looked just like his father. Pulling herself quickly together she smiled and swallowed hard, putting her little finger into the dimple on her chin and lifting her head, but blinking rapidly. She waved him away, and then walked slowly back into the house. Looking around the kitchen she gripped the back of a chair hard and took a few deep breaths to steady herself. She was all alone now. Taking a final calming breath and blowing it out slowly, she muttered, 'right then.' Picking up the list of numbers and email addresses that Marcus had gleaned from the internet for her, she stepped over a prostrate Barney who was lying flat out on his back with his tail wagging and his legs in the air in front of the Aga, 'What does Catherine do for diamonds?' she said wistfully, rubbing his fat belly on the way past, and walked across the room to pick up the telephone.

⭐

Having arranged an appointment with the chairman of the local allotments committee, an hour later, muffled sounds were emanating from the cupboard under the stairs in the boot room. 'Where are they?' she muttered crossly, 'everyone else's but not mine. I really must sort this cupboard out…Ah ha! Got one, now where's the other one?' then an 'Ouch!' as she hit her head on a shelf, followed by a triumphant, 'got it!'

She reversed out from the depths of the cupboard holding a pair of rather misshapen from years of neglect, trainers. One of them for sometime having been under one leg of the ancient wooden stepladder

Paul was photographed standing on, picking apples in Mrs Bennett's garden.

Having seen Jemmie off, Martin was loading his van with lighting equipment and preparing to set off on a job. 'Come on Dipstick!' he called. Dipstick appeared at his usual gallop from the back of the cottage, but instead of jumping in the van, through the door that Martin was holding open for him; he took off down the lane, barking.

'Damn it!' Martin shouted, slamming the door shut and taking off after him, 'Dipstick! Damn you, you stupid animal! You're going to make me late!'

Just around the next bend he heard the sound of a woman's voice, and Dipstick whining ecstatically. He was more than a bit surprised to find Jules in grey jog pants and an old t shirt, presumably one of Marcus' because it said *'Gun's 'n' Roses'* on the front and he couldn't imagine Paul being much of a fan, and a pair of lurid pink trainers, apparently out jogging. She had a very ethnic looking bum bag clipped around her waist, looked extremely hot and bothered and her hair was so frizzy it looked like she'd stuck her finger in a socket.

'Hi,' she panted, still out of breath, and grabbing Dipstick's collar so he couldn't run off again, '...thought I'd jog to the Post office, I need stamps....You just off?'

Handing her his back door key because she'd promised to keep an eye on things for him, he replied,

'I am.' Then, looking her up and down, said, ' er... Jules...?'

She waved one hand at him dismissively, putting the key in her bag.

'If I'm going to try and get a job I'll need to fit in something smarter than my usual wardrobe, so I'm going to try and get some weight off.'

She handed Dipstick back to him and he smiled, and gave her an oblivious-to-the-sweaty-t-shirt hug.

'Will you be gone long?' she asked, hugging him back.

'All this week,' he replied, 'then I'm picking up Jemmie and we're going to go away for the weekend together, assuming she can get the time off.'

'If she can't it won't be for want of trying,' she said. 'I'm so pleased this is working out for you two.'

He smiled. 'Thanks Jules,' and then kissed her lovingly on the end of her nose.

Waving him off with Dipstick's head poking through the open passenger window, panting happily and with his tongue lolling in the fresh air, she stood for a few moments with her hands on her hips. Checking her watch she breathed in for motivation and continued on her way up the steep hill to the post office.

✹

The village square in Frincham was actually more of a triangle. Dominating one side was the imposing wattle and daub fourteenth century Michelin starred and thatched pub and restaurant called the Royal Oak: leaning slightly drunkenly to one side from hundreds of years of subsidence and with its leaded windows glinting in the autumn sunshine. The oak from which it took its name had been felled many years ago with disease, and its remaining stump formed the centre of a mini roundabout in the centre of the triangle. The butchers shop, called Griffin's, stood on the corner of the second angle and had been in the same family for many generations, and its current custodian, Ken Griffin, waved to Jules as she approached. The shop was double fronted and still boasted its huge and Dickensian bow windows, through which she could see the array of meats, pies and pasty's that were temptingly on offer. Jules detoured briefly into the shop to buy a pasty for her lunch and some sausages. In doing so, as usual, she gained a large shin bone as a special treat for Barney too.

Leaving the butcher's she stood and took in the rest of the square for a moment. Directly opposite the Royal Oak, and on the third angle, stood a row of three terraced black and white 'chocolate box' cottages, thatched as one, and at the end, by the bakery and the grocer's shop, stood a much larger property set farther back and semi obscured by the cottages, and with a sweeping semi circular driveway. This was originally the manor house of the village, and was Jacobean in style with characteristic windows, lintels, and a huge front door right in its centre that must have had a key the size of a spanner.

The village's second, and most popular with the locals, pub, was called the White Hart, and stood to the side of the road just down the lane from the square, sitting comfortably between the village hall and the school. The square towered Norman church and its Rectory stood opposite the school, but set back with a slightly raised aspect of very old churchyard and a war memorial.

The bakery required the use of blinkers and a nose clamp to pass it without temptation and the grocers shop, called Mattesons, was also double fronted and boasted its original bow windows, which wore an array of posters and fluorescent 'bang' stickers indicating the special offers not to be missed inside. This was also the post office, and where Jules was headed. Outside the shop stood a Victorian red VR letter box, of which the village was very proud, and tended annually with a fresh coat of post office red paint. It was equally proud that it had managed to retain its old red telephone box too, that stood on the corner by the butchers.

Having passed the time of day for ten minutes in the shop and suffered the embarrassed looks that were obviously passing between the two assistants trying to decide whether to mention Paul or not, she was putting her stamps into her bag and standing right by the door, when it flew open suddenly, sending her sharply backwards to avoid it, and the sound of bickering children broke the air nosily, tearing into the shop like a whirlwind. 'Batty LEAVE IT!' yelled the child's mother, 'Looby Loo darling hold my hand...Tesco? Oh, there you are. Good girl!'

'Morning Dizzy!' Jules laughed, grabbing a child that was about to take the bottom tin out of a four foot pyramid of soup tins.

Dizzy Hardy-Mitchell was Jules' best friend in the whole world. Married to the local Rector, and herself fully ordained as a minister, she had undergone fertility treatment four years ago when a previous run in with breast cancer at 32 years old had made getting pregnant the usual way very unlikely. So now they were the proud, if frazzled parents of triplets, named after three of Thomas Hardy's best known characters, Tess, Liza-Lu, and (Lord help her) Bathsheba. Dizzy's assiduous determination to mess about with everyone's names meant that they had soon become known as Tesco, Looby-Loo and Batty, and were now almost three, and quite a handful. Dizzy collectively called them, 'The unholy Horrors.'

Baptised Gloria, Dizzy had also been a life long sufferer of Menieres, an inner ear problem that upset her balance dreadfully, and she suffered intermittent bouts of vertigo that laid her up in bed for days, but hence the nickname Dizzy, labelled at school, had stuck.

After her brush with death at 32, and having re christened herself 'The One Tit Wonder', somewhat defiantly, she had taken herself off on a trip to the Holy Land in search of some answers. Once there, she had joined a 'Chicken and Church tour', so nicknamed because people soon discover that all of the significant biblical sites now have churches on them, and that in the absence of pork, you eat an awful lot of chicken. The trip itself had been spectacular though, and she held rich and inspiring memories of the sites and places she visited.

Her most unexpected Epiphany moment came while standing on the top of Mount Tabor, the high mountain that Jesus ascended with the apostles Peter, James and John, and where he was transfigured before them into a shining vision, according to the bible. Dizzy later described her moment as not being quite so spectacular, but she had definitely glowed after the hairy trip up that mountain in a minibus driven by a servant of the devil.

She had however, become undeniably aware as she stood there looking down at the most spectacular view on what had been a very memorable trip all round, that she had been called to ministry. She described it as being nearest to the kind of feeling you get when the answer to a question that has been bugging you for ages, suddenly comes to you and you feel immensely satisfied and relieved. Free, even.

On her return home she quickly set about being accepted for training and subsequently attended Ridley Hall in Cambridge until her ordination.

She had also at this point given up all hope of finding her true love and getting married, because she had discovered the undeniable truth that men are more scared of lady vicars than they are of going to the dentist.

Her best friend at Ridley was a very tall girl with a shock of red frizzy hair called Sophie who, once ordained, went to work as curate in the parish of Cranbrook in Kent, and invited Dizzy to stay for the weekend one summer. The Team Vicar of that parish was one Hector Hardy-Mitchell, whose quiet and serious manner somehow managed to intrigue her in a Mr Darcy sort of way, and closer acquaintance proved him to have quite a gentle and dry humour, and just the hint of a twinkle in his eyes that grew to a distinct sparkle when he looked into hers. Her visits became frequent and they soon became close, and much to Hector's delighted amazement, she agreed to marry him about a year later whilst eating ice-creams on top of Beachey Head, sitting on the bonnet of his car, and staring out into the vast expanse of the English Channel; she being by this time thirty eight, and he forty. They had moved into the parish of Frincham soon after they had married, he as incumbent Rector and she working for the glory of God and expenses, because the Diocese didn't know what to do with double acts in a church that was not busy enough to stipend two clergy. The triplets had been born after a long battle to have fertility treatment at her age that was eventually won: big time, and virtually the whole village turned out the day the three girls were baptised by their very proud Daddy.

Dizzy had appeared at Jules' back door one day, hugely pregnant and ready to pop, gently begging for something to raffle for the church roof repair fund. Insisting that she come in and rest her swollen ankles, an instant connection was made and they quickly became firm friends. Dizzy was thrilled that she now had someone she could go to in the village and pour her heart out without having her vicar face on, and Jules was just thrilled to have someone genuine to talk to. When the triplets were baptised Jules agreed to become Godmother to all three of them, and she loved all three of them very dearly.

Back in the shop, Jules had retrieved Batty and had hoisted her onto one hip, while Dizzy collected her carrier bag from the till, simultaneously grabbing the other two girls, and motioned for them to go outside the shop and talk.

Once the door had closed behind them with a ping, Dizzy kissed her on the cheek and tilted her head slightly to one side, 'Ok Jules?' she asked, 'I'm so sorry

I haven't been over for ages, It's the end of the wedding season and then Hector's been to one of his runaway seminars and I've had them on my own all week....'
She turned away and was loading two of the girls into an enormous push chair that looked like some kind of military combat vehicle.

'Don't worry,' Jules smiled, 'I'm doing a lot better than I was!'

'He's home on Friday thank goodness... so how about I come over for coffee Saturday morning then? Then Oh Heck can take them out... he owes me!' she added with a puff as she stood up with a stretch and took the last child from Jules' hip.

'Lovely,' she said, 'I could do with a bit of a chat!' she loved the way Dizzy called him 'Oh Heck'. She said it was because she spent most of her time saying, 'Oh Hector!' and it sort of got shortened.

'You're on then... I'll be there, with kit-kats!' Dizzy smiled, holding the packet up as proof. There was a chorus of 'pleeeeease Mummy!' from the three girls and so she began wrenching the packet open with her teeth. 'That's if there's any left!'

'Great. Listen I must go,' Jules said, checking her watch again, 'I've got someone coming and I need to have a shower and change first.'

'See you tomorrow morning then Jay...' Dizzy kissed her again and then kissed the top of Batty's head, ruffling her hair, 'Come on Batty, in the Charabanc! Grief! We look like a travelling circus with this thing!'

She laughed, heaving her back into manoeuvring the mammoth pushchair into the homeward direction. Jules watched as they headed off towards the Rectory, all four of them happily, and peacefully, munching chocolate, and turned to go home.

※

With perfect timing she was just coming down the stairs from her shower and change when the back door bell rang.

Chris Palmer, the chairman of the local allotments committee, was about 35 years old and wore a flat cap, checked shirt, and green Wellingtons over his dirty mustard yellow trousers, topped off with a rather tatty waxed Barbour jacket; every bit the stereotypical country gent, and she smiled at his appearance through the door. Opening it, she introduced herself, grabbed her own equally tatty Barbour from a hook on the back of the door, and selected a large key from a bowl on the dresser.

They made their way over to the walled garden, and Jules took the key from her pocket and unlocked the padlock on the old wooden door.

'A good secure site, that's always a good start,' he said.

Jules stood to one side and let him go in first.

He looked around the site. It was a decent enough size; four or five good size plots, he thought. Needed clearing....

'We get lots of blackberries,' she smiled, seeing him eyeing the forest of brambles.

He smiled. Marcus would think he had nice teeth.

He had his hands on his hips as he scanned the garden with his eyes. 'I bet you do,' he said, 'I have a slight passion for blackberry and apple pie myself...' and then he smiled at her, and she began to change her opinion of him.

'The wall is in very good condition,' he said, 'I see there's been some restoration?'

'Yes,' she replied, 'my husband,' she paused, 'he... decided on a whim one day to get a pool and a gym put in here, so he had the wall repaired, after we spent weeks with the children combing the edges of local fields picking up flints. The farmers throw them to the edges of the fields as they plough them up you know, so they don't damage their machinery...'

'Yes I know,' he replied. 'They call them diamonds. 'So why didn't you get the pool and the gym?' he asked.

'Oh, lots of reasons', she said vaguely, 'we don't really get the weather for an outdoor pool do we? And the children just liked swimming in the lake; there's so much more to see and do out there. And as for the gym; well, he changed his mind.'

'Well it was a good decision for us,' he said, bending down and picking up some loose soil from a mole hill. Putting the handful of earth up to his nose, he sniffed, and ran it through his fingers. 'You have excellent soil Mrs Taylor.'

'Julie, please, or Jules. Well it would have been the kitchen garden for this house in the old days...' she said.

'Chris...' he nodded, 'Quite. 'Well we'll need to get it cleared: my committee loves a challenge.'

'You mean you're interested?' she asked.

'Oh, Definitely! Land is at a premium these days... Jules. Most of the allotment land in this area has been sold off for redevelopment, and privately owned allotment schemes seem to be the way forward now. We have a five year waiting list you know.' He looked around the plot again. 'You could have four or maybe five plots here,' and then, walking towards the tap, 'and you have a water supply too, I see. It is connected?'

'Oh yes,' she replied. 'We run a hose from there to wash the cars...'

'This is the perfect time of year for this kind of thing. The weather's still pretty mild; no frosts yet, so we should easily be ready for the spring planting.' He brushed his hands together briskly to remove the remains of the soil. 'Well then, shall we discuss the details?'

'Let's have some coffee in the house,' she replied, leading the way.

Back in the kitchen they discussed the terms of the allotments scheme as Jules made a pot of coffee. Marcus had done some research for her on the internet, and she was very satisfied with the annual rental figures that Chris came up with, that would keep the wolves from the door for a while. She had also spoken to the local council and they had been very helpful too; seemingly as enthusiastic to encourage private allotments schemes as she was to provide one.

'And you're sure about the clearance?' she asked him, placing two mugs on the table. 'Oh yes,' he said. 'That's nothing unusual. Like I said we love a challenge, and new sites never come ready for planting...and then of course there are the perks to consider too...' he looked across the table at her.

'Perks?' she said, eyebrows shooting upwards slightly warily, as his expression was giving nothing away.

He smiled. 'You'll get a constant supply of free vegetables,' he said cheerily, 'and soft fruit. If everyone gets a good crop at the same time they'll all be queuing up at your back door begging you to take some!'

Her eyebrows descended gratefully. 'Ah, yes of course! Well in that case I wish I'd thought of all this before!' She laughed, took a sip of her coffee, and there was a little pause.

'So...Chris, you have a family?' She pushed the tin of biscuits towards him and he took one, nodding his thanks.

'Oh yes,' he said, 'my wife is Sarah, she's on the Parish Council and chair of the Horticultural society... and in her spare time she runs the mother and toddler group in the village hall too.... We have three girls; ten, eight and five.'

Jules reached over and slid a cardboard box along the table towards him. He looked inside it. It was full of crisps, biscuits, and bags of marshmallows.

'Would they like these?' she asked. 'I had a clearout... because I'm kind of on a diet!'

'Great! I'm sure they'd love them!' he smiled adding, as he sipped his coffee, 'you sound just like my wife, with her never ending diets!'

She put down her mug. 'Well I'm trying anyway... so, tell me about your girls...'

'Well,' he paused, 'Amanda is five and loves any colour so long as it's pink.

Fay is eight and into Judo and has just got her yellow belt, and Amy is nearly eleven and completely pony mad. She has a little skewbald pony of her own now, he's called Whisper, but she's costing me a small fortune in fuel every a day because the world and his wife all have horses around here and the closest livery we could get for him was on a farm over towards Yattley...which is getting on for twelve miles away, and with her needing to be there twice a day there's lots of sitting around in the car for me or her mother!'

She picked her mug up again, and looked at him, 'and where do you live?' she asked him.

'Oh we live in the village, just near the shop; the Manor House. I'm planning to transfer my allotment plot as soon as we get things settled. I'll be able to walk here, it's much nearer than my existing one, and a much better site.'

'So might Amy,' she said, 'I have another scheme. Just come with me…' and she stood up.

Leading the way across to the stables Chris's face absolutely lit up.

'You're not serious?' he said incredulously. 'I've watched this all standing here empty so enviously for years when I walk the dog round the lake. I was trying to pluck up the courage to enquire but the feeling in the village was that your husband…valued his privacy, shall we say? This is just too good to be true!'

'Yes well let's just say his privacy isn't a problem around here anymore…' she said briskly, 'and I'll enjoy the… company. I'm being totally serious! The stables have been empty since my daughter went off to university and sold her horse on. She kept him in one and used the other one for tack and storage. There's power in both of them of course…but they're both full of all Marcus' junk at the moment. I could get it cleared easily enough if you'd really like them. I think the roof and everything is still sound, and the paddock fence looks ok… and there's the ménage for jumping practice if she wants to…and there's another field…just behind the house that has a bit of a slope to it… and with some trees for a nice bit of shade. You might want to check the all the land for nasty weeds though, that hasn't been looked at for a good while…'

'It's a fantastic idea Jules, I can't believe it… I'm so glad I met you today! She can fiddle about here with her pony to her hearts content and I can be doing something a lot more useful in the allotments.' He looked absolutely delighted.

'Well then, let me have a think about the rent and I'll give you a call,' she said.

'I don't care! Please let me give you a hug! Compared to our carbon footprint for the last two years we'll take it! *And* he can keep us all in organic fertiliser!' he laughed, pulling Jules towards him happily.

# Chapter twelve

Soon after, the kitchen garden was full of happy people covered in mud and making lots of noise. Men, women and children, in a bright assortment of coloured Wellingtons, passed by in a constant stream of happy waving to her at the bottom of the garden, en route to and from the new allotments. There was a roar of machinery, and a wide plume of smoke from a huge bonfire was doing its best to head for the sky, but being buffeted by the blustery November winds.

One of Chris' suggestions was to have a second gate put in across the other side of the garden, where the wall was adjacent to a car parking area for lake visitors, and then people wouldn't have to keep passing her house. One of the new tenants was a building contractor and had offered to do it in lieu of some of his allotment rent, so Jules had agreed and could just see him and one of his men making good the area around the new door, complete with key pad entry system for added security.

She had decided to strike while the iron was hot and had two days worth of excellent exercise shifting all Marcus' stuff up into the garage, and the rest of it that wouldn't fit, into Paul's studio; well he wasn't using it… and it wouldn't be there long anyway. Marcus and Sam were coming down again soon and she'd just tell him to hire a van instead of coming in a car and then he could do with it whatever he decided. She was sure that his boxes and boxes of dental books and models would be snapped up by some grateful dental student or other.

Looking across to the stables now, she smiled as she watched Amy Palmer and two of her friends fussing around Whisper the little skewbald pony as he fought to avoid his bridle. They had found some of Jemmie's old poles behind Marcus' junk and were setting up some makeshift jumps on straw bales in the paddock.

Jules was swept back in time to a similar scene, where Jemmie was the little girl in the paddock with her friends, and Sparkler, the slate grey pony with the blonde mane and tail had been her pride and joy. He used to bow most extravagantly with one front leg stretched out before him and the other tucked under at the knee, and had won many a prize at the numerous pony club gymkhanas Jemmie had entered; his favourite event having been the obstacle course. His fringe was very long and he had the most beautiful eyelashes, and Jules always thought he looked as if he'd been drawn for a cartoon by Walt Disney.

Oh how Jemmie had wept the day he was loaded into the lorry to be taken away to his new home! She'd thought her world was coming to an end and there had been no consoling her for many days, even though she had looked so comical riding him, having grown too tall for the little pony. She'd looked like one of those Thelwell cartoons that showed the rider needing roller skates for her long legs and huge feet.

And then there had been Troy, the chestnut gelding. He had lived with them and been Jemmies one true love until she was 15 and discovered boys, but that being said, if the boy didn't like horses he didn't stand much chance with Jemmie either. Troy would have Jules in hysterics when he tossed his head at the fence and smiled for an apple as she pegged out her washing on the line near his field.

When the novelty of boys had worn off a bit and Troy had gone the same way as dear little Sparkler, there had been Darcy the black stallion with the white socks and the velvety nose. He was a mighty 18 hands and as proud and arrogant as the man he was named after. He would strut around his field practising his extended trot technique, but was such a wimp that he would spook at a bee. Jemmie was the only one who could get anywhere near him, and Jules had missed dear old Troy, who was always so friendly, and would trot over to see her when she came to the fence with an apple or carrot as a treat for him, or even dance and sway with joy if she came up with a polo mint.

Darcy had been sold on when Jemmie went off to university because it was plain for her to see that he needed someone with a lot more time to work him.

He'd gone to an eventing yard in Kingsclere, not too far away, and Jules had seen him on TV, competing at Burghley and Badminton, and looking devastatingly handsome, just like his namesake.

✯

Jules checked her reflection in the full length mirror, 'hmm, well, that's a work in progress…' she said, out loud and a whole pound lighter this morning. Grabbing her bag from the back of the chair, she looked across at the red dress hanging on the wardrobe door. Paul had bought her this dress, years ago, and it was a Gianni Versace. It was also a size ten, and not a very generous one at that. Even when it had fitted she'd had to breathe in and skip dessert.

She might not get into it again, but this was her incentive.

Jules' wardrobe contents, she often joked, ranged in sizes from '*Wow*' to '*Woe* '. This one was way down at the *Wow* end of the wardrobe with a chair against the door that was perfectly imprinted in the carpet, so was obviously not used for regular access these days.

It was a gorgeous dress though; a timeless classic that was ballerina length with a very low back and hung in beautiful folds like something from a Hollywood musical. She pulled a slight face at the thought of how much she'd need to lose to get even close, and then running down the stairs to the kitchen, she picked up her car keys and her envelope of course information. Five days from 9.30am until 4.30pm; that should stop her brooding!

✷

Up in London and very early in the day for him, Paul was not having much luck deciding what to pack from the meagre collection of clothes he had taken when he had left Jules, allegedly just for a trip to Milan, and Catherine was supervising. Still in her satin robe and nothing else, lounging on the bed with one knee bent up and swaying slightly, she was watching him intently.

'How long will you be away?' she asked, pouting slightly that her efforts to lure him back into bed had failed.

'Five, six days...tops,' he replied, from behind the wardrobe door.

Coming out with two silk ties he held them both up towards her. 'Which one goes best with the cream linen suit?' he asked.

She rolled off the bed and stood in front of him, studying them. Pulling an impatient face she asked, 'Don't you have anything else in there? Where is that nice gold one I bought you?'

She went across to the wardrobe and rifled through his limited selection of clothes. It wasn't there.

She turned around and looked at him incredulously. 'I'm not surprised you can't make your mind up what to take,' she said. 'These are all your summer clothes! Where are all your other suits, and shirts and things?'

'Still in my wardrobes at ho...I mean, Jules still has them... I suppose.' He looked a bit uncomfortable. 'I only have what I'd packed for that last trip when I...'

Catherine pulled a face. 'Oh, honestly Paul! How on earth can you grace the galleries of Milan in any of these things! You're suit isn't even clean! What were you thinking?' She went in the bathroom rapidly and turned on the shower. Calling out over her shoulder she said hurriedly; 'give me five minutes and we'll hit the shops. I've been longing to get you up to date!'

A quick trip to the West End on what was a very gloomy and foggy Monday morning saw them returning to the apartment building in Eaton Square Kensington weighed down with a considerable number of upmarket stiff paper carrier bags. Once back inside Catherine set about removing labels with a pair of nail scissors and then began re packing his suitcase.

She stopped when her mobile rang in the other room and she ran to answer it. Vaguely listening to her increasingly loud ranting to the poor soul at the other end Paul felt even more uncomfortable looking at his new clothes. Catherine had picked everything out for him, despite his protests, saying it was time he came up to date, and he wouldn't have picked any of them for himself. And worse still he had felt a very definite but disconcerting pang that Jules would have known just what he liked. Catherine's tastes were much... younger. These clothes looked like something Marcus would wear. All crumpled up shirts that she'd said were supposed to look like that, and trousers called chinos with no creases down the front; and he hadn't worn jeans for anything other than gardening for decades. He much preferred the neat, Saville Row look.

He looked at these clothes with distaste; designer labels they may be but those trousers looked like they only came half way up to your waist and you could barely fit a hanky in the pockets.

Catherine came back into the bedroom looking far from happy.

'I have to go to bloody Manchester on a job... for three bloody days!' she said crossly. 'Karen, that idiot assistant of mine has messed up my diary and I thought the exhibition started tomorrow.'

'Don't worry darling; I'll get a car sent for me,' he said calmly.

She looked at him, puzzled at his comment, caught neatly in the act of not giving the fact that she was supposed to be taking him to Heathrow a thought.

She did her best to look contrite and full of apology in her time honoured fashion.

'What time is check-in for your flight again?' she said, in her best little girl voice.

'Five,' he said, looking out of the window. 'Assuming the weather doesn't mess things up, it's getting foggier by the minute out there. Anyway, ages yet. It's only...' he checked his watch, '11.15.'

'I said I'd be another hour before I could possibly leave,' she smiled, carefully lifting his bag of folded clothes off the bed.

※

In a much better mood, and nearer an hour and a half later, Catherine set off down to her car with a hastily packed Louis Vuitton bag. Throwing the bag carelessly into the boot and climbing into the driver's seat, she picked up her phone and scrolled down to a number from the memory.

'Hi,' she said, 'it's me. Great news, I'm coming up today instead of tomorrow... so I could see you this evening... if you can manage to get away?'

The person at the other end said something and she smiled as she put her key into the ignition and turned it.

'Good,' she said. 'I thought you'd be pleased...'

The person at the other end said something else, and she smiled again. Paul already forgotten.

'Me too,' she purred.

※

Paul was finishing packing his own bags with not very much enthusiasm when his own mobile rang; it was Hugo. Heathrow was now fog bound, the forecast was dire and no flights were arriving or leaving now until at least tomorrow morning. He had been transferred to the flight due to leave for Milan at 11.30.

Well that was just great.

He looked at his suitcase, and then his watch, and had a brilliant idea. Maybe it really was great after all.

Heading down the red carpeted staircase to the front door and nodding to the doorman, he walked just down the street to his car. 'A couple of hours in this weather', he thought, climbing in. Worth every second to get some decent clothes he wouldn't feel ridiculous in.

He checked the clock on the dashboard of his car as he set off. It was just approaching 1.15pm.

'I should be there and back by seven if I'm lucky,' he thought.

Turning off the M4 at junction 12 to join the A4, he was making fairly good time considering. The fog was awful but things were moving steadily, albeit very slowly and there hadn't been any hold-ups to speak of so far.

By the time he reached Newbury it was approaching 2.45pm and the fog had lifted a tiny bit. He'd tried ringing the house to warn Jules that he was on his way, but there was no reply. Pulling off what passed for a main road at Frincham and down the lane towards the lake he wondered vaguely where she could be on a Monday afternoon at this time.

Probably out with Barney.

The first thing he noticed as he entered the driveway was a skewbald pony in the paddock and three little girls wearing the village school uniform were sitting on the fence, watching it graze. Schools seemed to finish half way through the day these days.

Wait a minute…

Puzzled, Paul got out of the car. His ears quickly picked up the sound of voices, coming from…the walled garden if he wasn't mistaken.

Making his way past the paddock the three girls said hello to him and he smiled at them briefly but kept walking. 'If you're looking for my Daddy he's in the allotments,' called one of them.

Allotments? What on earth...? Now decidedly puzzled and opening the big wooden door to the garden he got the shock of his life. Though it was far from a pleasant day it was an absolute hive of activity; several rotavators were turning over the soil with men in green Wellingtons plodding along behind them and all shouting encouragement to each other.

There were other people industriously working in there too; men, women and children, all of them happy and chatting away nineteen to the dozen in their tasks. One of the men looked up and saw him standing there, and walked over, brushing off his hands as he did so.

'I'm sorry,' he said, 'I'm afraid all the plots are taken.'

Paul opened his mouth but nothing came out. He was mesmerised by what he could see going on all around him, and he closed it again.

'If you would like to go up to the house though, Mrs Taylor should be home from college soon and she's started a waiting list...' he went on.

'Mrs... A what? You say she's due back from where?' he said confusedly.

Chris Palmer started to look a bit worried. 'College... she's doing a course...she's started a waiting list... for the allotments; I thought you were looking to rent one... no?'

'No, he said, still puzzled.

'Oh.' Not really knowing what to say next, Chris introduced himself as chair of the local allotments committee, and put out his still very grubby hand. Paul looked at it a little distastefully but took it vaguely.

'And you are?' said Chris expectantly.

'My name is Paul Taylor,' Paul said, rubbing his hands together pointedly to remove any soil that might have been transferred; 'and I own this house... and you seem to be on my land...'

Chris looked more than surprised, having never actually seen the great man this close in the flesh before. 'I think you should discuss this with your wife, Mr Taylor... she would seem to have other ideas...' he said evenly.

✮

Jules had had a brilliant first day at college and was making her way home feeling buoyed up and positive, but turning off the main road and into the top of Clearwater Lane Jules looked down across the field and through the gloom to see the unmistakeable shape of Paul's car sitting like the black angel of doom in the driveway of the house. In horror, she shot into Martin's driveway and rested her head on her hands on the steering wheel for a minute.

It started to rain.

She did not want to face him now under any circumstances, with no one else around to back her up, and especially if he'd brought, as she suspected, Catherine with him, or worse still, divorce papers, or even both.

Standing up to him was much easier with Marcus around.

Thinking quickly she opened her bag and took out Martin's back door key, and running round the back of the cottage practically on all fours so she wouldn't be seen from below, she opened the door quickly and shot inside.

She stood panting in the tiny kitchen for a minute. What now?

Climbing the stairs at speed she went into the spare room and over to the window. It afforded and excellent view of her house and driveway down below when the weather was halfway decent, but today...?

Now, where was he? She squinted slightly, trying to focus through the fog.

'He' was making his way up the fire escape to his studio and looked as if he was selecting the key from the bunch he was carrying. So he must have been inside the house already.

She bit her bottom lip. Oops. Marcus' belongings were stacked inside - and there were a lot of them; even a canoe and two sets of skis... and she'd moved all Paul's half finished paintings and his easels up to one end. He wouldn't be pleased.

He wasn't, because no sooner had he gone in than he backed out again, relocked the door and ran swiftly back down the steps.

Jules had noticed a pair of binoculars in a box on the floor by the wardrobe, and went over to get them, shaking them out of their box impatiently. Focussing them on Paul, she was shocked for a moment that thanks to all the security lights at the house; even in the gloom she could see him as if he were less than two feet in front of her.

And he looked far from happy.

Despite the tension she found herself smiling slightly hysterically in her secret spy hole, and stifled a nervous giggle.

He went back over to the house and disappeared inside while she waited and watched, but he didn't reappear.

He's waiting for me; she thought.

Well then he could keep on waiting.

She watched as the workers in the allotments began to clear up and wend their way homewards, and then all the lights went out. Clearwater House was now in darkness apart from a single light shining like a lighthouse through the fog, in the kitchen.

Jules went back down the stairs and went into Martin's kitchen to put the kettle on and make herself a cup of tea. Then she looked in both the fridge and the freezer. Lunch had been hours ago and a bit frugal. She was getting hungry.

'Great,' she said aloud, pulling out a frozen packet of beef stew and dumplings. 'I'll hole up here for the rest of the day until he gives up and goes.'

※

Down in the house, Paul had gone up the stairs and into the bedroom; their bedroom, and the first thing he noticed with some surprise was the red dress hanging on the wardrobe door. He wondered why it was there, and remembered all too well her complaining that it no longer fitted her. He nodded to himself as he decided she must have got it out to give it to someone else; maybe Jemmie wanted it, or maybe she was sending it to the charity shop. It was a real shame; she had looked absolutely stunning in it, he thought, running the floaty fabric through his fingers absently.

But that had been years ago.

Pulling a suitcase out from a cupboard in his dressing room, he laid it open on the bed and proceeded to empty his wardrobe, actually quite relieved she wasn't home to cause any more awkward scenes.

Mind you, she certainly had some explaining to do with all that was going on outside, and about all the junk that had appeared in his studio. But he didn't have time for any of that now: that could wait until another time, and he continued with the task that had brought him down here.

Delightedly, he packed all the clothes he felt comfortable in: the shirts, ties, suits and jackets, and the trousers that fit to his waist with a belt, like they were supposed to. Thinking he might need some casual clothes too, he added a couple of pairs of his jog pants and some polo shirts; after all, hotels were bad enough and even he couldn't relax properly in a suit.

Then he noticed his blue hooded fleece hanging over the back of her chair, and thinking for less than a second, he picked it up, smelled it, and as his heart fluttered disconcertingly he added it to the rest of his belongings.

He checked his watch: almost five o'clock and totally dark outside.

Where on earth could she be? And what was all that about college?

Back down in the kitchen, Barney, though delighted to see his master again without being banished to the utility room, was hovering expectantly over his dinner bowl and doing his best to convey a message. Getting that message loud and clear, Paul went to the pantry to get his dog biscuits, and poured some into a dish, to Barney's tail-thumping delight. Then returning the box to the pantry, he couldn't help but notice that its contents looked a bit different to usual.

No crisps or biscuits, no cakes and, most significantly, no packets of the customary marshmallows either.

Opening the fridge he saw skimmed milk, fruit juice, cottage cheese, salad, fresh vegetables, and a bowl of chopped vegetables covered in cling film with a label on the top in her writing saying *'deliver us from evil!'*

He frowned, and thought again of the red dress on the back of the door upstairs.

So that was it. She's dieting and wants to get into that dress.

What on earth for?

Or, to put it another way, *who* on earth for?

He checked his watch again; almost 5.15 now. If he left now he could well be home by 7 o' clock and get a meal and a decent night's sleep before his flight tomorrow morning.

Grabbing a pen and pulling a used envelope from a bulldog clip, (Jules had always used the backs of these to write lists and things on, which had always annoyed him because they could well afford a note pad), he quickly scrawled her a note and let himself out, relocking the door behind him and slipping the keys back into his jacket pocket.

Up in Martin's cottage and still in her spy hole in the spare room: thanks to the outside lights that came on when he opened the back door, Jules saw Paul through the binoculars putting a large suitcase into the boot of his car.

So that was the reason for the visit. Well, at least Catherine wasn't with him.

Taking one last look around, he climbed into his car and set off down the drive and out into the lane.

Jules ran into Martin's bedroom, ignoring Jemmies night shirt and the unmade bed, and stood behind the pulled curtains, peeping through a tiny gap and waiting for him to drive past.

Making his way up Clearwater Lane Paul drove past the cottage but it was too dark to see his face, and she heaved an audible sigh of relief as she let go of the curtain.

He'd gone.

Then she heard his tyres protest as he braked and stopped suddenly, and backing up, he had another look.

Upstairs and back at the curtains Jules caught her breath and her eyes opened wider. She knew what he'd seen, and her hand shot up to her mouth in horror.

Jules' car was parked in the driveway of this cottage; Mrs Bennett's cottage.

So this must be *his* cottage now; he'd heard them talking about it before.

Looking up at the closed bedroom curtains, all at once Paul put two and two together and made five.

She was dieting; she was dieting because she really was having an affair with Martin Ryan. She wanted to look good for Martin Ryan, and they were in this cottage together, up in that front bedroom behind those curtains *right now.*

Surely she could see that Ryan was just using her to get back at him for taking Catherine - that was perfectly obvious. Why couldn't she see that? And what then, about Jemmie? Was he honestly having an affair with both of them? This was ridiculous! For a moment he considered getting out of the car and barging his way in there to... well, he wasn't entirely sure what really, but he stopped himself.

Jules meanwhile still up in the bedroom, was holding her breath and scared to move a muscle, for fear of what he might be thinking.

Paul's heart was beating very hard, his breaths were coming fast and he felt a powerful surge of something that registered in his brain as hatred for that... pond scum that was obviously going to hurt Jules.

But anyone else would have recognised it as green eyed monster of jealousy.

Thoroughly confused by his feelings and not really knowing what to do, with another screech of expensive tyres he put his foot down and took off up the lane, astonished to find himself almost blinded by angry tears.

In the bedroom Jules sank down onto the unmade bed, and burst into tears. Laying down she pulled the duvet up over her head, and sobbed herself into a fitful slumber.

She eventually woke up and pulled herself together enough to set off for home at about eight o'clock and, opening her own back door she was greeted by Barney, who after greeting her ecstatically in his own way with the news that he'd seen his master again, and that was why the kitchen light was on, and then he immediately went to stand by his bowl again. Well, it was worth a try.

Jules instantly saw the note on the table and picked it up, noticing that he got straight to the point:

*Jules. Called to collect rest clothes.*

*Studio-junk & chaos outside! What is going on??*

*Need to discuss.*

*Milan again tomorrow but will be in touch by 6th inst.*

*P*

Inst.? It was like he'd set her a telegram. She screwed it up and threw it at the bin; missing it by miles and sending it rolling under the dresser, where it could jolly well stay.

Upstairs in the bedroom his dressing room door was ajar. She could see that all of his cupboard doors and drawers stood wide open, and everything had gone. Even, she noticed, the blue fleece from the back of her chair.

# Chapter thirteen

Martin was working on an exhibition in a large gallery in Manchester's city centre. He was sitting in the gallery's coffee shop at 11am taking a break with a newspaper when, turning the page, he looked up for a second and was more than a little surprised to see a familiar figure walk past the door. For a moment he thought he could see what Jules meant about the clone thing... but as she turned to say something to her companion he could see that it really was Catherine. She was with a smartly dressed man in a grey suit, but it wasn't Paul Taylor. She was laughing, and his arm was draped around her shoulders.

Intrigued, Martin folded up his newspaper, left the coffee shop, and followed them discreetly out of the door, but he leapt back inside when he realised that they had actually stopped directly outside, and that the man was hailing a taxi. Once successful, she got in but he didn't, but he did reach in and kiss her goodbye;

and it hadn't been a peck on the cheek either. The taxi pulled away and headed off into the traffic, whilst Mr Grey Suit returned to the gallery, whistling slightly, and went across to speak to the receptionist. She smiled and nodded at something he said, and he looked very smug and happy with himself, Martin thought.

Not really knowing why, he took out his mobile phone and selected camera. Looking around to make sure he wasn't being watched, he took a photo of the man as he began to speak to someone else, but clicked just as the mystery man turned to walk back towards him.

He looked directly at Martin.

'Signal,' Martin said innocently, 'can't get one in here anywhere!'

The man smiled knowingly and nodded, but kept walking, and headed for a door that declared 'staff only.'

Martin went across to the reception desk.

'Excuse me? That man who was just talking to you, who was he?' he asked. 'He looks familiar.'

'Oh that's Daniel Makepeace,' she said. 'He's with the Manchester Chronicle. He's the chief executive, and he's on the board of trustees here.'

Once back in his room at a little dog friendly hotel Martin opened his laptop and Googled Daniel Makepeace at the Manchester Chronicle and found a profile article from a recent colour supplement. He was forty six years old. Well enough qualified, having started on the news desk, but seemed to have found himself at the top of the board room in a remarkably short time and without too much in between. That seemed odd. A member of the Rotary Club, married to someone called Sabrina, whose father was quite the newspaper magnate and owned the paper. That explained that one then. Promotion by nepotism; he'd married the owners daughter. They had two children, a boy and a girl; the perfect package. He wondered if Sabrina and her dad knew about her husband's obvious 'friendship' with Catherine.

Talking to Jemmie on the phone later that evening he said, 'guess who I ran into at the gallery today?'

'Not my father,' she said, 'he's in Milan at the moment: he emailed me again, trying to win me over.'

'While the mouse is away the *Cat* can play...' Martin said mysteriously.

He heard a sharp intake of breath at the other end of the line.

'You saw Catherine? Did you speak to her? What did she say? What did you say to her? ...Martin?' She was flustered.

He laughed, 'Whoa! Down girl! Calm down! No, I didn't speak to her, she didn't see me either; she had a much bigger fish to fry.'

There was a pause at the other end. 'Meaning?'

'She was with another man.' He emphasised the word 'with' so she could not mistake what he meant.

'What do you mean with another... who was it?' she said. 'Do you know who it was?'

'No, but I found out,' he said. 'His name is Daniel Makepeace and he's the chief executive of the Manchester Chronicle: I Googled him, just out of interest.'

Jemmie took another breath and let it out slowly. She wasn't sure what to think. Sorry for her father, smug for her mother, or worried that Martin had seen Catherine again, and had Googled the man she'd been with to find out who he was.

'No, I didn't...' he said, when she hadn't spoken for a full minute.

'Didn't what?'

'I didn't Google him because I wanted to know for myself. I did it so I could tell you. I love you, remember?'

'I miss you,' she said simply.

He smiled, 'I'm very glad to hear it. Listen, I have to go back and do some work now. Have a think about what we should do with this and I'll see you at the weekend.'

'Ok. I can't wait.'

'Neither can I!'

Jemmie hung up and sat thinking for a while. She logged into her laptop and repeated Martin's exercise of earlier on and she sat looking at the photo of Daniel Makepeace. He was certainly handsome; like a cross between George Clooney and Paul Newman. What was she playing at? Martin had said she was a gold digger, and it was certainly starting to look like it. Maybe she didn't get off on actually getting the prize; she got off on the hunt for it. Or then again maybe he was an old flame and she just ran into him... she thought generously. After all Martin only saw a kiss, even it was a passionate one; but then he of all people would know what he saw.... Either way the problem was what to do with the information now if anything, and if she did tell her mother, what this would ultimately do to her father.

Meanwhile Paul was now with Hugo in Milan spending a few days doing what Hugo called Air Kissing in a select few of its prestigious artistic venues: attending exhibitions and generally raising his own profile by appearing in the press. This was by far one of his least favourite activities, and what's more, this particular evening he was visibly not in the mood to be either agreeable or amusing: indeed, his mood was positively grumpy, and petulant.

Whilst artists in general are often assumed to be somewhat unpredictable, Paul Taylor had always had the reputation of being the exception: well mannered and courteous, though well known for not suffering fools gladly and, always, always impeccably turned out.

This particular evening he had only managed to fulfil one of his virtues, thanks to his trip to Frincham, but he had not been his usual self by any stretch of the imagination. Hugo had therefore spent most of it calming ruffled feathers; explaining in his flawless Italian, as best he could, that Paul was having, 'a few problems with his latest piece.'

If only he knew!

Back in his hotel much later, in a suite which was considerably larger and grander than Martin's back in Manchester, Paul loosened his tie slowly as he poured himself a neat single malt whisky at the lavishly stocked bar. Hugo had given him quite a lecture on the way back and now he was feeling like the world and his wife… literally, were against him.

Propping up his ridiculously plush pillows he kicked off his shoes and sat up on the bed, crossed his still-socked feet and took a sip of his drink. Picking up the remote control as if it weighed three tons and pressing a little red button, the flat screen HD television slid noiselessly down like magic from its slot in the wall unit, and he flicked it on. Scrolling through a series of loud Italian voices intermittently and disjointedly singing, shouting crying or laughing he couldn't find anything to entertain him, so he switched it off again and waved a half hearted goodbye to it as it re ascended, dropping the remote disconsolately on the bed beside him. Looking around the room he pulled a face. On top of everything else these days he was heartily sick and tired of hotel rooms that looked like he'd fallen headlong into the pages of some glossy lifestyle magazine. In fact between the numerous hotels, and the half equipped apartment in London, he felt displaced, nomadic... adrift.

And he really needed to talk to someone.

Getting off the bed again he reached into his jacket pocket and took out his mobile phone. He chose Catherine's number from the menu and pressed call, but her phone went straight to voicemail.

He even thought of ringing Jules, but couldn't face another row.

And even Hugo was in a hiss with him, and he was being paid.

Only slightly mollified by the sound of Catherine's voice, even if it was only telling him to leave a message, the phone went the same way as the remote control.

He looked at the clock. 10.45pm; 9.45 on his body clock, and he wasn't even a little bit hungry.

Disconsolately he let out a deep sigh as he removed his tie, and then the belt from his trousers, then he reached over to turn out the light, and lay down fully clothed.

✶

Jules loved the early mornings. A lifelong early bird that had always driven Paul mad; her parents had always said that even when she was a baby in a cot in their bedroom, she would make them feel quite sick because she could open her eyes and sit straight up, raring to go. She wasn't quite that enthusiastic these days, but she still couldn't stay in bed once she was awake unless she was ill.

It was just before the dawn now, and she was absolutely wide awake. Jumping out of bed and dressing quickly, she decided to go for a walk: this was turning into a bit of a habit.

Collecting a somewhat startled Barney from his bed, they set off into the gloom down the garden path, and once he was outside, Barney set off at a fat trot to see what scents were around at this time of the morning.

He trotted off in the direction of the allotments; nose to the ground and scenting; Paul had always said he was doing the dog version of, 'reading the morning papers.'

Since the morning she had met Martin, she had never met anyone else out this early, so she was surprised to see that even at this time of the morning on a cold day in November, with her breath clearly visible ahead of her, and the days had reached that point where night and day spread closer together without much day in between; there was someone in there. Someone had left the new gate propped open, and she could see the headlights of a vehicle in the car park across the other side of the garden, illuminating a man. He was using the lights to assist him carrying what looked like the makings of a shed from a trailer attached to the back of some kind of four wheel drive monster, parked adjacent to the new door. He was busy in his task and couldn't see her in the early morning mist and murk, and jumped visibly when Barney went up to investigate him. He turned and saw Jules approaching, breathed in and smiled; his hand on his chest in mock relief.

'It's Mrs Taylor isn't it?'

'Yes,' she said, 'I'm sorry we made you jump, he's very inquisitive.'

She thought he looked familiar but couldn't place him. He wasn't as tall as Paul, and rugged in a Daniel Craig sort of a way. His hair was a sort of pewter grey and his eyes, as far as she could make out in the light from the monster, were pale blue. His accent was northern.

'I hope I didn't wake you making all this noise?' and then thinking he should have introduced himself first, added, 'I'm Ben, by the way, Ben Robinson: I've got one of the plots here.'

'I guessed,' she replied, nodding slightly, 'call me Jules...please.'

'I've seen you around and about,' he said, holding out his right arm, and they shook hands briefly.

'You're up and about early?' she said.

'I haven't been to bed,' he smiled. 'No point now though. I've been up all night with a cow over at Yattley; the Preston farm, with a breeched calf. I had these on the trailer back at the yard so I thought I'd do something useful and unload them before going back to the surgery to collect my morning list.'

'Oh of course!' she said recognising him at last. 'You're the vet aren't you?'

'That's right,' he smiled, 'I'm a partner with Lawson's, in the village.'

'Ah yes, I know it well... Barney here usually sees Mr Lawson. Not his favourite place I'm afraid.'

On hearing the word vet, Barney had slunk rapidly away and headed for the original doorway.

Jules shook her head and smiled after him.

'I specialise in the big stuff really,' Ben continued. 'I'm the horses and farm animals and Stan concentrates on the family members like Barney there... I like being outside.'

'Me too,' she said. 'When my daughter had a horse here we used to have Peter Metcalf.'

He nodded. 'That's right. I took over from him when he retired, about four years ago.... So Jules... what about you? Do you work or...?'

'I'm doing a college course at the moment,' she said. 'I've been away from work for quite a few years but I'm thinking of going back to it and doing a teaching assistant job now. I'm interested in special needs.'

'This place is not enough to occupy your time then?' he said, looking around.

'More of an economic necessity really...' she replied. Feeling the need to elucidate she continued. 'My husband and I have separated and...' she tailed off, unsure how much more she wanted to say. Noting her discomfort, he butted in. 'Oh I know a song about that one!' he smiled, nodding ironically. 'I'm divorced myself. Four years ago. My wife ran off with our best man. Should have guessed really; the clue was in the name.... That's when I upped sticks from Stockport and moved down here.'

Hence the accent, she thought. 'There's a lot of it about I hear,' she replied politely, and began to turn away from him, feeling a bit uncomfortable now and not wanting to discuss it any further. 'I'll leave you too it then Ben,' she said carefully, 'nice to meet you.'

'You too, Jules,' he said, and watched her for a minute as she called Barney out of the bushes where he was scenting a rabbit, before going back to collect more of his shed panels.

※

That same morning up in London Marcus was doing his best to concentrate on the task in hand. His emergency patient, an extremely big man with teeth like an old graveyard and breath that could strip paint, was in the process of having a large and irretrievable lower molar extracted, largely due to his addiction to toffees, and the crown of the tooth had just snapped off, making the process a lot more difficult.

He was now experiencing some difficulty in negotiating his patient's enormous frame to get near enough for a decent angle with his forceps. This wasn't being helped by Sam, standing behind the patient and doing her level best to stifle a giggle by stuffing her fist in her mouth, because Marcus had just almost put one leg across the top of his patient, looking like a snooker player going for a tricky angle.

In the pocket of his jacket on the back of the door, his mobile phone began to vibrate, and Sam jumped with some relief to go and answer it. Not wanting to disrupt proceedings in the chair, she left the surgery and stayed on the step just outside the door, but Marcus could still hear enough to realise that she was talking to Jemmie. After the initial greeting Sam became very quiet as she listened; only making the occasional comment. Jemmie obviously had a lot to say, and Marcus was doing his best to both listen, and concentrate on the job in hand.

Asking his patient to have a quick rinse and handing him a glass of pink water, he opened the door to the surgery and stuck his head out, looking at Sam in silent query. Sam's eyes were wide open as she listened to Jemmie on the other end of the phone. She put up her hand as if to say, 'it's ok,' but it was obvious to him that Jemmie was telling her something very captivating. Going back to his patient, after a few more minutes he heard her say goodbye. She slipped quietly back into the surgery and went across to her desk, wrote something down on a post it note and then stuck it on the work surface behind him. Winking at him as she returned to her desk and continued her task of filling in the patient's notes on the laptop.

Wheeling his stool around with his feet in order to pick up some cotton wool rolls from the box behind him Marcus looked sideways at the post it note. It said, *'guess who Martin saw in Manchester playing cosy twosomes with another man?'*

Turning back to attend to his patient, he looked across at Sam, his eyebrows knitted together and his mouth said a silent, *who?*

'Cath-Rine!' she mouthed with some exaggeration so that he could understand.

Marcus' pursed his lips as he then smiled, snorted slightly and nodded in a 'well, well, well...' sort of a way. He removed his patient's blue bib with a cheery, 'Well Mr White, you'll be glad to know we're all done. Just keep biting on that pack for an hour or so, no rinsing until tomorrow and I'll see you in a couple of days.'

# Chapter fourteen

On the dot of eleven o'clock that Saturday morning, as arranged, Dizzy appeared at the back door, minus the unholy horrors.

'Hector's taken them swimming,' she said, as Jules enquired after them.

'Swimming?' she said incredulously, 'that's a bit ambitious isn't it?' as she moved across to put on the kettle.

'He stopped off to pick up Amy and Fay Palmer first. He won't take them in the men's changing rooms any more since the willy incident...' she continued over her own shoulder while hanging her coat on the back of the door.

'The...? Oh do tell!' Jules laughed.

Dizzy sat down. 'Last time he took them on his own, he went to the loo in the changing rooms and left Ben Robinson the vet in charge of them because he'd met him in there too, and while he was in the loo he could hear all these hoots of laughter. It's always Batty you see, she's too clever for her own good and she leads the others astray. When he went back to them he found Ben nearly on the floor in hysterics, because Batty was corrupting the other two into counting men's willies while they changed...'

Bursting out laughing, Jules wiped away a tear. 'You're such a tonic Dizz! You always cheer me up!' and she handed her a mug of coffee as she sat down.

They sipped quietly and said nothing for a moment, and the atmosphere changed.

'So,' said Dizzy, reaching across the table and laying her hand on top of Jules', 'bring me up to speed. I'm obviously up to date on the more salacious village gossip but now I'd rather have it truthfully from you.... What's going on?'

Jules sat back in her chair and traced one finger slowly around the rim of her coffee mug. 'Straight to the point I see...' she sighed.

'Shoot from the hip Jay, no blindfold. I'm a vicar, I can take it...' she said lovingly.

Dizzy was only person in the world that had ever called her Jay and got away with it, and as a wife, mother, and minister, she was the epitome of her husband's description of her; as provided by Thomas Hardy of course...

*'She was the stuff of which great men's mothers are made. She was indispensable to high generation, hated at tea parties, feared in shops and loved at crises....'*

The last shining talent being what came into play on this particular morning.

Jules took a deep breath. 'Ok. The abridged version and hopefully without the snot then.... He's been having an affair for a year behind my back, and even had the audacity to bring her into this house while I was away, so now I can't sleep in my own bed anymore... and now he's left me and gone to be with her, holed up in the apartment in London. She's of course your average nightmare with long blonde hair, but the jury's still out on whether her collar and cuffs match... and he's not saying, obviously. She's slim, tall, successful, and she's got legs to rival Julia Roberts and her forty four inches from hip to toe, apparently. Oh, and by complete coincidence her ex boyfriend has moved into Mrs Bennett's cottage on the hill. He's called Martin and he's been lovely to me... though I can't say I've always treated him so well. And to complicate things even further he's now fallen head over heels in love at first sight with Jemmie... and she feels the same way about him.'

Dizzy's eyes were wide. 'Cripes Jules! I had no idea! So... what about Paul now then... what's the latest...?'

'He sneaked back here the other night while Martin was in here with the rest of us... well, Marcus and Sam, and Jemmie, all came running to my aid you see... and there was the most almighty row....'

She decided not to point out why at that moment.

'Then he sneaked back again, and cleared his dressing room of everything he owns and took it away with him, so I guess he really means it. Will that do...?'

Dizzy nodded slowly, and took a good two minutes to decide what to say. And within the next hour and a half, a box of tissues and a whole packet of kit kats they talked through marriage, fidelity, betrayal, and trust: and had just arrived at the ultimate challenge; forgiveness.

'The bible is full of acts of forgiveness Jules, you must know that...' Dizzy said, pouring out some more coffee.

'And I do but right now that's not at the top of my list Dizz... and I'm not sure I'll ever be able to do that.... To be honest with you, where I am now is more like I'd quite like to clean the toilet with his toothbrush and cut one sleeve off all his suit jackets.... Maybe that's why he took them all....' Taking the mug back from Dizzy she continued sadly. 'You see, even before he... I knew it Dizz. He changed. I've never said it before, but... even before I knew for sure about the affair... well, when he kissed me goodbye in the morning or something, I just felt there was no kiss behind it... like I was kissing the back of my hand... and if there was some element of committal during ... well... you know... I just knew that in his mind he was with someone else because he was... well... he was different... he wanted different... things we never... did.... And even if by some miracle he ever did see the light and want to come home to me at some point... well then, lying is an easy habit and I'd always wonder, you see... always doubt him. I'd be paranoid, I know it... and I don't know how to get around that feeling... I couldn't trust him.'

Dizzy passed her a crumpled tissue from up her sleeve once the box was empty. 'Don't worry it's clean. Jules, that's because you're misunderstanding what forgiveness, really is...' she said gently. 'You're obviously not ready to tackle this now anyway my darling, but this is what you need to consider for the future... some time in the future...whether he wakes up and misses your perfume or your home cooking again or not, you'll need to do it so your life can move on so just hear me out, yes?' She reached across and took her hand. 'You need to understand it Jules. It isn't dismissal. Forgiveness doesn't mean it didn't matter. It doesn't mean that the fact you've been hurt as profoundly as this is unimportant... or insignificant. It means it did matter, and he did hurt you, but it means that despite that, you have reached a point where you can see the way forward with strength and determination, because you don't want to feel wretched like this anymore. Trust me darling, you don't want to be, because despondency breeds from itself: you feel bad and then you feel bad because you do, see..? It's a huge step forward because in reality it means that from the moment you make that decision, you're not reheating last night's argument into today's row. It's finished. Done with. True forgiveness is the place in your heart where you can find peace again.'

Jules wiped her eyes and looked at her friend. 'So what do I do?' she asked.

'Take it slowly, one day and one step at a time... and don't be scared to pray,' she said, patting her hand gently, 'you'll know when it's time... you'll feel it. And it might help, even in the short term, if... what I mean is... a change of scenery might be a good idea too.'

'I'm not leaving this house if that's what you mean...' she said defiantly.

'No of course not... I wouldn't dream of suggesting that, Jay. I was thinking more along the lines of... I just really think you could do with... you really need a holiday...' she said gently, but Jules looked doubtful. 'Not this side of Christmas maybe, but soon. Give yourself a break. Breathe some different air.... You might think a lot more clearly after that.'

'I can't afford a holiday, and anyway where would I go on my own?' she said.

'You'd feel so much better being away from here for a couple of weeks Jules, and as for affording it... open those gorgeous eyes of yours and look around you, you nit!' She waved an arm expansively, 'paintings... paintings everywhere! Possession is nine tenths of the law... you could easily sell one, or better still sell two and go around the world a few times!'

'I'll think about it...' Jules said, with the merest hint of a smile.

Putting all thoughts of a holiday on the back burner so she wouldn't have to think about selling paintings and facing the row that doing that would undoubtedly cause, Jules set about applying for jobs, knowing that if she was busy she'd have less time to dwell on things. She found one in the Newbury Weekly News that she really liked the sound of at a school in Yattley, which was a small village about twelve miles from Frincham: fifteen minutes drive and just about far enough for a little anonymity. They had advertised for a teaching assistant to work in both the Infant and Junior classes for 30 hours per week during term time and starting immediately.

Having already been on the internet to design her CV, such as it was, and as if anyone actually remembered O Levels anymore, she duly posted off her application and metaphorically held her breath. A couple of days later and considerably sooner than she expected, she received a phone call from an efficient sounding woman called Sonia Reed, asking her to attend an interview, and she ransacked her wardrobe to find something suitable to wear that actually fitted.

'Mum, stop panicking!' Marcus was on the phone the night before the interview.

'But I haven't been on a job interview since you were tiny!' she wailed, her confidence at an all time low.

'Just be yourself Mum, and you'll be fine! You've done your course, you know what to expect don't you?'

'I know, but...'

'But nothing...' he interrupted her before she could persuade herself to sink further. 'They'll be stupid not to take someone as clever as you,' he said encouragingly.

The next morning Jules stood in front of the bedroom mirror tugging and twisting her outfit into submission and towards some attempt at a suitable appearance. Then combing her hair into a low pony tail and securing it with the silk headscarf Dizzy had given her for Christmas last year, she looked at her reflection in the mirror one last time, and recited to herself what Marcus had said last night. Then she turned away to head downstairs, and out.

# Chapter fifteen

Yattley School was a Church of England school, and was a fairly imposing old Victorian building that had had a few unsympathetic additions since its birth.

To get to the main entrance, and presumably then to her interview location, Jules had to walk across the playground, conscious of many pairs of easily distracted eyes watching her as she did so. She pressed a buzzer attached to the wall by the front doors just as several children passed by and looked inquisitively at her from inside. A distant voice that sounded not unlike one of Dr Who's Daleks, spoke out of a box on the wall beside her, and asked her to come on in once she'd introduced herself. At which point the door emitted a sharp buzzing sound like and angry insect and one of the doors released itself slightly with a clunk. Two boys of about six years old were sitting on a blue rug at a small library area in front of the door, and she smiled at them.

'Good morning,' she said brightly. 'Could one of you show me the way to Mrs Reed's office?'

The boys looked at each other and then one of them stood up.

'This way miss,' he said, leading the way through a set of double doors that opened into what was obviously the main hall, where a cacophony of sound hit them clashingly between the ears because a PE lesson was in noisy, whistle blowing progress. Jules followed him as he marched confidently and importantly in his smart grey uniform, down one side of the hall and towards the opposite doors, one half of which opened suddenly and a tall woman with short blonde hair met him coming the other way.

'Mrs Taylor?' she asked, and Jules nodded. 'Pleased to meet you, I'm Sonia Reed,' she said, holding out her arm, and they shook hands warmly. 'Thank you James,' she said, turning to the boy, indicating that his job was done.

He turned to look up at Jules and gave her a cheeky smile.

'Good luck miss!' he said, and ran off back the way he had come.

Jules smiled, 'not lacking in confidence, is he!' she said.

'James is the youngest of seven children in his family, to parents that are both consultant surgeons,' she smiled. 'They get through nannies like the Von

Trapps and if you have something to say you have to get in fast or you don't get in at all at his house!'

She opened one half of the swing doors she had appeared through and allowed Jules to go through first. 'He had his birthday last week,' she continued. 'When his mother asked him what he would like for his birthday treat he said he wanted to go to the supermarket with her on his own and have a doughnut together in the café afterwards... makes you think doesn't it? My daughter asked for party in a club with a DJ... and she's only thirteen!'

Reaching another door at the foot of a flight of stairs, she opened it and motioned Jules through first.

'Straight up the stairs, they're waiting for you, and good luck...' she nodded, and then she turned and disappeared back the way they'd come.

Jules made her way up the dark, creaky staircase surreptitiously straightening her skirt, and then checked her hair for the sixth time since she stepped out of the car. The only door that was at the top of the stairs was closed, but she could hear low talking from within, at the end of which someone male laughed.

She closed her eyes to say a silent prayer and then knocked at the door in a way that was intended to be somewhere between polite and confident.

At her knock the door was wrenched open suddenly, taking her by surprise and sending her two steps backwards, and precariously near the top of the stairs. Regrouping rapidly she smiled a little nervously and accepted the request to enter the head teacher's study.

Peter Hammond, Head Teacher at Yattley, was tall and wirily thin, with a wide friendly smile, fair hair, and a very think Midlands accent that put her completely at ease because it gave him an air of fun. This was helped on closer inspection by his Mickey Mouse tie and, she noticed when he sat down in a shabby black swivel chair, his Daffy Duck socks. Also in the room was another man, introduced as Matthew, or Matt, Cooper, chair of the school governors.

A hand bell sounded the beginning of break time from somewhere in the distance, and the sound of doors banging and children shouting to each other filled the air outside, so Peter stood up to close the window. A knock at the door then signalled the arrival of two women, who were introduced as Christine Steele and Gill Jordan; the two teachers she might be working with, if successful.

Jules immediately felt comfortable at the friendliness of the teachers, and this was further helped by the arrival of a tray of coffee mugs with Sonia. A chorus of approval by the assembled group greeted the accompaniment of a plate of custard cream biscuits, which seemed to have a particular, but as yet unknown to her, meaning among them, and a few minutes were spent in informal chatter. She was asked about herself, and told them why she had been so long out of the workplace, skipping a few of the more delicate recent details and not mentioning Paul at all, other than to say that she and her husband were currently separated, and to her relief nobody asked anything more about it, or him, thankfully.

Coffee over, she was told about the position and what would be expected of her, with the explanation that the recent addition of a new classroom and teacher, Gill, gave rise to the necessity of a permanent classroom assistant in school, who would float between classrooms on a regular timetable of classes and tasks. Jules then explained about her recent college course, which seemed to be very well received. She took the required criminal record check application form from Peter and slipped it into her bag for filling in at home, and Gill and Christine shook her hand enthusiastically as they disappeared when the bell rang at the end of break time.

Before she knew it the interview was over, without any difficulty at all on her part, and there had been no tricky questions for her to answer. Sonia then reappeared as if by magic, and offered to show her around the school before she left.

Shaking hands with the remaining group she followed Sonia down the stairs and back into the hall, which was now being laid out ready for lunch. Jules remarked that she couldn't actually smell anything cooking, remembering her last job where the smell of cabbage or fish had hung around the school all day.

'That's because it's not here yet,' she said. 'We don't cook here anymore, the meals get delivered hot, in big metal boxes, and our dinner lady... sorry, Lunchtime Controller, just serves them up. Honestly the titles we all have these days! I used to be a school secretary but now I'm a School Finance officer, and Fred the caretaker is now the Site Manager!'

Opening one half of the doors at the other end of the hall, and passing the now empty library area by the main entrance, Sonia led the way down a wide corridor lined with coat pegs on each side, each one holding a coloured and bulging pillowcase with a plaited rainbow of wool string pulling it tight through the top, presumably to keep the owner's belongings all in one place and tidy. Jules thought they looked like regiments of pregnant women awaiting inspection, but liked the look of the assorted pillowcases with their mysterious bulges, and noted that each one had the owner's name embroidered in chain stitch across the bottom. This school obviously had some traditional values, and she imagined that there would be high competition among pupils to have the best bag.

Down three wide steps now, Jules found herself at the door of the infants' class and peeped in through the toughened glass panel at the top of the door. About twenty children were all sitting on the floor by a very large window, on a brightly coloured green carpet that looked as if it was patterned with roads and road signs, and it appeared as though Christine had just begun to read them a story. Jules was enchanted at the scene and smiled at Sonia as they turned away.

Turning a sharp left and down a slightly wider corridor with similar colourful pillowcases on each side, they arrived at two classrooms with their doors directly opposite each other at the end. 'These are the two junior classes,' said Sonia, pausing at the first door. Peeping through the glass Jules saw Gill with her class, noisily preparing some kind of science lesson with leaves and flowers all over the tables. Peering in the other door she saw Peter, the head teacher, now in place and writing something on a whiteboard while his class listened to him quietly, pens in hands and books open.

Leaving the school and feeling very happy, and nervously excited, Jules drove home but couldn't settle to anything. In the absence of anyone else to talk to, she told Barney all about her job interview, who sat with his head on her knees as he listened to her with adoring eyes, rapt with interest as usual. Having waited in all afternoon for the phone to ring and sure they would have rung by now, and therefore beginning to feel a bit concerned she picked up Barney's collar and was just setting off for a walk at about four o'clock when the phone finally began to ring. Ignoring Barney's noisy protest at her about turn she picked it up on its third ring a little breathlessly, and found a slightly amused Peter

Hammond on the other end as she tried to quiet the dog and listen to him.

'We would love it if you came to work with us Jules,' he said eventually, and a grin lit up her face as she accepted his offer joyously, put down the phone, and then tackled Barney over onto his back for an ecstatic tummy rub, before resuming plan A and heading out of the door.

# Chapter Sixteen

The next few days passed in a bit of a blur as she readied herself to start work on December the first and everyone had been really supportive. The five allotments tenants all adored Barney when he dropped by to visit, and had agreed to set up a rota to ensure that he was let out during the day. Jemmie, Dizzy and Marcus were thrilled at such a positive move forward, Martin promised to keep an eye on things when he was around and Paul… well he'd find out at some point, she supposed.

Her first day dawned cold and very frosty as she set off in the early dawn to walk Barney around the lake and her white and steamy breath mingled with his as they walked down the gravel path and through the gate. Not much wildlife about this morning either, just a moorhen and a couple of ducks that moved slowly but purposefully in her direction in the hope of a tasty early morning treat. She drew a stale bread roll from her pocket, broke it into pieces, and threw them lightly into the water, much to the delight of the birds, at having the whole meal to themselves for a change. Jules shivered a little and pulled her grey scarf a little tighter around her neck as she watched them, looking at their feet under the water's surface and marvelling, as always, at their ability to withstand the freezing water against their naked little legs.

Continuing on her way as Barney sped ahead, nose to the ground and panting, she looked up the lane towards Martin's cottage and found herself wondering if one day Jemmie might live there too. Now there was an interesting thought. They were certainly made for each other, anyone could see that. Despite Jemmie's punishing work schedule they still managed to see each other as often as they could and had even managed that mini break Martin was hoping for.

Back at the house an hour later Jules, now post shower, was drying her hair in front of the mirror and applying a little makeup. She had chosen to wear a pair of black trousers and a red polo neck sweater, and was going to tie her hair back in a low ponytail with a jaunty red and black retro patterned head scarf, that Paul always said looked like his parents kitchen floor lino in the 1960's, but she had always liked it despite his sarcasm.

By 8.20 she was scraping the car windscreen with a metal fish slice from the kitchen and the engine was running to warm up and de-fog the inside. One day she would make sure that all the junk in the big-as-a-four-bedroomed-house garage would be distributed to its rightful owners and she might even have the luxury of a frost free windscreen occasionally.

Another project to add to the list, she thought, as she drove slowly out of the gates and set off up the lane to the main road.

The school playground was very busy when she arrived. Parents stood in stamping huddles and chatted, shoulders up, heads down and gloved hands thrust deeply into coat pockets against the cold. Children ran this way and that way with their coats flapping open; and hand-free gloves danced, suspended from elastic tapes pulled through their sleeves.

She pressed the front door bell and it buzzed open immediately, allowing her in. Peter Hammond appeared to greet her with a wide and welcoming grin on his friendly face, and carrying a large pile of blue exercise books under one arm, presumably en route to his classroom. Christine appeared at the door of the Infants' class and greeted her warmly, and holding the door open for her, followed her into the classroom.

'We do an activity called Show and Tell on Mondays, and then we do reading first every morning,' she said. 'It calms them down before we try and tackle anything else.' A smile lifted the corners of her mouth. 'Prepare yourself for anything in Show and Tell though because I'm quite sure some of them think it's called Show and Shock!'

A hand bell sounded enthusiastically outside. Children began noisily pouring through the front doors, hanging up their coats, rummaging in pillowcases and shouting to each other as they parted company to find their different classrooms. The Infants lined up outside their classroom and waited for Christine to let them in, with the child holding the hand bell securely by its clapper so it would stay silent, at the front of the queue. It was Christine's way of demonstrating the difference between behaviour outside and behaviour in the classroom, and it seemed to work very well. They all stood quietly, eventually, and waited for her to beckon them in, and as she did so she had her other index finger pressed vertically to her lips. As they came into the classroom the bell monitor placed the bell on Christine's desk, and then they all went straight to the carpet and sat cross legged and expectantly on the floor. About forty excited looking eyes were on Jules as she sat herself down on the edge of a very low table and was introduced to the children one by one. Christine was holding a small box of cut up coloured name stickers that the children had obviously prepared earlier, and as each child was called out, she handed them their sticker so that Jules would know who they all were by the end of the day.

Show and Tell, as Christine had told her, was a first thing on a Monday morning activity that enabled the children to talk about things that had happened at the weekend; birthday's, visits to relatives, gory playtime accidents recalling bloodied knees and grazed elbows, taking the dog, the cat, the rabbit to the vet; Grandma coming to stay; anything at all really, and the children obviously loved it.

Reading time involved changing home reading books for the next one in the series, and transferring them to and from the red Velcro sealed book bags they all carried, to listening to older ones read from a book of their choice from the assortment of titles on the library shelves by the front doors.

The first half of the morning absolutely flew by. Coffee was drunk from thick mugs held tightly in both hands to keep them warm, while supervising break time with Christine. Jules had been asked to bring in a mug for herself, and its familiar pattern seemed somehow unfamiliar and odd now, in these brand new surroundings.

Soon afterwards, lunch was eaten in the hall from very hardy looking plastic plates, and plastic beakers of water were distributed from a huge jug. Not bad at all really, but Jules made a mental note to bring a packed lunch tomorrow, like the rest of the staff, because the children's portions hardly constituted her own main meal of the day, and if she was going to get any weight off she didn't want two dinners five days a week!

The lunchtime controller was a large and mildly intimidating woman called Margaret Fletcher. She could plough fearlessly into any situation in the playground and had a shout that could halt a parade ground of new recruits, whilst simultaneously comforting any shy infant sucking its thumb at the boisterous antics of the rest of the school in one arm, and stopping someone's nosebleed with one of a huge ball of tissues she always carried in the pockets of her pink gingham overall, with the other.

After lunch, the first activity of the afternoon was called Circle Time; a time where all the children sat in a circle on the carpet and basically had an opportunity to say sorry or thank you to someone else in the class. A small teddy bear, who was apparently called Geoffrey, was passed around the circle, and the children were only allowed to speak when they were holding him. Jules was captivated by the simplicity of this most valuable activity, and sat on the edge of a desk and listened to the solemn Sorry from Myles to Edward for tripping him up in the playground and making his knees bleed, and for the sparkly eyed Thank You from Tara to Jessica for the invitation to her birthday party on Friday after school.

Before she knew it the school day was over and the children were pouring out to the playground carrying their book bags.

Standing at the low sinks washing up paint pots, Jules noticed out of the window that, unlike that morning, there were not many cars outside, and the reason for this soon became obvious to her. Four women, presumably from a rota of mothers and all sporting high visibility yellow jackets, were waiting by the gate while the children lined up noisily in front of them. She continued to watch as one of them gave the first child the end of a roll of coloured thick string, with equidistant knots tied in it, to pass back up the line until all of the children were holding on to it by a knot. Another woman handed out fluorescent yellow bands for the children to wear diagonally over their coats.

So this was a Walking Bus!

Obviously much practiced, the 'bus' set off in the direction of the village square with one mum at each end carrying a huge torch, and two along the line carrying smaller ones. Jules watched as the bus snaked its way and disappeared around the corner to the village square, and then into the dusk of the winter afternoon and out of sight.

She was hugely impressed with this school; with the happy staff and contented children, with their good manners and polite ways. There was really quite an atmosphere here and she knew what it was. It was respect. With set boundaries and gentle discipline the children all knew exactly were they stood, and it showed in every one of them.

After enjoying a much deserved cup of tea and a debrief with the rest of the staff, Jules set off for home at four thirty with a huge smile of satisfaction on her face, but soon became pensive when she arrived back at home and turned her key in the lock, reminded with a jolt at the darkness inside that there was no one but Barney to tell about her first day at work, on this day on or on any other day.

# Chapter seventeen

She settled in at school quickly, and her days were thankfully filled with noise and sometimes frantic activity to take her mind off her problems and, very soon the sole topic of conversation and brain capacity overload was Christmas.

Preparations were well underway for the annual carol service in the church, which of course included the Infants' Nativity play, and the juniors' medieval Mummers play.

Jules had always adored working in a school at Christmas time, and now found herself spending all her previously long and lonely evenings at home making angels wings with halos of silver tinsel, kings turbans from cardboard, scraps of material, and lots and lots of staples...and shepherd's costumes; plaiting old pairs of coloured tights for headbands, and hunting out gingham patterned tea towels for their headdresses. Her rag bag was also almost empty now that she had been making Mummers rags costumes for the juniors too. This was a great way to while away the otherwise lonely evenings when Martin was away working, and she looked across the floor to where Dipstick, banished from this particular trip, was stretched out contentedly in front of the fire, while Barney still preferred to lie at full stretch by the Aga in the kitchen, on his own.

Thankfully, there was a lot less time for her to dwell on the more confusing things....

Paul had arrived the previous weekend, just behind Marcus in a rent-a-van, to help him move all his stuff up to London. Though Marcus had warned her he had been on the phone offering to help, presumably in order to get his studio cleared, she'd really bristled when he'd arrogantly blocked her own car in with his, and it looked so huge and alien sitting there after so long an absence. He marched into the kitchen as if he was still lord of his Berkshire manor as well as his London one too, and she'd pointedly said she'd prefer it if he'd knock in future. Neither of them really knew how to greet eachother now; what to say, or how to be, but underneath it all, if she were being totally honest, it had still felt weirdly better somehow, to have him there. Kind of like the sort of better you know you'll feel once you've actually plucked up the courage to pull a plaster of the sensitive hairs on your arm. She'd even caught her breath when she'd seen him through the sitting room window, actually laughing when the bottom fell out of the heavy cardboard box he was carrying; the contents tumbling down the fire escape steps and past Marcus who was carrying another box, with a loud clatter against the metal. Not so long ago, he would never have found that funny.

And then he'd stayed up there for a while once it had been cleared, and she could see him through the enormous picture window, wandering and touching things, moving them back to where they'd originally been, as if he'd really missed it, and going through some of his canvasses with a critical eye.

She'd made them all lunch too, and they'd sat at the kitchen table together just like old times. Except that when his eyes had eventually clashed with hers, they'd looked very quickly away again. Clearing his throat to break the tension he remarked, 'The lock on the studio door needs lubricating, it's very stiff... and that tap is leaking annoyingly Jules....' He used his head to indicate the kitchen sink. 'I'll see if I can find a washer and get that fixed for you. And the grass is too long outside. I'm sorry I missed its last cut before the winter... but it's dry enough today...I'll get the tractor out and cut it after lunch... which is delicious... by the way....'

Jules nodded slightly but said nothing, and her face flushed slightly.

Marcus had been sitting and quietly watching him. What a hypocrite! Putting down his knife and fork slowly, he said evenly, 'I'll do all that, Dad. I'm taking care of

Mum's problems now. You don't live here anymore, remember?'

Paul had left soon after that, making his self conscious excuses and performing a very awkward goodbye, and without a backward glance he walked to his car.

Pulling out of the driveway however, he stole one last look back up towards the kitchen window, to see Marcus pulling Jules towards him. Her head was down and she had one hand up to her face.

✫

Jules moved the pile of finished costumes from the floor beside her chair in the sitting room and, folding them into a big clear plastic box she carried them through the house and put it on the dining room table, ready to put in the car in the morning. Going through to the kitchen she ignored the urge to open a second bottle of wine and flicked the switch on the kettle instead. Wine contained so many calories after all, and the bathroom scales had held no nice surprises just lately.

The dress had gone back in the wow end of the wardrobe: too high a mountain to climb at the moment.

Coffee now in hand, she picked up a small carrier bag from the counter, sat down at the table, and sighed with an audible little groan as she opened the bag. Christmas cards.

She'd been dreading this.

So many cards received already, and all to either Paul *and* Jules or Jules *and* Paul depending on from which side of the family they'd come from, and she hadn't even started yet. Thanks to Gill's suggestion when she'd started working at the school she'd quickly discovered how to do her food shopping online, so someone else did it for her and it magically appeared on Saturday mornings. She'd even discovered the pleasures of Christmas shopping on the internet, as a vacant bedroom floor carpeted in boxes upstairs could now testify.

So why hadn't anyone come up with a Christmas card writing service?

She had underlined Jemmie's birthday on the wall calendar two weeks ago, in red marker pen, so she'd remember to find a birthday card and wrapping paper before all you could find in the shops were Christmassy ones, but writing Christmas cards truly was a pain in the rear.

At least this year she wouldn't have to fold one of Paul's pretentious letters in with them all. All full of horrible smarmy comments about how well he and everyone else had done that particular year, apart from her of course. Her only mention in his letters was usually, 'and Jules sends her love'.

She could now pretend in her literary silence that she'd ended world poverty by her self this year if she wanted to. A small shred of silver in the approaching dark cloud, but not nearly enough.

She closed her eyes, and made the box go away momentarily, but not effectively.

Pulling her address book from her handbag that was hanging on the back of the chair, she made a half hearted start by flicking through it, wondering if *they* were sending out joint cards this year, to confuse everyone even more.

Picking up the pen, she wrote the first one. God, it was so humiliating just putting 'love from Jules'.

And what if he'd written one of his letters to put in with their cards?

*'I'm sorry to report that Jules and I parted company this year but are still on very friendly terms.'* (yes well...) *Catherine and I look forward to seeing you again in the near future.*

*Best wishes for Christmas and the New Year from Paul and Catherine...*

Maybe she'd just hibernate through Christmas and just wouldn't bother this year.

The dim but precious glimmer in her Christmas plans to keep her from the hibernation idea was that the children were coming home, obviously worried about her being left alone.

Poor old Mum; such a liability these days...

She slid the lid back onto the box and pushed it away decisively. Then she stood up and went to the fridge and pulled out another bottle of white wine.

'What the hell, it's Christmas,' she said out loud. Barney opened one eye and looked up at her critically but, seeing no food appear from the fridge along with the bottle, his head sank back onto the rug.

## Chapter eighteen

And so the end of term arrived and school was over until 6th January. The Nativity Play at the Carol service had been a triumph of gaffer tape and safety pins over all unscheduled evils, the congregation had, in most cases, stifled the urge to burst out laughing when the Innkeeper's loud proclamation, (his head having appeared around the very substantial vestry door), of; *'I'm sorry we have no room here,'* was met with Joseph's response of; *'but Richard I haven't knocked yet!'* and the Mummer's play was much enjoyed, but left most people completely baffled, as usual.

Jules was now at home for the duration and had little time to dwell on her first Christmas without Paul during the hours of daylight, however brief they were, being swamped under a mountain of three days worth of meat and vegetables to prepare. Night times were a different story though, so no change there then. Christmas or not, once the house was quiet, and she'd locked all the doors and crept upstairs to bed, it was then that she discovered what loneliness really felt like.

The Saturday before Christmas, and after waking up and biting the bullet to get the tree up and the rooms decorated, for the children if not for her, she pulled the tatty wicker basket of Christmas decorations backwards down the loft ladder, which had been a bad enough experience on her own, but opening it and taking out the tree decorations had been ten times worse. She had never been one for fashionable Christmas tree dressings and in latter years Paul had really resented that, but instead, she had gradually built up a large collection of heart warming and nostalgic treasures over the years. Things like the two glass bells carefully wrapped in tissue paper, which had belonged to her grandmother. The little fat fairy from the Christmas fair at the children's junior school so long ago. The lopsided snowman made with cotton wool and the middle of a toilet roll. The star made from modelling clay that was so heavy it drooped the top of even the most robust tree, and had to be propped on the mantelpiece instead.

When the children were really small and they'd had no money, she'd bought a big box of cheap red and gold baubles from Woolworths, and Paul and the children had sat in their tiny kitchen one afternoon and transformed them into the most beautiful ones she'd ever seen; the children's ones twinkled in the light of the fire with glitter and stars, and Paul's were so delicately painted with snow scenes and fairies.

As she sat on the floor by the tree now, she lifted one out of its tissue paper carefully, holding it up into the light of the fire. So wonderfully realistic, it had a snow covered church on it, and a little choir in Victorian costumes all holding candle lanterns in the shape of little bow windows. He'd copied the lid of the Quality Street chocolates tin, and it always made her laugh.

Not anymore. She swallowed hard.

Then she lifted out the one that had Marcus and Jemmie's tiny cameo faces painted onto it, and the death by a thousand knives experience was complete. She crumpled into a sobbing heap on the carpet.

※

The day before Christmas Eve now and up in London, Marcus and Sam were enjoying an evening out at a prestigious hotel in the company of a lot of other dentists and their partners, courtesy of one of the big dental supply companies. Marcus was really enjoying himself. The round tables were all set out for twelve so that there were plenty of people to talk to, the food had been wonderful and Sam looked stunning in a strapless silver evening gown that clung in all the right places and shimmered as she danced. He had to admit he was enjoying the envied glances of his colleagues when his arm slid around her waist possessively too. She was in a terrific mood and her eyes sparkled with fun. In fact the evening was going swimmingly. His new suit trousers had a thirty two waist, business was booming and, apart from worrying about his mother and not really speaking to his father, he found himself totally content with his life.

Among the party seated at the table right next to them was a woman with a little boy of about two years old, who was actually the only child in the room of any age. The child was obviously tired and fractious, squirming and wriggling like an over excited puppy, and the parents were beginning to get embarrassed at the glances they were getting from the occupants at the other tables, as well as their own.

'Oh for pity's sake take the little demon home to bed! Why on earth don't they take it to bed?' Marcus hissed at no one in particular.

'Quite right Marcus! Kids shouldn't be allowed at this sort of do...' replied Angus Campbell, an overweight and obnoxious Scotsman from Middlesex who'd been leering at Sam all evening: plenty loud enough to be heard, and also seated at their table.

Marcus knew the child's father vaguely. His name was Tom Williamson and he was an associate partner in an NHS practice not far from his. He had also known him before he married the wife that now sat with the demonic child. He'd played rugby on Sunday mornings, and played just as hard on Sunday evenings in the rugby club bar. He had met Patsy, now his wife, in that same club bar where she was working at the time. She had been quite a looker in those days too, and gave just as good as she got in the ribald atmosphere, he recalled. She had long black hair with a fringe just brushing her brown eyes, and a very fine pair of boobs nicely displayed in the low cut tops she used to wear.

The change in both of them tonight was quite shocking.

Hearing Angus, Tom took the child in his arms and stood up, turning around to face them. 'I'm sorry if he's being a bother to you all,' he muttered nervously, 'he's teething you see and the babysitter couldn't...'

'Do spare us the gory details dear boy...' said Angus, rudely.

Tom flushed crimson and swallowed hard. Turning away quickly, and taking the child away from the table, Patsy stood up to follow him, straightening the skirt of her dress self consciously and over a very noticeable stomach. With tears in her eyes she turned and looked straight at Marcus. 'It's so hard for us to get out now we have him Marcus,' she blinked. 'When the sitter couldn't come we... well we were both so looking forward to this. I'm sorry, but we thought it would all be ok...'

'Well it's probably better off in bed at this time of night anyway...' Marcus replied, but he was already reaching for the wine bottle.

'I'm sorry if you're evening has been spoiled Patsy...' Sam interrupted, embarrassed at Marcus' frequent use of 'it' to describe her son, and by his rudeness towards her now. Patsy looked at her and tried to smile but her bottom lip was quivering, so she simply nodded, turned away and sped off after her husband.

Angus continued annoyingly in the same vein for quite a while longer and Marcus, Sam was shocked to see, was still agreeing with him. They were saying that children had no place at corporate events like these and if the parents should want to go out sometime they should either get a sitter or Patsy should have stayed at home with him and Tom could have come along by himself.

Marcus also said he'd sooner stay unencumbered personally, and he'd gone on to brag that he and Sam had an understanding and both felt the same way about it.

He'd put his arm around her and squeezed her shoulder at that point.

Nobody said you had to have them. Children were for other people. Like marriage was for other people. Those things change everything, and Tom and Patsy were a prime example of that change. Sam took care of herself and always looked sexy. He and Sam were perfectly content they way things were.

Life was perfect.


Sam was quiet all the way home in the back of the taxi but Marcus was asleep with his mouth open and snoring anyway so didn't notice. She looked across at him; maybe things were not quite as perfect as he thought, and a huge bombshell was about to hit him.

She was late, very late. She'd been surprised by her own reaction at being beside herself with excitement when she'd done the test this morning, and then seen that little blue line of fate, but after hearing Marcus tonight, she was no longer in such an excellent mood and her eyes weren't sparkling with fun anymore.

She was scared.

※

Marcus meanwhile was blissfully unaware of the impending bombshell and continued to be incorrigible at Christmas as he always had been.

Presents had to be hidden in ever more inventive places in order to beat him at snooping to find them. When he was a little boy, and after many spoiled surprises, Mrs Bennett used to keep all the presents up in her cottage and poor Marcus would spend hours ferreting around at home trying to find them. So it was with some frustration that he loaded up the car in London that Christmas Eve morning, because there was nothing for him from Sam to shake and squeeze and sniff, amongst the other presents in any of the bags. He'd been so certain he would see it once the car got loaded, but there truly was nothing; he'd looked, twice.

She'd been like a cat all morning too. At first he'd put it down to her having a bit of a hangover, but then he remembered he hadn't seen her partake of anything stronger than fruit juice all evening. He had no idea what he'd done but it must have been something bad, and although he'd had a lot to drink it wasn't as if he couldn't still remember everything, and besides, she'd been really happy at the party.

She'd been snappy and tearful since she got up though, but when asked, had said 'I'm fine!' in a voice that meant she clearly wasn't. Doors and drawers slammed when she packed their bags, saucepan lids crashed as she unpacked the dishwasher, and she looked thunderous…

So maybe it was so awful she hadn't bought him a present?

She was really quiet on the journey too. Marcus surreptitiously looked sideways at her from the driving seat several times, and each time she was either chewing her bottom lip, or biting the side of one thumb, which she always did when tense.

Something was definitely wrong.

'Sam? Ok?' he asked tentatively.

'Fine,' she said. 'Watch the road,' and that was it. The sum total of her conversation for the best part of the journey was those four words, and as soon as they arrived in Frincham, Sam disappeared off to find a loo. Jules, extra sensitive to emotions these last few months, and feeling the atmosphere between them asked Marcus if everything was alright, and he'd shrugged.

'We're fine apparently,' he said.

Jemmie, Martin and Dipstick came over just before dinner time, having been for a walk around the lake to burn off some of Dipstick's boundless energy before he saw everyone. It didn't really work because once he and Barney had said their doggy hello's both dogs took off to chase each other round the dining room table, hopelessly over excited by all the visitors, and by all the interesting goings on and tasty smells in the house.

After all the human greetings were done, and the dogs separated and calmed down, Jules chivvied everyone to the table for dinner. The kitchen smelled absolutely gorgeous because traditionally at home, Christmas Eve dinner was always gammon and she had been at it all day, soaking, rinsing, scoring, and boiling the huge joint. She always finished it off by roasting it off coated in brown sugar, honey and cloves, and Marcus just adored it. She served it up with roasted root vegetables in a special sauce and crispy baked potatoes from the Aga with lashings of butter.

Hang the diet.

There was a bit of an uncomfortable pause when she sat down and left the joint at the end of the table for the non existent Paul to carve, as he had done for the best part of thirty Christmas Eve's before this one, but Marcus saved her humiliation by leaping up to carve it, over exaggerating the knife sharpening process to cover the awkwardness.

Despite her own fragility, all through the meal Jules was watching Sam. She had gone straight up to their room when they'd arrived, and hadn't come down again until dinner was ready, saying she was still tired from the night before, but when she did appear she looked pale and her eyes were puffy, as if she'd been crying.

It was a real puzzle. She never did have a huge appetite but she'd always loved Jules' Christmas gammon, and yet she was just picking at her food, and then left most of it. Jules wondered if they'd had a row in the car. Catching Marcus' eye she nodded towards Sam to get him to look at her too, her brows meeting with concern, but he'd just shrugged his shoulders slightly. When he'd quietly asked her again if she was alright, she'd said she had a headache, that's all.

Jules offered to get some Paracetemol tablets from the kitchen for her but she said she was fine and not to worry.

She did seem to realise that people were becoming concerned though and so managed to eat some of the pudding that Jules had made, and helped to clear the table once the meal was over.

In the sitting room to sounds of the clatter of the dishwasher being loaded in the kitchen, Marcus was secretly searching through all the presents under the tree, looking for Sam's, and got caught out by the eventual arrival of the others from the kitchen, carrying a tray of coffee.

'You won't find it down there Marcus!' said Sam, sitting in an armchair and turning sideways, kicking off her shoes so that she could hang her legs over the arm and face the sofa.

Everyone else was in high spirits which was quite contagious. Jules undid the button on the waist of her next size down but a bit hopeful jeans and groaned as she sat down, and even Sam seemed a little brighter once away from the intensity of the table.

They all flopped into the various other chairs around the sitting room and Jemmie was teasing Marcus as she sat down beside Martin cosily on the sofa.

'So what did you get him then?' she laughed across to Sam.

'More importantly where did you hide it?' he asked her, 'I've looked everywhere...'

'Everything comes to he who waits...' said Jules, taking a mug from the tray on the coffee table.

'He'll be waiting quite a while then,' said Sam, very quietly.

She was definitely trying, but whenever Marcus stole a look at her, there was that tense thumb chewing again.

At 11.15pm they all donned their coats and gloves and set off with torches into the moonless night for the church, and to the midnight service.

Jules had always loved the midnight service at St. Mary's; well, until she walked in through the south door this particular year and took in the sideways glances from those who knew *about* Paul coming thick and fast, and the backward glances *for* Paul, from those who didn't. And then there were the cringingly hideous, 'How *are* yous', with the sympathetic head tilts; along with the, 'I'm *fines',* with the slow nod routines. Rector Hector though was in excellent form, and timed the last verse of O Come all ye Faithful for exactly one minute past twelve. *Yea Lord we greet Thee, born this happy morning...* and Jules felt horribly like she was going to cry. Blinking hard and swallowing a lump in her throat the size of a cricket ball, she found she just couldn't stop it and her eyes began to betray her. Loud whispering from the pews behind and in front made it even worse as she fumbled in her pockets for a tissue, but then she felt a gloved hand take hers and squeeze.

It was Sam, and she was crying openly too, but Jules could see instantly that this was for more than just missing her mother and lamenting for Christmases gone by.

'I don't know what to do!' she whispered, her head leaning in to Jules' coat sleeve.

'About what?' she whispered back, her own urge to cry ceasing instantly.

'Marcus,' she sobbed. 'It's all going wrong!' and she buried her head into Jules like a little girl.

Marcus looked horrified as Jules sat back down and pulled Sam with her.

'What is it darling? What's wrong?' she whispered anxiously. Sam shook her head and tried to dry her eyes with the back of her hand. Marcus' hand appeared beside hers and slipped his handkerchief into it. Taking it gratefully she looked up at him and then her head went down and she sobbed into it uncontrollably.

The Carol finished and Hector was now in the Pulpit and just beginning his sermon having successfully regained the attention of the congregation on the right hand side of the nave back to the matter in hand, and Marcus, now re seated, tried to slip his arm around Sam's shoulders but she pulled away and leaned harder into Jules.

People were thankfully beginning to lose interest in them and listen to Hector as Jules continued to hold Sam, gently rubbing her arm until she calmed down, and once the offertory hymn started and the opportunity arose, she stood up and took Sam's arm, leading the way out of the pew and motioning at Marcus to stay put. This was obviously something she had to say without him.

Ignoring the rekindled interest from the pews near the back, they made their way out into the churchyard and took advantage of the exterior lighting to lean against an ancient table top tombstone that declared for all eternity;

*'Sacred to the memory of Charles Edward Whittaker*

*Rector of this Parish for forty three years*

*Died 14th January 1879 aged 73 years*

*"Well done Thy Good and Faithful Servant"*

'What is it Sam, what is it that's all gone wrong?' Jules asked plaintively.

Now outside, Sam let herself really go and was only able to tell her in short bursts about the dinner the night before and what had happened with Marcus over Tom and Patsy's little boy.

'Oh Sam,' she said. 'He'd been drinking! I'm sure he never meant anything by it…he just…'

'You weren't there Jules! You never saw him! And he never has *that* much to drink! He never wants to have children… he said so… he said we were perfect the way we are.'

'And you're not happy about that… obviously. Is that it Sam?'

'I was happy Jules, I really love him. We were so happy… but the thing is we never talked about wanting children… and I always assumed he did… like I do… but we never actually discussed it… and now… and now I've… now it's…'

She started to cry again.

'Oh Sam…' Jules pulled her into her arms and hugged her tightly. 'Most men think like that at first!

They're just like little boys who never want their summer holidays to end!' She rubbed her shoulder comfortingly. 'You'll see.'

Sam shook her head sadly.

'Yes he will, you'll see. Talk to him about it. Get this out into the open. Talk about how you both feel about this... there are two of you in this relationship remember... and you're both young yet... there's plenty of time for him to get his head around it.'

She looked up suddenly and straight into her eyes. 'Oh no there isn't...' she sobbed.

'Just tell him,' Jules said, as the penny dropped. 'You definitely need to tell him. You'll see.'

'Do you really think so?'

'I do...' she said, standing up and taking her hand.

'Maybe you're right Jules...' she whispered.

✤

'Sam, please talk to me, tell me what's wrong?' Marcus was whispering to her back in the darkness of the bedroom a little later, but she pretended to be asleep.

Not yet... but it was going to be alright; she was plotting the perfect way to tell him.

Christmas Day was so hectic, and being Jemmie's birthday as well, the focus of the breakfast table had traditionally been given to her and her presents, so that Sam and Marcus' problem remained mostly unnoticed to all but themselves and to Jules.

After the breakfast of cold gammon ham and fresh eggs, for which Sam didn't even appear anyway, everyone ploughed through to the sitting room to open the Christmas presents, to the musical accompaniment of the Vienna Boys choir. Marcus went up to fetch Sam and brought her downstairs to join everyone. She looked a lot more cheerful and was carrying a small gift wrapped present about the size of a fountain pen, so he guessed that that was what it was. Like he really needed another fountain pen… and he tried to hide his disappointment.

Jules was thrilled with her trolley case from Jemmie and Martin, so that she could carry all her things to and from school without hurting her back, and she was over the moon with her long weekend travel package to London from Marcus and Sam and was already planning which show to see and which shops to mount an assault on in the New Year, and there was a hotel too so no more humiliating surprises by staying in Paul's London apartment: not that that was even an option…

Martin bought Jemmie a notebook computer so she could carry it around without the theoretical aid of a winch like her old laptop, and for her birthday he was taking her to Paris for a long weekend in the spring. Jemmie bought him a driver's dream day with a Ferrari and a Lamborghini that made his eyes twinkle with excitement.

Marcus made a great show of his gift to Sam which was a delicate and obviously expensive gold bracelet in a red leather box, and then all the present giving was seemingly over. Jules began gathering up the sea of wrapping paper from the floor, and Jemmie got up to get some more drinks.

Then Sam took a mammoth deep breath and stood up. 'Don't forget me!' she said, 'Just one more gift...' and the room fell quiet once more. Then because they were in fact all aware of the funny atmosphere between Sam and Marcus, they all sat down again and looked at both of them expectantly.

'Marcus,' she said, with a little nervous smile, 'here is your present...' and she walked across the room and handed him the fountain pen. He opened it very impatiently, feigning excitement, but then he found himself longing for another fountain pen, for inside the gift wrap and selotape package was the positive pregnancy test. The rest of them erupted into hoots of laughter and congratulations, and only Jules and Sam caught the horror in his eyes as he stared at that little blue line, looking for all the world as though straight down the barrel of a loaded twelve bore shotgun.

The rest of the day was a testimony to faux happiness, with a forced smile fixed on Marcus' face and a brittle one on Sam's, and so inevitably, in the early hours of Boxing Day morning and after the horrified Marcus had finally confronted her with a barrage of his true feelings once they'd gone up to bed, and consequently choosing to sleep in his old room, Sam crept fully clothed but carrying her shoes, into the kitchen, having left a letter on the mantelpiece addressed to Marcus. Then she slipped out of the back door with her bag, and drove away into the night.

Upstairs and asleep in his old bedroom Marcus stirred at the sound of the car starting outside and just below his window, but not enough to absolutely wake him, and he turned over with a slight snore and drifted back to sleep.

✵

Sam's absence was noticed once the relatively apologetic Marcus had tried to deliver her a cup of tea in bed in the morning, only to find that the bed had not even been slept in. Jules eventually found him sitting in his father's study, looking thunderous, and a mirror image of the man himself. He'd just slammed down the phone and still had her letter in his hand, which was positively shaking as he seethed. 'That,' he said shortly, 'was Sam, but she obviously thought you would answer the phone because she wouldn't even speak to me....'

'Marcus, let's go for walk,' she said, in a mother's tone.

Knowing that particular tone very well indeed, he knew that argument was futile, so he got up and followed her out through the kitchen. Once outside and leaning on the fence and watching Amy's pony graze on a pile of hay, she waited for him to say something first.

'Sam told you I suppose?' he said eventually.

'She did.'

He nodded slightly, and drew in a deep breath, letting it out quickly. 'I just don't know how she could do that to me! In front of everyone like that! It was so humiliating!'

'For you or for her?' she said.

He glared at her, and again she swallowed at the likeness she'd never really noticed this much before.

'I don't know how this could have happened!' he continued lamely, but seeing her look of incredulousness he shook his head impatiently. 'Not that Mum! I'm not stupid! ...we never thought we were cut out to be parents I... I mean we never wanted children...'

'That was maybe a bit of an assumption on you're part Marcus, because it seems apparently Sam did...' she said quietly.

His head dropped.

'All this talk of 'we' never wanted children... but you never actually discussed it with her though did you?'

'She never said... we never...' he turned his back to the paddock and leaned against the fence heavily, and began to kick at the ground. The pony raised its head at the sudden vibration in the fence, but seeing nothing of interest, quickly returned to his breakfast. 'I just don't know how we got here... she should never have let... She should never have let it happen without consulting me... I should have had a say in this! And the thing is... I seriously...*seriously* don't know if I can do this Mum.'

Just like his father. Not his idea, therefore not his problem.

'So you're saying the relationship is over then Marcus?'

'I...'

'You're saying that you're going to leave Sam to do this alone?'

'No! I mean... I don't know Mum! I just don't know... maybe she won't want to have it now...' Seeing his mother's eyes almost pop out of her head at that, he began to walk away slowly. She followed him and they walked along the bank towards the woods.

'Do you love Sam, Marcus?'

He looked impatient again. 'Of course I do! She knows I do! Loving her is not the problem here is it?'

'Well if you love her Marcus, and if as you say, she knows that, then why do you suppose she left?'

He shrugged. 'Beats me... maybe she's testing me...' he stopped walking. 'She thinks that by leaving like that she'll shock me into submission. Well she won't.'

She stopped walking too and turned to face him. 'You sound just like little Markie, Marcus.'

'So now you're saying I'm being childish?'

'I'm saying you're acting with a generous chunk of it. You feel as if a decision has been made without consulting you and now you've gone straight for the feeling threatened option instead of really thinking it through, and I'm saying that because of that, and because of your very audible tantrum last night, Sam feels vulnerable and humiliated and that's why she left: she couldn't face any of us after that. She didn't trick you Marcus, and she's not testing you. You know her better than that darling.'

He sat down on a fallen tree and pulled his fleece tighter around him, folding his arms and hunching his shoulders defensively.

'I don't want things to change. She knew that. I like our life as it is. We have money, we go out, we go on great holidays... we ski... we have a good social life; loads of friends... I don't *want* it to change. You can't do any of that with a kid in tow... and I don't want Sam to change...'

Jules continued to stand, and looked down at him. 'You can't stay hold of your youth forever you know, any more than Sam can... however hard you try. Every parent in the world has been there before you... the *am I really ready for all this?* routine....' She smiled and touched his arm. 'Marcus this *is* real life, not the one you're still grasping hold of with the tips of your fingers. And you must understand that real life, real maturity and a real... committed relationship can't be sustained if one of you still thinks differently on such a huge issue. Or, if one of you still thinks that despite having a partner he's still young free and single. Where's the stability and where's the commitment in that?'

'We have stability! We have commitment! We live together... we share a home...'

'That isn't commitment sweetheart, that's playing house, and as for stability, what just happened here?'

He drew a breath and bit his lower lip, 'I know you've never approved of us living together Mum...'

'True, but that's not what I mean here and you know it. You need to make a decision here. Sam is having a baby now whether you think it was planned or whether it wasn't, and for what it's worth she told me it wasn't and therefore I believe her. Having a baby is what being together is all about in the grown up world; it's what we're put here to do, and what's more it won't go away now it's happened... however hard you kick and scream to try and make it. So ask yourself; do you really love her or not? That's the real test here. This isn't Sam testing you, it's you testing yourself.'

He put his head on her shoulder as she sat down, and she kissed him on the top of his head, finally able to reach it.

'When I told your father I was expecting you he acted just the same way...'

'I'm not a bit like him!' he sat up suddenly.

'You are you know. More than you know it.'

'I'm not like him. I'd never treat Sam like he's treated you!'

She ignored the urge to correct him.

'I mean you're like him as he used to be, before...'

His head went back onto her shoulder and she slipped her arm around him and rocked him gently, just like she used to when he hadn't been so tall, and his problems hadn't been nearly so complicated.

'He wanted us to stay the same forever too. He worried about suddenly being responsible for another human being; he worried about me loving you more than I did him. He worried you'd be born with two heads and three legs...'

Marcus smiled, despite himself.

'He worried about money... we never had any then. He worried about everything! It's perfectly normal to be worried Marcus; it's all part of life's rich pattern... but it's so worth it... really. Just wait until you see your *baby*... the perfect miracle that will be *your* baby... yours and Sam's... and then you'll see what it's really all about... Life, the universe, and everything...'

He smiled at her quote from his favourite set of books as he'd grown up; the Hitch Hikers Guide to the Galaxy, but then he frowned again. 'I'm just not ready...'

'Nobody ever is darling. Not really. The decision may have been made for both of you sooner than it might have been, but it has been made nevertheless, so now you need to deal with it.'

'I don't even know where she is...'

'Yes you do Marcus. She said in her letter she was going home. So go and find her and put this right, now.'

'And in the meantime I suppose you'll have to tell Dad about this too?'

'That's for you to do Marcus. It's not for me to tell him your news... though what he'll make of becoming a Grandad is anyone's guess at the moment! Sort Sam out first and then tell him.'

'I can't. I don't want him to know. I don't even want to talk to him after that last visit here when he had the downright guile to try and control everything... I just can't deal with what he's done to you... or to us. I hate him.'

'No you don't. Don't let him and what he's done cloud your own good judgement. You might resent him for what he's done to me and the rest of our family, but he'll always be your dad. His problem is with me, not you.'

'Don't you hate him for what he did to you? Splashing your marriage all over the papers and everything?'

She thought for a moment and smiled a little. 'I thought I did, and maybe I really did for a while... I know I should. I have every right to. But I don't. I think

I hate myself for still... Well It's not something you can just switch off is it? Not when he's been half of me for thirty years... and so... while we're speaking truthfully darling, I miss him like hell.'

# Chapter nineteen

Marcus left straight away in Jules' car and with a plastic box of turkey sandwiches to sustain him on the journey, not that he could eat them, and having tried Sam's mobile number again at least twice more, but her phone was switched off and she'd disabled her voicemail.

Arriving at the apartment soon after one, it was apparent even before he'd even looked under the fire extinguisher to get the spare key, she was not there; he could not feel her there.

Dropping the car keys on the coffee table, he sat down on the sofa heavily, put his head in his hands, and then shocked himself by bursting into tears: great wracking sobs that came from nowhere and shook him to the core. Suddenly she wasn't pregnant Sam anymore, she was just Sam, his Sam; he had betrayed and humiliated her in a most terrible way when she'd needed him so badly, and now she'd gone. And he had no idea where.

He spent the rest of the day in a complete daze of phone calls to friends and pacing of carpets, and fell eventually into an exhausted sleep on the bed, fully clothed. He awoke the next morning when it was still early enough for the pigeons on the roof to be quiet, and with his mouth feeling like he'd swallowed a pub carpet and it had got stuck half way down his throat.

✷

It was breakfast time back at Clearwater House when the telephone rang in the kitchen. Jemmie and Martin had left early and Jules was emptying the dishwasher in search of a cereal bowl, and wiped her hands on a tea towel quickly before picking it up.

'Oh Marcus...' she gasped at his despair. Hearing her child crying at the end of the phone still made her blood run cold from when he and Jemmie had been at university and had occasionally rung home in a state over results and things. Back when, over the top of every sensible suggestion it was her motherly duty to make, her every instinct had really screamed *come home to Mummy* as much then as it did now. 'Think about it darling... it's so obvious I thought you'd have guessed. Where do you and Jemmie always come when you're in trouble?'

'We come home to you...' he said, and then he had it.

Tearing back down the stairs to the car park and leaping into the car he headed west, towards Barnes.

Sam's family home for her whole life up to Marcus had been in the London suburb of Barnes, at Spencer Road, which was a typical leafy London street, made up of an assortment of post war 1950's and 60's houses and flats. At the very end of the road and near the playing fields stood a double fronted 1950's house with mock Tudor beams above the front bedrooms, leaded windows throughout, and a crazy paving front driveway that was undergoing a constant fight for supremacy against nature through the cracked and flaking cement between its slabs.

On the driveway of that house sat his own car, sitting patiently behind her dad's orange Austin Princess that he'd had since it was new, and he knew he'd found her.

Upstairs, a curtain moved in the window of Sam's old room as he walked up the path, and the front door opened before he'd even reached for the bell chain.

Sam's mother had died tragically in an awful train crash when Sam was just was thirteen, and it was her father, whom she absolutely adored; and really it should have been much easier to guess that of course she would run to him when she needed help, who stood in the open doorway now. He stood aside and allowed Marcus into the house without a word being said. In fact the whole sequence was completed virtually without words, there being precisely three, which were 'Tea?' and, 'Yes please'. He was then shown into the sitting room which was a tribute to 1970's retro chic, and he sat nervously on the orange and brown stripey sofa while her father disappeared into the kitchen to make it.

Then Sam appeared at the open door, his Sam, and the very first thing he noticed apart from the look on her face was that she was still wearing her bracelet. She was quivering with nerves, but she was wearing his present, which was possibly a good sign; he hoped.

He stood up shakily. 'I love you Sam. Oh Sam I'm so sorry. I'm such an idiot… I love you… both of you…' he said quietly, choking with emotion.

'We need to talk Marcus,' she said, turning in one movement and heading for the front door, grabbing her coat from the newel post at the bottom of the stairs on the way. In the kitchen, Brian Mason turned off the kettle at the wall switch and looked at the front door as it closed behind them, entirely unsure whether to be worried or relieved.

They walked to the end of the road and through a little gate onto the playing fields, and then on into the parkland beyond. Marcus took her hand and they walked in silence towards a wooden bench under a large horse chestnut tree. She smiled, just a little, knowing exactly what he was going to say.

'You brought me here the first time I came to meet your dad...' he said quietly.

She nodded and sat down on the bench, shoulders hunched and knees firmly locked together against the freezing cold. Marcus continued to stand because his eyes were now drawn to the tree, his head darting from spot to spot, searching for something.

'Trees grow Marcus... it was a long time ago.' She indicated something about eight feet from the bottom of the tree; nearly three feet higher than it had originally been. 'It's way up there now....'

Above his head was a little heart carved into a round, naked spot in the bark that marked where a branch had once been removed.

It had *'M T loves S M'* in its centre.

'You already found it...'

'Yesterday; I came here yesterday, just after I arrived.... Dad wasn't home... he was at his bridge club Christmas party at the pub...' then she smiled again, a little sadly. 'That was the first time you told me you loved me...' she said, as he sat down and turned to face her.

'I remember. Not very original, defacing an ancient oak tree was it?'

'It's a conker tree Marcus... look at the ground... there are still bits of squashed conkers everywhere.'

He used one finger to move a strand of hair from across her eyes. '...It's a tree... same difference.... But I still do love you Sam, so much... I don't know what I'd do without you...'

She looked away from him and into the distance, focussing her gaze on a young couple with a little boy, throwing a stick for their dog.

'I thought I'd really blown it this time...' he continued, then, changing tack he became serious. 'Listen... I know I've been an idiot and...'

'Stop... Marcus don't... I know what you want to say, but...'

'Please Sam, let me...'

She looked down and then back up at him under her lashes in a movement that had made his heart flutter the first time he'd seen her do it, sitting right on this bench under this very tree, in the summer that she'd proudly taken him to meet her father; and after it had done the third somersault he'd told her there and then that he loved her.

And in that instant he knew.

'Marry me?' he asked suddenly, as her mouth fell open and her eyes almost popped out of her head.

'M... Marcus... I... What did you say? But you don't believe in... *What?*'

'Marry me. Samantha Nicole Mason... I mean it... I want you with me... I always want you with me... I want... I want us...' he placed his hand gently against her stomach, 'I want all of us... to be a proper family....'

'Marcus... are you quite...?'

'Yes, Sam, I am sure. I've never been more sure of anything since the last time we sat on this bench. Just say yes, Sam... say yes.' He slipped down on to one knee in the wet grass among the squashed conkers and took her stripey gloved hand in his own very cold, pink one. She looked at him for at least ten years before whispering, 'Yes... Marcus Paul Francis Taylor,' as her voice broke and her eyes filled with tears. 'Yes!'

He kissed her then, long and passionately, just as he had back then, and also just as he had back then, knowing he'd finally got the right girl. And the couple with the little boy and the dog were the first to offer their congratulations on what they had just witnessed, as they walked past them, the man bouncing his little son on his shoulders.

'I can't wait to do that with our son...' he murmured, as he watched them continue on their way, holding hands, the little boy laughing and giggling as they went.

'Or daughter...' she smiled, kissing his cheek.

Standing up finally and pulling him with her, the wicked twinkle had returned to her eyes, and she said seriously, 'we'd better go and tell Dad now Marcus, so he can put his shotgun away...'

He looked at her for a moment and then seeing the twinkle, laughed, slightly nervously.

'Oh I'm being perfectly serious...' she smiled. 'You're lucky he let you past the front door... he hadn't even twigged we have sex!' and then she pulled her hand away and ran from him, shooting down the slope and across the park and howling with laughter.

'Sam you shouldn't be running! Not in your condition!' He tore after her and caught her, still giggling, and pulled her back towards him, determined to never let her go again.

# Chapter twenty

Blissfully unaware of the traumas in Frincham, Paul's Christmas with Catherine was somewhat different. Not for them the excitement of a traditional family Christmas in their apartment, for there was only the two of them; and their history wasn't anywhere near old enough to be called tradition.

They'd gone Christmas tree shopping far too late so that the only ones left were the really spindly ones, so they'd actually bought a made up display one from a shop window that arrived complete with twinkling lights and un customised baubles; no fat fairy, no snowman, no character whatsoever, and just sat in the corner.

His present to her was the pair of diamond earrings from Hatton Garden that he had actually bought for Jules' birthday some time previously. Diamonds are forever... but that had seemed so hypocritical at that time he'd kept them and given her a bottle of her favourite perfume instead. His present from her was an extremely sexy and very sheer black silk negligee that she promised to model for him later.

That was the presents done then.

No CD's or funny book from Jules, no brew your own beer kit or rent a vine of grapes for a year from the children... and no giant toblerone from Barney either.

And there wasn't any gammon; far from it, because Catherine hadn't done any food shopping, assuming that they would be eating out all over the holiday. So when he'd arrived home far too early on Christmas Eve after the reception he'd gone to had fizzled in everyone's eagerness to rush home to their families, the best he could rustle up, because she wasn't even home so her party must have been much more successful, had been beans on toast; which had really pulled at the heartstrings of his taste buds for the Clearwater gammon and baked potatoes of so many previous years. He tried hard to call it fun and convince himself that Christmas was bound to be different because he was building a new life with a girl he was head over heels about, but at the back of his mind there was a distinct ache of yearning for tradition... and history... and family.

What was it about Christmas that did that?

On Christmas Day they had spent most of the morning in bed, snuggled up together in between bouts of mind blowingly sensuous lovemaking that had made his senses reel. They hadn't booked anywhere for lunch either, but Hugo had come up trumps even on

Christmas Day, and got them in by mentioning Paul's name, and the promise of a very fat tip for the restaurant manager, at one of the capital's top restaurants. Once there they had, thankfully, met up with some of Paul's celebrity friends who had brightened things up a bit, on the surface at least, and they ended up spending the evening, and eventually the night, at a house party in Bayswater at the home of one of the country's most prestigious young film directors.

After arriving back at the apartment on Boxing Day morning with the hangover from hell, Paul had made his excuses and gone for a very welcome lie down, but on closing the bedroom door, instead of lying down on the bed he reached into his jacket pocket and pulled out his phone. With his heart pounding with nerves, but so very desperate by now to hear a familiar voice that would give him the tiniest glimmer of a traditional family Christmas, he selected the number and listened as it dialled. But it had been Marcus who had picked up the phone on its first ring, as though he'd been waiting by it.

'Sam?' He heard him say anxiously, 'Sam is that you?'

So he disconnected the call without saying a word, wondering where Sam was and why on earth would she be ringing the house?

# Chapter twenty one

December became January, life resumed to its empty self and Jules returned to School. By now it was dark when she set off in the mornings and dark when she returned home, so she bought a plug with a timer on it to bring on a house light once it got dark, to at least give the appearance of someone other than Barney waiting for her to come home, and she started preparing her evening meal in the mornings and leaving it in the slow oven in the Aga, so that something would smell comforting and good when she opened the door. But none of it helped. She was still lonely as hell and hating every minute of living alone.

Travelling home one dank and gloomy Friday afternoon just as that bleak January was morphing into an even bleaker February; she arrived home from school and was surprised to see that Barney wasn't in the house. It was pitch dark and raining hard so, cursing a little and dropping her keys onto the counter, she went through to the boot room and grabbed a huge golfing umbrella from a bin by the door. Pulling up the hood on one of Paul's huge waxed coats and holding the only torch she could find in there, she walked over to the allotments. Using the somewhat feeble light from the torch she negotiated her way carefully through the ruts and the mud and called out to him, but he wasn't in there either; in fact nobody was in this kind of weather, unsurprisingly. Going back into the kitchen and now becoming slightly concerned, she shrugged off the coat and went over to her bag to get her phone and call Martin to see if he'd got him for some reason: maybe he'd wandered off from the allotments unnoticed, and along the lakeside to find Dipstick. At that point she realised that her phone was flashing like a little blue beacon out of her handbag, and on closer investigation discovered three missed calls from the same person, but she didn't recognise the number at first. Then she recognised it as Ben's number at the vet's surgery. Pressing, 'return call' she held her breath. Her worst fears realised, the receptionist told her that Barney had been hit by a car in the lane by the new allotments gate, apparently having been following one of his new friends, who hadn't noticed him. Jules let out a moan of despair and sank into a chair. Barney was in the operating theatre as the receptionist spoke, and could Jules please come over to the surgery now?

Grabbing her car keys Jules was out of the door like a flash. No umbrella, no coat, no nothing.

Arriving at the surgery car park a few minutes later she saw Ben's gas guzzler 4x4 parked haphazardly by the front entrance, and thought surely he hadn't been the one that hit him?

Inside, she was told that Ben had actually been the one who found him lying at the side of the lane when he'd gone to his allotment with a sack of manure from some stables he'd just visited, which had been just after lunch, and had brought him straight in.

That had been almost four hours ago now.

Stan Lawson had been out on an urgent call to an Irish setter that was trying to give birth to at least ten puppies, so Ben was operating, and she wasn't sure of the extent of his injuries but thought one of Barney's hips or legs had been broken and that he'd lost some blood. Just at that moment Ben's head and shoulders appeared round the door behind the reception area, still in his green theatre cap and disconcertingly blood spattered tunic, and with his face mask hanging loose around his neck, asking her if she'd managed to get hold of Mrs. Taylor yet. And then he saw her standing there, soaked to the skin and shaking like a leaf. He motioned her through to one of the vacant consulting rooms and then came in to meet her by coming in from a door at the other end of the room. She noticed he'd changed his tunic on the way.

'What… happened Ben?' she stammered, 'is he..? Will he be… I mean I…'

He interrupted her. 'I'm going to keep him here for a few days just to keep an eye on him,' he said. Then, more softly, 'I'll be totally honest with you Jules; he's been pretty badly hurt I'm afraid. I would guess that he got hit on the rear end as he ran across the lane. One of his back legs was pretty badly broken and his hip. He'd lost quite a bit of blood before I found him… but he was unconscious so he didn't know how much it hurt, honestly, that's the body's way…. At first sight I thought he was…'

'Did you see who…? Did anyone else see…?' she interrupted him, unable to bear the thought of his next word.

He shook his head. 'I'll ask around at the allotments tomorrow.'

She leaned against the examination table for support and began to cry.

The way cars whipped up and down that lane to and from that car park sometimes; and a loose black dog on a murky day… it could have been anyone, and he wouldn't even have been wearing his collar. Ben put his arm around her shoulder to comfort her as her heart continued to pound, and gently massaged his fingers on the soft skin just where her neck met her shoulder. The shock of what had happened and the sudden overpowering need to be held and comforted by a man was too much for Jules, and she turned and leaned in to him, slid her arms around his back, clung on for dear life and let herself go. Ben responded, wrapped her in his strong, rugby playing and used to wrestling with farm animals arms, and just held her. Then when she was ready, he took her hand and led her through the back way and to the recovery room to see Barney.

In a large room with harsh overhead lighting and machines beeping in assorted cages containing recovering animals of all shapes and sizes, Barney was lying on a bed of towels and newspapers in large, shiny metal cage at floor level. He was attached to a drip, which Ben told her contained a sedative that was calming him from the shock of the accident and keeping him asleep. His broken leg was encased in dressings, covered with a vivid blue rubbery bandage, and there were two metal pins and some contraption joining them together, sticking out of it; securing his broken bones together.

She could see that all the hair on his hip on that side had been shaved off, and thought he looked so strange with no hair; his naked flesh looked so pink and alien, with its shadow of black hair follicles visible just below the skin. He was fast asleep and looked very peaceful, with just the merest hint of a twitch from his top lip as he slept, just as if he was chasing rabbits in his dreams.

'I know this looks pretty awful,' Ben said, 'but he's a big strong dog and he stands a good chance of a full

recovery you know, and he can come home in a few days but he'll need quite a bit of care. You'd best keep him in one of these cages so he doesn't move around too much... I'll bring one over to you. Then in a while you'll see... he'll be able to go for gentle walks again.'
She nodded her head and, placing one hand on the bars of the cage, she lowered herself to Barney's level on the floor.

Kissing her finger tips, she slipped her shaking hand through the cage and placed the kiss on his sleeping face, and then stood, still looking at the sleeping blissfully, and totally unaware of what was going on, Barney.

'Shall I run you home Jules?' he asked quietly.

'No... no, it's alright... I have the car,' she whispered. Placing her hand on his arm she added; 'thank you Ben... thank you.'

He smiled slightly and nodded just once. 'I'll call you tomorrow morning.'


Back at home Jules was shocked by the gaping emptiness of the house with Barney missing and, with a jolt, she realised she hadn't been alone all these months as she'd thought, she'd had him for company. She had taken for granted the extent of his powerful and loving presence, offering stability in this house that was otherwise so changed now. She had grossly underestimated how much she needed to see his big friendly face, and hear his tail thumping against the kitchen table when she came home from work every day, and how much she needed his unconditional love that did not lie or betray her, but was simply content to know that she was home again.

Sniffing the air and looking across at the Aga she pulled a face, unable to eat the casserole that she'd put in the slow oven that morning, however good it smelled.

Picking up the telephone from its cradle she sat down at the table and closed her eyes for a few moments, running her hand through her wet hair and willing herself brave enough to pluck up the courage to make the call she knew she had to make. Paul may have left him as well as her, but Barney was still a member of this family.

※

Don't be Catherine.

Don't be Catherine, she prayed silently, and as if in answer to her prayer it was Hugo who had picked up the telephone, which was a relief, but he'd called Paul to talk to her as soon as Jules had started to tell him what had happened.

Brusque and defensive and distant as ever these days, Paul became much softer when she told him, and she'd agreed to his coming over before she'd even realised what she'd said. Hanging up, she turned to put the phone back in its cradle and looked at a large brown envelope that was lurking menacingly on the counter. Just yesterday when she'd got home from school the long expected and dreaded divorce papers had finally arrived from Paul's Solicitor.

One way or another it was going to be a dreadful weekend.

# Chapter twenty two

Ben called the next morning just after 9am. Barney was awake but very weak, was now on a drip feed as well to stop him becoming dehydrated, and he'd suggested she stay away so as not to excite him, promising to call her after he had checked on him again, after his list and before he went home.

Paul, and Catherine, arrived at 10am on the dot. Jules had been dusting and polishing frantically in an effort to keep calm, and the shock of seeing Catherine getting out of the car, and now sitting there so smugly, in her home; her safe place, up close and personal for the first time ever, was almost too much.

Noticing that Paul, though still standing, had dandruff flakes on the collar of his coat, she resisted the urge to dust him too, on her way to the kettle.

He only got dandruff when he was stressed; she knew that. Well what was this then, if it wasn't stressful?

Circling each other like a couple of prize fighters, Paul had been most put out at not being allowed to visit Barney at the vet once she had explained everything that Ben had said. She asked him to sit down and offered to make them both some coffee, mostly because he looked so tall and intimidating, just standing there, and Catherine was just so frosty and smug sitting there like the cat that got the cream. She was looking around critically and as if she was thinking of paint and wallpaper... well if she thought she was getting her house as well as her husband she could think again.

The silence was screaming as, once the coffee was made, they all awkwardly pretended to drink while it was still far too hot, and then they had jumped a mile when the kitchen phone suddenly burst into life and trilled loudly.

It was Martin, checking up on Barney. Paul pulled a face when he realised who Jules was speaking to, and Jules turned her back on him, determined not to be intimidated, but her heart was thumping painfully. She never got a chance to see if Catherine looked uncomfortable that her ex was on the phone and, much later, considered that that was a good chance missed.

Ending the call and putting the phone back in its cradle she sat down again and waited, though she wasn't sure what for.

'So Jules... how are you?' he asked her softly.

'How am I what?' she replied.

'How are you... you know, coping here, on your own?'

This was too much... now he was paint and wallpapering too!

Chin jutting out with pride just like her father's used to, she asked incredulously; 'How am I coping on my own with what Paul? Knowing Barney is lying half dead at the vets because thanks to you, I have to go out to work now to keep this roof over my head, which I will, incidentally, and I wasn't here to watch him properly? Or how am I coping on my own having received your surprise package from the solicitors the day before yesterday, and having to deal with the fact that now it's official my husband doesn't want me anymore and has thrown me out like one of his old paintbrush rags... and for... this?' She indicated Catherine with as much venom as she could muster, which in fact was quite sufficient for the purpose.

'You can keep the house... Jules, I just...'

'You just want a divorce... It said.' She turned and took the papers from the counter and pushed them towards him disdainfully. 'I get it... and you're damn right I'm keeping this house... but getting someone else to tell me you want to end our marriage? How typically *you* Paul!' Her voice cracked, and he bit his bottom lip. She knew that look. He loathed confrontations: all front; that was Paul, all over.

His breathing was becoming heavy and he had begun to shake. 'Jules, please... I...' he stopped short and shook his head slightly, regretting having asked the question of her in the first place and regretting bringing Catherine with him to see it, coming in a close second.

Seeing him sitting there at that table in that kitchen, in their house but with Her, had given Jules a kind of déjà vu but somehow backwards feeling, sort of like waking up in the middle of a film and trying to remind yourself of the plot:

*What happened? How did we get here? What did I miss?*

Seeing the look on her face, Catherine slid her arm through Paul's possessively. 'What ever you may think of all this Jules... it's all turning out for the best...'

'Best for who? I'm sure you think that way Catherine, and maybe he does too, but then again, we all make mistakes.' Jules sounded considerably calmer than she felt. 'In doing this he is making the biggest mistake of his life... he's being a fool and he'll realise that one day.'

'Oh granted we all do make mistakes... but it's not with me...' Catherine hissed. 'I'm the best thing that's ever happened to him and he knows it. It's you Jules; and whether you like it or not, he *told* me... you're the worst mistake he ever made.'

Tears sprang to Jules' eyes and she swallowed very hard and it hurt. She looked to Paul for some kind of retraction, but he had merely put his hand on Catherine's arm, to stop her.

Changing tone to cover her distress and determined to see what would happen, however humiliating, Jules went in for revenge. Indicating Catherine with her head she almost whispered; 'Tell me something Paul. Before I found out you were having this... what should we call it, your midlife crisis fling? ...did you ever bring her here when I wasn't around?'

Sweetly put, but a trick question nonetheless, for she knew perfectly well that he had.

'No... of course not...I...'

Catherine looked down but it was plain to see she was loving this.

Jules' green eyes blazed. 'I'm not stupid Paul so don't treat me like a fool. Don't you *dare* lie to me! I am still your wife at this moment in time and you are still accountable to me. I am not an idiot. I know you brought her into our home *and* had sex with her... committed *adultery* with her... *here*, and in *our* bed...'

He looked dumbstruck; Catherine embarrassed herself by going as red as a beetroot. Jules had guts and Paul was speechless.

'Why take her in our bed Paul? Or did she choose it, like a cuckoo does a nest? Couldn't you have distracted her from there and chosen a different one? Or didn't you care? We have six bedrooms here after all! You had several others to choose from!'

'I'm sorry Jules, I... think... I just didn't realise quite what all this would do... to you... I never meant to hurt you...'

She stood up and pointed at him, her hand shaking. 'Do you really want to know what you've done to me? Do you too?' She looked at Catherine. 'You've made me wrong Paul. In doing this you've made more than half of my life wrong. Everything I've worked for, everything I've believed in, wrong. And there's no click undo for me... I can't go back and try again.'

He shook his head and attempted to take the easy way out and deny it again, but one look in those eyes and he knew there wasn't any point.

But he still wondered how she knew.

As if telepathic she continued, with her icy stare aimed at Catherine. 'I think you should see a doctor!' And then turning back to him as Catherine blinked disbelievingly; 'She must have Alopecia Paul. She left far too much of her bottle blonde hair in my hairbrush to be normal, and in the shower drain... and on the headboard...'

Paul's chin sunk down to his chest.

'You thought you'd got away with changing those bed sheets that time Jemmie and I went to France didn't you? You thought you'd been so clever. But you shouldn't have underestimated how well I know you Paul; don't you ever underestimate that. In twenty eight years when did you *ever* change a bed? You, who dropped half a bowl of cornflakes in bed once and left it for me to find the soggy mess when I went upstairs, hours after you'd gone off somewhere without even having mentioned it. But then again why would you? Once you made a name for yourself and got used to staying in plush hotels you treated me like the chambermaid as well.'

'I honestly never meant to hurt you,' he mumbled pathetically, 'I didn't realise... I was confused... Catherine was... a...'

'What? She was what? Available? Around? A total slut?' Jules shook her head angrily.

'I'm no slut!' said Catherine, shortly.

Jules ignored her and continued to focus her eyes on her husband. 'You were always weak Paul; it's always been your downfall. But it wasn't weakness that made me choose you. I loved you. And it wasn't weakness the day you said you loved me and asked me to be your right shoe. You said your heart missed a beat whenever I came near you, and you couldn't wait to get me into bed.

Did he say that to you too?' she looked at Catherine but was sneering. 'I expect he did....' She looked back towards him again. 'But the difference was that he respected me... at least he did then. And so we got married, didn't we Paul? We did it properly. We got married first, and before your family and mine; and we got married before God, and as far as I was concerned that wasn't supposed to be a gamble. And then I gave you two beautiful children. All together I gave you thirty years of my *life* Paul. I never once regretted that either, even when your star was soaring and you were off somewhere courting the groupies and the press, while

I was left behind being the dutiful wife and mother... never once regretted it... until now. You're damn right I want to know what happened in my home! You owe me that. You owe me a hell of a lot more than that!' She sank back into her chair to draw breath.

He still said nothing.

'What changed Paul? When precisely did you discover that you don't love me anymore? Or did you lie about that too, about ever loving me?'

He stood up and turned away from her, unable to look at her. His left arm fell to his side and his fist opened and closed, in and out, in and out, and Catherine was watching him.

'Of course I loved you.' He said quietly.

Walking across to the sink he leaned against the counter and ran one hand through his hair, and a little flurry of dandruff flakes snowed to the floor. 'I think it was... once it was just you and me Jules, when the children were grown and gone, and I was away working so much... I can't really explain... but one day I came home and I just looked at you... you were telling me about something that had happened in the supermarket car park and then it was if I could see your mouth moving but there was no sound... and I realised I didn't feel it anymore, and it's not like I could remember when it stopped. The times when I woke up and looked for you next to me; the times when I would never dream of walking down the road without holding your hand; it was just gone... and then I met Catherine... and I felt... It didn't feel *wrong* you see. I just felt... I'm so sorry Jules...'

'Sorry?' she shook her head and sighed. 'You think '*sorry*' makes it all better again Paul? Is that one little word the best you can come up with?'

'No of course not, but I... I just wanted to say it...'

'Not this time. You can't make it all better this time Paul, with one of your apologies. We are your family,' she said resignedly. 'You've betrayed me... all of us... in our own home, and you did it for someone shallow like her. There's more to her than you know Paul. You couldn't have sunk lower than her.'

'You don't know me!' Catherine hissed, and again Paul's hand went to her shoulder.

'Oh but you forget, Martin does miss...' she was deliberately patronising in pointing out her still single status: 'Jemmie told me he saw you in Manchester back before Christmas when Paul was in Milan. You were at the Guildhall Gallery... with Daniel Makepeace, so he followed you both and saw your passionate kiss in the taxi... and then Googled him to find out who he was. Another married man with children? Tut tut Catherine. Is he the next one on your list of men you want to sleep your way to the top with? The next family you want to destroy? Because I'd watch out for Daniel Makepeace if I were you... you're too much alike... he slept his way to the top too... he married the boss's daughter!'

Her face was ashen and she looked absolutely horrified, 'Don't listen to her Paul! She's lying!'

Pulling the papers back towards her Jules reached for a pen, and Paul looked across to her and over to Catherine, and then back to Jules again, and his heart felt as if she was ripping it out with her bare hands. What was this she was saying?

'You say I never really knew you, but I do. The real you that is, so I know that it's you that's changed and not me, and what's more I don't like this new version of you Paul. Not the immoral, conceited and arrogant version of you that she's helped you become, and the one that you think is the real you now... and I'm really not sure I want to. Whoever you are is of no interest to me now.'

She signed the papers with a confident hand and slid them back towards him. 'Go now, I want you to leave my house and take your slut with you. I will contact you when I know more about Barney, but through my solicitor... oh, and I'd like your keys before you go this time. You said it yourself. This is my house now.'


Less than twenty minutes after they had gone, Ben, on his way back to the surgery from a call nearby and wanting to see how she was, knocked at the back door and walked straight in to find Jules in a heap at the table with her head on her arms, and sobbing her heart out. Bringing her head up sharply and seeing him standing there, she ran headlong into his arms, and before she knew it she found herself kissing him, hard and impatiently, and she realised with a jolt that he was kissing her back. Pulling away suddenly, her hand shot up to her face in horror. 'I'm sorry Ben... I'm so sorry!' and she ran out of the room.

Mightily confused, Ben waited for a few minutes, unsure whether to go and find her or leave well alone, but guessing that it was best that he leave her, at least for now, he picked up his phone and his keys from the floor where he'd dropped them, and left quietly.

# Chapter twenty three

Almost a week passed before Barney was allowed home, and Jules had been grateful to Ben that he had stayed away once she had bitten the bullet and phoned him to explain herself, burning with embarrassment and saying that, whilst she thought she liked him, she could not deal emotionally with another relationship while her life was such a mess, because it wasn't fair on him.

She had put Barney's cage next to the Aga, in his favourite spot, and he was confined to barracks until he could take some gentle exercise. His head was encased in a huge lampshade like device that was to stop him worrying his leg, and he looked extremely resentful and sorry for himself in his solitary confinement.

It was the first day of the February half term the day he came home and so Jules was thankfully able to care for him through the worst of it, and she discovered that if she bent herself into an impossible shape she could get into the cage with him to change his dressings and keep him clean. His eyes looked with such adoring ecstasy whenever she gently scratched the new hair growth on his naked hip for him, and with such relief the day the lampshade was removed and he took his first tentative steps across the kitchen.

Considering the extent of his injuries he did begin to recover quite quickly. Dipstick was allowed to visit the following Saturday morning, and was surprisingly gentle in his greetings to his friend, as if he knew, and Martin, having no work on for a few days after Jules went back to school, temporarily moved into Jemmie's room, in order to keep an eye on Barney until it was safe to leave him.

As Barney's health improved he had so enjoyed all the attention the day that Jules arranged to take him into school to see the children, after they had made him a Get Well Soon card and had all signed it. After all the giggling as he sniffed his way around all the children and their classroom, he settled down on the carpet by the window for story time and was fast asleep by the time the bell sounded for the end of the day.

Jules had a little trouble the following morning getting out of the door without him, as he plainly thought he was going to school again too, and had looked quite disgusted when she shut the door on him and left alone.

Dizzy appeared late one afternoon a couple of weeks later, and things had returned pretty much back to normal by this time, with Barney if with nothing else. She arrived just as Jules arrived home from school, and immediately noticed that she looked absolutely mid OFSTED school inspection shattered.

Putting on the kettle to boil as Jules went to check that Barney was ok and then slip into something a bit more comfortable; reaching for the teapot Dizzy looked at her as she walked back through the doorway. 'Well darling, you look pretty well, considering, but you also look exhausted...' she said, tipping out the warming the pot water into the sink and then making the tea.

'Be nice Dizz...' Jules said, sitting down, it's been a long week.'

'Getting any easier?'

'Barney's doing really well... school has been like walking on a carpet of upended drawing pins all week with inspectors leaning over everyone's shoulder and tutting with a notebook... but if you mean the other thing... it's all gone a bit quiet.'

'Not settled yet then?'

'I've signed everything at the solicitor's so now I'm just waiting...'

'Well when it's all sorted... did you think any more about my suggestion? About taking a holiday?'

'I know, I know... but I'm not sure I can afford it yet...'

'Of course you can! Go on splash out... do what we talked about last time... sell that painting you hate... the one in the dining room you've always hated.

Now... what was that quote I saw in the paper the other day...? Oh I remember... it was Arthur C Clarke... *'Art cannot be enjoyed unless it is approached with love...'* Don't leave it hanging over the table in there like the spectre at the feast... ditch it and enjoy the spoils!'

The next morning Jules was on the telephone to Paul's old boss, Victor, and he set the wheels in motion on her behalf to put the painting up for auction. Paul was away, a fact she'd discovered after ringing Hugo in a slight pang of conscience. As expected though, Paul rang almost immediately in high dudgeon from wherever he was, so Hugo must have told him, and to find out why she was selling it. In the absence of anything better to say she re quoted Dizzy's Arthur C Clarke but added, 'you figure it out!' and then slammed the phone down on him.

But the blank space on the dining room wall was like a metaphor for the empty space where their marriage had once been: their divorce was finalised, the decree arrived in the post by recorded delivery the previous day, and like it or lump it she was single again.

✷

Paul got himself a phone link to the auction so that he could keep tabs on the sale of the painting without being seen.

It was sold at Sotheby's to an anonymous telephone bidder from Japan. Jules hadn't gone to watch, but Marcus and Sam had, and though it was an early work it had fetched more than enough to fund a good holiday and get someone in to fix that front porch light.

She had no idea what Paul thought of the fetching price.

Then before Jules knew it Easter arrived in a blur of confused life, and after a hectic week that involved three school trips, steering little people around a Sealife Centre, the Bovington Tank Museum and Monkey World, she finally conceded that Dizzy had a point. She had spent the entire first day of the school holidays doing the laundry and housework, and realised that what she really needed at this point was to get away from the house and her troubled life for a while. She'd had one idea already. When the children were small and they'd had no money they'd stayed at Victor's Spanish villa a few times and she considered calling him to see if she could slope off there. But that was no good; too many memories. She needed somewhere sterile.

The coast was clear. Paul had apparently gone to America so she knew she could safely leave the house without finding he'd been back without her knowledge, and Catherine had apparently gone to Scotland on a job for a couple of weeks. Also, Barney was completely recovered, so she was unfettered and finally able to think about a holiday. Heaving herself up from the sofa with a wide yawn she slouched through into the kitchen in her flip flops and placed her empty coffee cup on the kitchen counter for a refill from the pot. Then she took it through to the study to turn on the computer.

It only took her a few minutes to find the site she was looking for, details of villas for rent in the south of France. She tapped in her needs, which were pretty basic; peace and quiet, solitude, no memories of any kind whatsoever, sun and a pool. A few villas came up, but the one that took her fancy was called '*Le Petite Cachette*' – a little hiding place- she translated, and was in a small town called Fayence, about half an hour from the airport at Nice, and nestled in the surrounding hills near Antibes.

A hiding place...perfect.

She clicked, *contact*, and sent an email to the owner requesting booking details as soon as possible, then went back to the utility room to swap yet more washing around and peg some out on the line before it rained again.

She was very surprised on her return a few minutes later, to hear her email beep she hoped, with the reply.

Sure enough, an email had arrived from the owner, someone called M. Robert, with details of availability of the villa she was interested in and, better still, it was available immediately for ten days due to a last minute cancellation.

Jules took the bull by the horns and booked it, and spent the next couple of hours online sorting out a flight to Nice, and car hire. Then she spent the rest of the day packing and doing other useful things like hunting out her passport and checking to make sure it hadn't expired.

By eleven o'clock the following morning she was on the right plane having found the right check-in desk, and the right gate, with a great big smile on her face, having been driven to London Luton airport by a rather surprised Martin. It was the first time she had ever booked herself a holiday and made all the arrangements, and to her sheer delight she was beginning to feel quite strong and empowered…

✯

Nice airport was swarming with people when she arrived, and was also surprisingly hot. She made her way through to the car hire desks, and did her best to look cool and calm like everyone else around her as she filled in all the paperwork and took delivery of her car, a little blue Peugeot. She spent a few minutes familiarising herself with the controls, and setting up the Sat Nav, using the postal code of the villa in Fayence, before setting off on her journey driving on the wrong side of the road for the first time in her life. Her heart was pounding, but she soon found that it was quite easy really once she got the hang of it and anyway, the motorway seemed no different at all unless she looked across the central reservation and saw the cars going in the opposite direction in the wrong place.

As soon as she arrived in Fayence itself, she turned into an Intermarche supermarket to stock up on supplies. She happily filled her trolley with long baguettes and smelly cheese, and lots of wine and, having been told about the villa's large freezer, lots of pre cooked frozen meals so that she wouldn't have to bother with much cooking. Thanking the government at home silently for introducing chip and pin cards, she even managed to pay at the checkout with her credit card without attempting anything more testing than *Merci.*

Back on the road again, things got a lot more hairy as she came off the main carriageway and started to climb up into the hills on a single track road with a sheer drop on one side and very deep ditches on the other. There were virtually no fences on either side, just intermittent white lines painted to show where the edges were; for in the dark, presumably, because there were no street lights up there either. In fact there was a distinct air of, *'well, 'ere is zee edge, stay between zee lines or you will fall off zee road!"* and she made her way up the succession of hairpin and totally blind bends praying audibly that she wouldn't meet anything coming the other way. Hector once said that God got more prayers about driving and parking than he did for anything real…

Luckily all she met was an elderly man with a dog who waved his walking stick amiably as she slowed, even more, to pass him safely.

The Sat Nav was telling her that she had reached her destination but all she could see was olive trees; hundreds of them. She carried on slowly up the little road, which was by this time an even narrower dirt track, definitely more suited to ambling along than driving along, until at last she came to a gateway and was hugely relieved to see that it had, *'Le Petite Cachette'* carved into a piece of weathered grey olive wood that was attached to the opened gates.

There was a very shiny looking new silver Mercedes convertible in the driveway, and as she drove through the gates, the front door to the villa opened and a man appeared to meet her: the villa's owner presumably. He was tall and dark, and tanned, in the kind of way that people living on the continent are: looking inherent rather than attained. He wore cream coloured cotton trousers and a crisp pink shirt. A thin, primrose yellow cotton sweater was tied around his neck by a loose tie in the sleeves at the front, and he wore soft brown leather shoes. He wore no socks.

He looked very French, and very glamorous, just like his car. He introduced himself as Michel Robert, the villa's owner indeed. She thought he must be in his late forties or early fifties, as his full head of hair was pepper and salt and he had an attractive fan of laugh lines around his eyes as he removed his sunglasses. She considered that he might be called devastatingly handsome by both sexes; granted by one grudgingly and the other thankfully. Someone else obviously thought so too, she noted absently, because a wedding ring glinted on his left hand as well.

His English was very good, but had the typical French speaker's absence of '*th*' which was substituted with a '*z* ' as he showed her around the terracotta painted villa. It was all on one level, and open plan throughout its dining room, sitting room, and kitchen; all decorated in the Provencal style. The two bedrooms both contained enormous beds and the rooms themselves were enormous too, one with an ensuite bath, and one with an ensuite shower.

Outside there was a decent size swimming pool and a typically roof tiled and arched pool terrace with two day beds for relaxing in the shade. There were several padded lounge chairs around the pool too, all placed so that they were shaded under the branches of olive trees.

Surrounding the villa on all sides were woods of tall elegant pines, and numerous olive trees stood in groves of straight lines originally planted with military precision. The view through them took in the hills and woods that swept all the way into the distance, and to the Mediterranean.

She was in paradise.

Michel finished his tour and said goodbye, and Jules set about unloading the car and putting her shopping away. She decided that whoever had decorated this house, Madame Robert presumably, had got a definite flair for interior design because there were stylish little touches everywhere and all done with flawless taste- until she went into one of the cloakrooms with some toilet rolls. On the wall behind the door was a print of one of Paul's paintings and she caught her breath for a moment as he succeeded in invading her secret hiding place in the sun. She gazed at it: it was an early one and very well known. Called 'Bather' it was painted in simple black strokes of one brush, that made your own eyes fill in the spaces. A rear view of naked woman sitting on the side of a bath and putting her hair up in a towel, she remembered it well. He had been so proud of it, and she'd annoyed him by asking if his bather was getting in or getting out. Outwardly, the only sign to anyone that might have been watching her that she had been affected by this picture in any way was that her lips were parted, and they had been previously closed. She shut the door decisively behind her, and closed her eyes, quietly relieved that there were other cloakrooms she could use.

Later that same evening Jules finished her unpacking, poured herself a glass of cool white wine and took it out to the poolside. Flicking the switch for the pool lights, the water shone a rich turquoise and ghostlike shimmer into the dusk. The cicadas were chirruping noisily, *'come out! come out!'* and a myriad of flying creatures were skimming the surface of the pool; attracted by the iridescent light. Jules settled onto a comfy day bed under the terrace to watch them, and tucked her legs up beside her. Tiny geckos were also attracted to the light and scurried towards it, nervously tasting the air with their little tongues and with one front leg lifted as if in suspended animation.

Her eyes were drawn upwards by the sound of movement in the pine trees, and she looked up to see a pair of pine martens playing; their elongated bodies bounding effortlessly across the branches as they leapt between the trees. She was mesmerised at the beauty of the scene as she sipped her wine.

The evening was warm and she lay there for a couple of hours, in silent appreciation of the show that nature had provided, before the air cooled, and she went back inside in search of a light supper.

✯

A couple of days later, after settling in, and having had some decent sleep for the first time in many months, Jules was getting decidedly bored. She had come to this conclusion after she found herself counting how many steps it took her to walk from one end of the house to the other, (fifty three). Knowing that the same operation at home took sixty eight steps, (but you had to do this outside because there wasn't a direct route indoors) she decided that *Le Petite Cachette* was a lot more square than Clearwater House.

Bored.

She was lying on her favourite canary yellow day bed that had enormous yellow and white striped cushions, in the shade of the pool terrace. Her book lay open and abandoned on her lap as she dozed, listening to the sounds of distant birds of prey calling wheezily to each other in the thermals above the hills, and to the wind in the palm trees, whooshing like an approaching aircraft down to the valley below. On a rattan and very weathered little table to the side of her lay the remains of her bread and cheese lunch, and while she slept, a little bird was cheekily picking up crumbs as they blew from her plate to the ground in the gentle breeze.

Eventually, she became aware of the sound of a gently humming machine, and someone wearing flip flops was walking on the tiles around the pool edge. She turned her head suddenly: her hand shooting up to guard her eyes against the sun as she fumbled for her sunglasses. Michel Robert had returned and was cleaning the bottom of the pool with the aid of a long handled device that looked a bit like a carpet sweeper, attached to an even longer blue stretchy hose, which was sucking and filtering the water as he worked. To the side of him lay two containers of chemicals.

'*Pardon Madame*! I did not mean to wake you. I come to service zuh pool,' he said apologetically. His voice startled her as it broke into her silence: she hadn't spoken a word to anyone for nearly three days, but she smiled at him forgivingly.

'It's nice to see you Michel,' she said. 'I feel a bit like a hermit here all alone…'

'You mean you 'aven't been out yet?' he looked shocked. 'You should get out of 'ere and see somesing Madame! Zere is a lot to see, no? What is stopping you?' he shrugged and looked so French she couldn't help but smile at him.

'I haven't driven in France before this… and I'm a little nervous of the car.'

'Ah, Madame Taylor! You must! Zees area- it is beautiful.' He put down the pool cleaner, brushed his hands on the front of his jeans, and joined her by settling down on the edge of the other day bed in the pool terrace. She pulled her towel up over her legs, self consciously. 'I'm a nervous driver I'm afraid, I don't like driving in unfamiliar places and the thought of going into Cannes or San Tropez with what I recall of its narrow streets terrifies me!'

'Do you never go on 'oliday alone before?' he said, looking puzzled.

She shook her head. 'I used to go with my husband and children,' she began, finding that the knives didn't cut quite as deep when she said that these days, 'but the children are both grown now, and my husband and I are recently divorced... so now there's just me.'

'And you are a little new to zees single life, yes?' his head tilted to one side as he looked at her.

'Yes I am,' she said, 'but I'm getting better at it, slowly.'

There was a pause and she was embarrassed.

Both hands slapped against his thighs decisively. 'I will take you,' he said, and she looked more than a bit surprised. 'No, no, is ok! I will take you on a trip - tomorrow. We go to see Verdun Gorge... is very beautiful... you must see. Is like zuh Grand Canyon in America, but it is in France.'

The thought of getting out for a change of scenery was tempting. 'Is that ok? I mean, won't Madame Robert...?'

He threw his head back and laughed. 'My wife lives in Paris wiz a young man who is far too handsome for his own good, called Antoine. Unlike you Madame I am quite an old 'and at zuh single life!'

The following morning Michel arrived on the dot of 10am and they set off on the road to Verdun. It was a very hot day and Jules was glad the change of scenery and the fresh air as the wind whipped through her hair; and glad of the scarf that was tying it back too, or there would be no calming it later. The conversation flowed as the Mercedes swept its way up, and up, and up and her ears popped continuously. They purred expensively round numerous hairpins with sheer drops on one side and vertical cliff faces on the other, and then on into the stunning gorge, until he pulled into the car park of a viewing place called *Plas Sublime,* where the view through the gorge was absolutely spectacular.

As they left the car to have a look at the scenery the ground underfoot was very uneven and with a lot of loose shingle. Jules slipped as she tried to clamber up a rock towards a telescope, excited because she'd seen a vulture. Michel, behind her, grabbed her around the waist to stop her from falling over and she withdrew herself from his grasp with a slightly embarrassed laugh, but she was tingling all over from where he had touched her.

She felt an almost static tension in the air as they returned to the car, and as he held her door open he guided her to her seat by slipping his arm around her shoulder as she climbed in. She found herself wondering if he had an ulterior motive for this trip, or if he was just an excellent example of the infamous French gallantry. And then she found herself wondering how she felt about that, either way.

The road through the gorge was truly breathtaking, with overhanging rocks carved out to form a kind of bridge on one side in many places. There were a lot of cyclists and motorbikes tearing along the road, apparently timing the journey from top to bottom, and more than once they were overtaken by people on huge motorbikes, taking their own lives in their hands as they sped past, and the sound of their engines ripped through the gorge like the Red Arrows were flying through. Jules was amazed to see that many of the cyclists looked quite elderly too!

Michel pulled into another, much quieter, parking area and pulled a picnic basket from the boot of his car. 'Zis way Jules...' he said, walking round to open her door for her. It was the first time he had used her name, and the J was soft as he purred it. Her heart beat nervously as he put out his hand to help her from her seat, and she took it gingerly. Heading for a grassy area he spread a large blanket on the ground in front of them, then sat down and opened the basket. He removed a bottle of wine and two glasses, two baguettes, some cheese, some little plum tomatoes, a little jar of *cornichons* and some pâté: The classic French picnic.

'Sit,' he said, patting the blanket beside him, and she sat down, taking the glass of wine he offered her. He took out some plates and a knife, and proceeded to tear off some bread and prepare lunch. She was transfixed by his attention to detail, whilst at the same time making the whole thing seem completely effortless. Patiently waiting for him to pass her the knife so he could start his lunch and she could prepare her own, she was taken completely aback when he passed the plate he had prepared to her, and then proceeded to start preparing his own. This was heady stuff! Paul loathed picnics, and they hadn't had one since the children were small.

Even then it had been sandwiches, and tea in a flask, no matter how hot the weather. And the sandwiches, wrapped tightly in cling film, had to be egg mayonnaise so that nothing would fall out and make a mess. No cucumber, no tomato, and definitely no cress, which he loathed even more than sitting on a hairy blanket and eating from a floppy paper plate.

This display was really something else. She could hardly take her eyes off him as he ate either, with his obvious French passion for food and wine; completely ignoring the breadcrumbs that cascaded around him like confetti, and she smiled at the comparison to Paul. He noticed her smile and smiled back.

'You like?' he said, with his mouth full of cheese.

'I love it!' she said. 'This is the best picnic I have ever had... and this place...' her arm spanned the view in amazement.

'Ah! Is very beautiful, no?'

'It's breathtaking!'

'I'm glad,' he said. 'I make you happy now?'

'I feel much better, thank you Michel.'

'Is my pleasure.'

He continued to look at her and tipped his head slightly to one side. 'You know, you should smile more. You 'ave a beautiful smile. You look so beautiful when you smile, Jules.'

Not a phrase that anyone had ever used to describe her before, she blushed visibly, and then turned crimson as he took her hand when she passed him her empty glass for a refill, and kissed the back of it gently.

⭐

On the way back towards the villa Michel turned the car towards Cannes.

'Is still early, I show you Cannes,' he smiled. 'You like the water?' She nodded, excited and pleased that this perfect day would last a while longer.

On arrival in Cannes he drove down towards the marina, and steered the car smoothly into a parking space. He jumped out, opening her door for her and taking her hand again, but this time keeping it in his. As they walked slowly along the quayside Jules became totally absorbed by the yachts and boats moored there, reading their names and their exotic registration ports: Cape Town South Africa, Kingston Jamaica, George Town Camen Islands; the list went on and on. Row after row of them moored tightly together, glinting whitely in the sunshine, and many of them absolutely huge and highly glamorous, as were the people in and around them; the beautiful people. Men who all looked like they should be in a film, and tall skinny girls with long, long legs and absolutely no body hair…

Catherine would fit in here…

'Stop it!' she said under her breath.

Michel stopped walking and Jules turned around to see why.

'You like zis one?' he said, indicating a large boat with a slight jerk of his head. She was equal in size to her neighbours, registered in Cannes, and she was called *Gi Gi.*

Jules clapped her hands together, 'Oh! I love that film! Lesley Caron... Maurice Chevalier...*Thank heavens for little girls...* it always cheers me up when I'm feeling down!' She smiled, but he didn't move, he just continued to stand there, looking at her, before singing in an exaggerated French accent *'Zose little eyes so 'elpless and appealing...'*

She continued, *'One day will flash and send you crashing through the ceiling...!'* He still hadn't moved.

'Don't tell me... she's yours!' she joked.

He nodded.

She blinked.

As she stood with her mouth open he took a key ring from his pocket and opened a small remote control fob. Pressing a little green button, *Gi Gi's* gang plank slid gracefully towards him and stopped neatly at the edge of the jetty. Bounding up the plank with well practiced effortlessness he called; 'Come on!'

Still a bit speechless she carefully took hold of the rail, shoes now in hand, and joined him nervously on the bridge.

An hour later they were anchored out in the bay after Michel had negotiated a marina that looked like the car park at Waitrose on Christmas Eve. It was extremely hot, but there was a very pleasant breeze playfully lifting the ends of the headscarf that was still restraining her hair.

She was sitting with her legs dangling over the edge of the deck, her hands holding the guardrail that was just above her, and looking down into the water at a shoal of tiny fish when Michel appeared from the galley carrying two bottles of glistening ice cold beer. She took one gratefully, and they clinked their bottles together in salute as he sat down next to her, putting his legs and his bare feet over the edge of the deck next to hers as she sipped from her bottle.

They were silent for a moment.

'So,' she said, breaking it. 'What do you do to live this kind of a life Michel?'

He smiled. 'Nossing much, I retired two years ago.'

Her eyebrows went up.

'I just 'ave my four villas now, and one business interest in Spain. Before zat I was in zuh real estate business here. I sold villas and apartments to very rich people for lots of money...' he smiled easily. 'Millionaires mostly... excellent commission rates.'

She looked around at *Gi Gi's* glistening deck, 'I'll say!'

'So most of the year I live in Cannes apart from when I live in Barcelona while I look after my business there...'

They were quiet again as the boat gently swayed in the current.

She yawned widely, arching her back and stretching her arms high above her head. 'This is blissful Michel, I don't even know what day it is...'

'Ees Sursday I sink...' he said, catching the contagious yawn.

She started to yawn again but stopped short and laughed instead, 'it's what?'

'Sursday I sink... why do you laugh?'

'We really need to sort that out!' She laughed, and pulling her legs up on to the deck and kneeling up, rested herself back on her heels. She patted the deck in front of her. 'Come on Michel.'

He turned and did the same; facing her on his knees.

'Ok,' she smiled, 'stick your tongue out...'

'What?'

'Come on, I'm going to teach you the '*th*'- stick your tongue out.'

He poked it out at her. 'Not like that you fool! Relax it... that's it.' She took hold of his tongue gently, but it shrunk straight back inside his mouth.

'Come on, out with it!' She took hold of it again, more firmly this time. 'Now, put your teeth near the end of your tongue. No, don't bite it, and mind my fingers! Just rest them there gently. That's it. Now, blow a little air out through the gap under your teeth... no, just a little. You're not shooing a stray cat!'

He made a slight flat hissing sound, like a tyre going down.

'That's it Michel! Perfect. Now let's try it. Say 'The''

'The!' he said. She let go of his tongue and clapped.

'I did it!' he said, eyes shining like a little boy who's just realised his daddy has let go of the back of his bicycle.

'Now, you try it on your own this time... take your tongue back in at the same time as you blow the air under your teeth.'

'That! This! Then! The! Thursday! I can do it! He jumped up to his feet, pulling her with him and swung her around in his arms. 'Today is Thursday! Thank you Jules, Thank you, thank you, thank ....' Then without warning his lips were pressed against hers, and then he stopped just as suddenly, though not quite as surprised as she, and looked deep into her eyes, still holding her. She realised why; he was asking her for permission. Having already reached the point where her thoughts and her intentions had reached the irretrievable point of fusion where reason and consequence cease to exist, the next thing she knew her arms were around his neck they were kissing long and hard, before falling slowly backwards onto a long white leather seat.

# Chapter twenty four

She'd seen so many films and read so many beach novels on this theme, and they all either said or referred afterwards to something along the lines of; *'she couldn't remember how they got into the bedroom...'* but Jules did. He'd taken her hand, kissing it both tenderly and persuasively, and turning and kissing her all the way as he led her down the steps leading to the cabin, before laying her gently down on the bed and lying down next to her.

This didn't feel like love, this felt like sex... and she'd never had sex in her life before. And this couldn't possibly feel like ordinary sex: this felt like sex in a film.

They said nothing at all at first, but his actions were those of a very skilled and practiced lover. He undressed her slowly, kissing her body between each button on her thin cotton shirt, and she was completely naked before he would allow her to undress him, teasing her. She was embarrassed that her skin was so white against his, but he kissed and caressed her as if she was made of the finest porcelain. He slowly untied and pulled the scarf from her hair, letting it skim over her body tantalisingly as it fell to the floor, and fanned her hair across her shoulders like a mane, before kissing that too, and playing with it, running her tight curls through his fingers, as far as they could get without resistance.

He was wondrous. He took her into shadows of passion within her own body that had been previously unknown or explored; even in her wildest fantasies. And when it was over he held her; his arms wrapped right around her body as if he feared she might run away, gently stroking her shoulder with the tips of his fingers, and whispering sweet French Nothings into her ear as she fell asleep.

※

Back at the car and a very long time later, Michel was talking to a security guard at the marina car park and Jules was listening to the radio in the car while she waited for him, in a haze of post incredible sex floatiness.

Suddenly and without warning, Michael Bublé's voice filled the air around her, tormenting her with the song that still tore her apart; 'Home', and she started to cry, without warning and visibly. Michel got into the car, shocked by her tears as she groped somewhere for a tissue, and she quickly explained why she was upset.

'You know Jules, there is something I don't understand about you...' he ventured, handing her a crisp white handkerchief from his pocket and turning towards her. 'I meet people like your ex husband all the time, successful and rich, surrounded by sycophants who tell them they're great when they so much as fart... and they only mix with other people who are the same as they are... and lose track of reality.'

She looked down into her lap as he continued. 'And this Catherine, she probably spent weeks persuading him that she was the best thing since sliced brioche and that he should leave you, with the same lack of conscience as the rest of his dinner when he's full... and what I don't understand is... if you still love him so much, why you just lay back and took it...?'

She was weeping quietly and playing with his rolled up hanky in her hands, but she said nothing.

'Where was your fight Jules? Where is it now?' He started the engine and flicked on the CD player rather than the radio. A deep base guitar sound filled the air, and Michel smiled a little as he turned towards her, and Billy Idol started to sing. 'Where is your... *Rebel Yell?*' he said, gracefully sweeping out of the marina and pulling out onto the main road. 'Come on Jules! Sing it! Don't make me... Claudia says I sound like a pig in a corner when I sing!'

She smiled a bit, and bit her lip, grateful for the change in tempo and cheered up by his enthusiasm. By the time he joined the motorway he was singing his head off, very badly, but with a definite rebel yell; and the wind whipping through their hair as they tore along.

Jules suddenly realised they were going the wrong way.

'Michel! Where are we going?'

'All the bloody way to Calais unless you start singing soon!' he laughed. 'Come on! Let it go! Let it all out! I want to hear your *Rebel Yell!*'

He had pressed repeat when the song finished and so it went on and on, and before long she gave up and was singing at the top of her lungs and even playing air guitar with gay abandon. He was right, it was very exhilarating, tearing along the motorway, wind in your hair, arms flailing, and laughing at the funny looks they were getting from the other drivers.

'You're wrong about one thing…' she shouted above the CD. 'You don't sound like a pig in corner when you sing…'

'I don't?' he laughed.

'No… you sound more like Paul when he does!'

✯

His visits to the villa were frequent now. Sometimes they just talked for hours and sometimes they went to bed. But he always treated her like a queen, never just a lover. One night after the sun had sunk to another land he persuaded her to join him in skinny dipping in the pool. She had been so nervous, and as her hair spread across the surface of the water as she sunk tentatively down, he told her she looked like a beautiful mermaid in the iridescent turquoise light, and then she had been embarrassed.

He took her in his arms: 'You are very beautiful Jules, why do you not believe it?'

She pulled away from him, but he pulled her back.

'I can't... I'm not... I... Paul never said...' she flustered but the words wouldn't come, and she looked sad again. He took her face in his hands and looked into her eyes. 'You know, all women are beautiful, like diamonds Jules. You have just forgotten is all...' he kissed her gently. 'You must trust me. I am French after all....' He smiled seductively. 'I will remind you that you are a diamond, and then you will know it again.'

'Flatterer!' she was joking to hide the depths of herself esteem.

'No! It is true! When a woman is confident with herself and feels beautiful she *becomes* beautiful, you see?'

'Not really Michel, no.' She pulled away from him, climbed up the steps out of the pool and wrapped herself in a towel. 'You can't tell me that that I'm the same as those beautiful women in Cannes, Michel, you just can't... I'm not... I'm getting old, I'm overweight... I've tried losing weight and it just won't budge. I've got cellulite on my cellulite and my bum is enormous... look!' She slapped her behind in the towel.

He pulled himself up onto the side of the pool and stood up, looking at her, and picked up a towel. 'Jules, you are as lovely as a diamond, and the only difference between those women and you is that they know that diamonds come in all shapes and sizes; fat ones or thin ones, tall ones or short ones. So they take care of themselves and hold their heads very high so people can admire them as they twinkle in the sun. You, my darling, have lost your twinkle, and think you are a pebble. You think you are a pebble so you act like you're a pebble. Pebbles just look at the ground for somewhere to roll and only show their true beauty when they're wet... like you are now. Do you know that there is nothing more captivating to a man than a woman who is confident with herself? She shines like a diamond because she knows she is one... you see? Women of all shapes and sizes can be sexy. They just need to be confident with themselves.'

'You think I'm a diamond?' she smiled, ever so slightly.

'It's not a question Jules, it's a fact. Look at your reflection in the water. Say it and mean it.'

'I'm a diamond...' she said, peering down at her face as it wobbled and distorted in the movement of the water. 'In the rough, maybe.... I'm sorry I just don't feel it!' she shrugged.

'Well we need to work on that my darling, and I have a plan...' he said, sliding back into the water and holding up his hand to take her back in with him. She let her towel fall to the ground and took it.

He was fascinated by the way her hair moved in the water as she swam, and he dived under the water to see it swirl this way and that. Inevitably his lust for her overcame him at that point and they made love in the pool then, and afterwards he wrapped her in a towel and laid her on a daybed, while he went inside to fetch them a drink.

The air was cooling and the breeze was getting hungrier, and she looked up at the sky. Menacing dark clouds were visible in the moonlight, sweeping their way over the hills, bringing with them the winds that whipped through the surrounding pine trees: their cone heavy branches fanning their faces as if in panic at the impending storm, and a sudden rush of dry leaves tumbled hurriedly across the terrace, many of them falling into the pool, and dancing a Viennese waltz in the windswept eddies on its surface. A distant rumble resonated around the valley, and she shivered as he returned, bringing her robe draped across one arm as he carried the drinks tray.

'There is going to be a storm I think, are you scared of the thunder? Shall we go inside?' he said as he poured her a glass of wine.

She pulled the robe on gratefully and patted the bed beside her, 'Oh no... let's stay here and watch, I love a thunder storm; it's so dramatic.'

'You surprise me! My wife and son are terrified and run for cover at the first hint of a rumble....' He smiled, sitting down and pulling her close to him in a big manly hug.

He hadn't mentioned having a son before this, and she looked at him for a moment, watching his face. 'He is probably scared because his mother is. Children pick up on fears and phobias in their parents and so they become scared themselves.' This was the job training talking.

'True, I suppose. I am scared of spiders and he doesn't like those either!'

'I rest my case then! Paul and I...' she checked herself, 'we... used to sit the children at the bay window in our bedroom to watch the storms at night if they were frightened and came in to us. One time...' she laughed a little at the recollection and looked down into her lap, 'there was a lightning bolt that landed so close to the house, the force of it blew all four of us off the window seat we were kneeling on, and backwards, onto the floor... we were all in hysterics!'

A flash of silver dagger cracked the dark sky, illuminating the clouds in every tiny detail. Like the sky itself was on fire, the clouds became clouds of smoke billowing up and up, and a few seconds later there was a deep and menacing rumble. Michel remarked that it didn't seem possible that sounds and sights such as these could have come from God; they looked and sounded so evil.

'My mother used to sit me on her lap and tell me it was the sound of the angels moving the furniture in heaven,' she smiled, 'and if there was a really loud bang she would say they had dropped something heavy...'

He laughed, and kissed the top of her head, 'you have good, strong parents by the sound of it.'

'Had,' she replied, as another flash lit up the sky, 'they're both gone now.'

'They died young?' he seemed surprised.

'They did.'

'That is very sad. Here with me you must not be sad.' He pulled her face up towards his, very gently with his finger tips, and kissed her.

The rain began then. Big, heavy drops began plopping noisily into the pool and onto the roof of the pool terrace. A huge bang and rumble of thunder brought them apart in sudden shock.

'Well, there goes the wardrobe!' she laughed, as they jumped up, grabbing their glasses, and ran inside the house.

✺

'I can't think why your wife would ever have left you,' she smiled dreamily, flat out on the sofa with him as she sipped her wine, 'you make me feel so special; like a film star.'

'She didn't leave me,' he said.

'Oh, I thought....You mean... you left her?'

'No, we didn't leave each other at all. We just don't live together...'

Jules sat up suddenly. 'But you said... you told me she lived in Paris with the toy boy, Antoine?'

'Antoine is our son. They live together, in Paris, like I said.'

Her heart was pounding. 'Then...?'

'We are still married, yes. I never said we were divorced.'

'But...'

He sat up and faced her. 'Jules, calm down. It's different here. We are Catholic. We do not divorce. Claudia and I can't live together; we want different things, so we choose to live apart. She takes lovers, I take lovers, I look after them financially when necessary, and also she has her own career. And when we see each other, we get on very well... just no sex... it is an excellent arrangement.'

She shook her head in disbelief. 'And your son, Antoine?'

'He takes lovers too I expect. He's twenty nine. Like I said, he is too handsome for his own good.'

She wasn't sure whether to be angry with him or laugh. She knew she didn't love him, but the thought that he was married unsettled her. What did that make her? An adulterer?

Just like Paul.

'Jules, this is not a problem... we are having fun together aren't we?'

'Yes, but...'

'But nothing darling. Let's just be together, now. I can't help being me... it's who I am. For me the past is yesterday and the future is tomorrow, there is nothing else...'

'I wish I could think that way Michel,' she said ruefully.

'Well while you are here with me, you can!' he smiled. 'Come on, *ma cherie!* All this decadence has made me very hungry, and it's almost nine o'clock. Let me take you out for dinner. It has stopped raining now, listen. There is a very good restaurant in Fayence and I want to feed you lovely things, *Madame Rosbif.*'

He stood up and pulled her to her feet.

'Much as I would like it if you went out like this I think you should go and at least put on your panties my love or you may get arrested!'

※

Following an exquisite meal of langoustines in whisky and lamb in a delicious red wine sauce at the softly lit restaurant in town, Michel was kissing her goodnight in the car, back at the villa. Her senses reeled when he kissed her like that, and she kissed him back enthusiastically. Eventually they parted and said goodnight. 'Tomorrow, I will make you shine, my diamond in the rough. I will come and we will go shopping together, my treat. Tomorrow you will bury that dusty pebble back in the garden where it belongs!'

Jules climbed reluctantly out of the car and he clicked the ignition, taking off down the lane in a cloud of dust.

Jules went inside and kicked off her shoes. What on earth was he planning now? She passed a mirror and paused to look at herself. It was true he did make her feel like a diamond, but the mirror on the wall told a different story, as mirrors usually do.

She sat down a few minutes later with a mug of coffee and thought about the differences in their two sons as she curled up on the sofa and got comfortable. Marcus, thankfully now settled with Sam, engaged to be married and expecting their first baby; and Antoine, a chip off the old block by the sound of it, and knocking the mademoiselles of Paris clean out of their 'oh so skinny' jeans and stilettos, from what his father said. What a fine example of marriage for him they were setting. She wondered for a moment as she sat, if she and Paul would have been better off with an arrangement like Michel and Claudia. He could live in London and she could live in Frincham… that might work.

It was working.

And did it hurt?

You bet your life it did.

So what was the secret to this separate but companionable living?

Stop loving your husband, obviously.

Easy....

※

The next morning Jules woke up with the usual lack of any idea what the time was because closing the shutters at night plunged the room into such complete darkness that it was impossible to see when the morning came. The cacophony of birdsong drifting through the house informed her that it was most probably sometime after she should have got up, so she rolled over to see the clock on the bedside table. It said 9.45 and Michel was coming at 10! Throwing off the sheet that had been her only necessary bedclothes she ran into the bathroom and looked in the mirror, and a plump middle aged frump with an imprint of the crumpled sheet up one side of her face and frizzy hair looked back at her... which was not a good start. She turned on the shower and jumped inside, crying out with shock as stone cold water turned to a temperature worthy of tea making as it sorted itself out, and grabbing at the shampoo and soap, tried to carry out simultaneous ablutions at breakneck speed.

She was out again, and attempting to pull a summer dress over her head while she was still damp when the doorbell rang. Grabbing the towel she wrapped it round her head and went to let him in.

'Good morning!' he kissed the tip of her nose cheerfully. 'Running a little late are we my darling?'

'I'm sorry Michel I overslept! I'll just be a minute…' she started frantically rubbing her hair dry.

'Don't worry it will dry in the car on the way,' he said. 'Come on… rise and shine my little rough diamond!'

The car swept towards Cannes, and having driven down the main shopping area lined with trees in full blossom he pulled into a space opposite a row of very elite shops. Her eyes scanned the street in front of her nervously; Chanel, Hermes, Gucci, they were all there, their windows discreetly and minimally dressed and their interiors dim and intimidating. Opening her door for her gallantly he reached for her hand and they headed for the first shop of the day: lingerie. Jules instantly looked horrified and tried to go swiftly into reverse but he smiled reassuringly.

'The secret of a shiny diamond is that she will dress for the man she wants, not the man she has, even if she is blissfully happy with the man she has. That way she keeps her man at her feet and begging for mercy, and that, my dear Jules means attention to detail, so we have to start at the very beginning. It's a very good place to start, so I've heard.'

She smiled, doubtfully.

'Come on, I don't mean tassels and bells my love, but you can't look good on the outside without feeling good on the inside. And the way to achieve that is to feel some silk against your naked body first thing every day; trust me...' he took her hand and almost had to drag her into the shop. 'Progress and preservation do not make good bedfellows my darling and you need to throw out all that 'orrible grey underwear of yours and think again.'

Deftly, and without a hint of embarrassment he picked out delicate panties and bras, petticoats, suspender belts and stockings. Once again her mind drifted to Paul, and the Christmas he'd given her lingerie that was *'she's about your size'* too small, edged with scratchy black lace and with a red ribbon running through it... and she smiled at the memory of the look on the face of that Mothers Union member who had opened that bag of jumble come February.

Meanwhile Michel was now heading purposefully towards the nightclothes.

'Likewise,' he said as he picked out a beautiful jade green set, and another in black, 'you should always sleep dressed like a lover, not like a wife.'

She thought of her favourite nightshirt; the pink one with the strawberries on it that was fraying round the neck and the hem had come undone, and when she stood up, the side seams were so twisted that one of them was just about level with her navel.

Not once did he look at the prices. Jules surreptitiously looked at a label on a pair of silk panties on display and swallowed suddenly. 'Michel I can't possibly afford...'

'Nonsense! My treat I said.'

'But I couldn't possibly...'

'Be quiet, I am polishing you!' he smiled, putting the whole pile into her arms and taking her by the shoulders, he aimed her towards the fitting room. 'Claudette here will assist you,' he said, indicating with polished authority to the assistant, who leapt to attention as if she'd been stung by a bee at the thought of this much commission on a single sale and followed Jules into the fitting room.

Having discovered she'd been wearing the wrong size bra for most of her adult life, the next stop was for shoes.

'It is very important that your shoes fit well,' he said, his eyes already scanning the shelves.

Now beginning to enjoy herself, Jules loved shoes.

'Bette Midler once said that with the right shoes a woman can conquer the world...' she said, trying not to be intimidated by the shop assistant watching them closely, attracted by their impressive carrier bags.

'Exactly. A classic court shoe I think...' he replied, picking out a pair of elegant black leather shoes with a fine detail across the heels and toes and a heel of about two and a half inches. 'Try these first...'

She tried them on: they fitted like a glove and she felt as if she was walking on feathers as she walked around the shop.

'And some flats too, for comfort.' He passed her a pair of gold Gucci pumps, and a pair of leather thong sandals. She tried them all on, her wide eyes beginning to relax and she was really beginning to smile. She'd never experienced shoes like these: It felt like they had been made to measure.

Leaving the shop, Michel looked at his watch. 'Come on, time is getting on! We will do your top layer now!'

He grabbed her hand and headed towards the clothes shops.

'They won't have anything in my size!' she wailed. 'These shops only sell clothes for stick insects!'

'Shut up!' he smiled. 'This way!'

Two floaty summer dresses, some tailored crop pants and some very good jeans later, they headed back towards the car, but Michel took a sudden detour when his eye caught something, and he pulled her into Hermes.

'If you must tie your beautiful hair back it should be with something special and not those horrible elastic things.' Taking a colourful silk scarf from a rack he headed for the cash desk, grabbing a large gold tote bag on the way, saying, 'this will go very well with your pumps!' She was delighted with them, but still speechless with his generosity.

'Are we going back now?' she asked, as he piled the bags into the boot of the car, rummaging around and consolidating some of the items into three bags, which he then handed to her.

'No. This is where you really have some fun. We are going to see my friend Amelie over at the Givenchy spa. She is going to do some treatments for you to make you glow....'

She looked worried again.

'Don't panic, she's half English!' he smiled.

✶

Amelie was waiting for them in the very plush reception at the spa that was a huge expanse of white marble, brass fixtures and very high ceilings. After greeting her warmly, she took her bags and put them into a locker behind the desk, giving her the little gold key, and then Michel handed her an envelope and spoke to her rapidly in French for a few minutes. She looked towards Jules, and then back at Michel. 'I'll take care of her, and I'm sure this will cover everything you've asked for,' she said, indicating the rather fat envelope, that Jules realised with a jolt, was full of euros.

Turning back towards her Michel took her hand and smiled.

'Meet me at the marina when you're all done here,' he said, then, looking at his watch and kissing her lightly on the lips, 'I have to see a man about a mooring licence.'

Jules had looked a bit like Antoine had at eight years old when he realised he was being left at boarding school on his own as Michel left, and after he'd gone her stomach gurgled in protest at her lack of breakfast.

'Come with me Mrs. Taylor,' said Amelie respectfully. 'First things first, I'll show you to the dining room. You're going to need a full stomach for this!'

Amelie's mother, Jules learned on her way to the restaurant, was from Bordeaux, and her maternal grandparents spoke no English at all, so consequently Amelie was bi lingual by the age of three. At the age of eight her family had moved to England for her father's job: he was in computer electronics, and then she went to school in Reading. She passed her French A level with flying colours when she was sixteen, and earned a degree in Beauty Therapy at Reading University by the time she was twenty.

She moved back to France to pursue her career as a top rank beautician and was extremely popular with the clients in the spa because she spoke both English and French perfectly, and after two years dating a German hotelier a few years ago, she spoke pretty decent German too. She now lived in an apartment above a Boulanger in Cannes with her French partner Jean, who knew Michel very well through the real estate business, because that was his business too, though not quite as successfully yet.

Jules enjoyed a very fine lunch of grilled sea bass in a heavenly dill sauce and steamed vegetables, and was feeling pretty good and ready for her make over, so Amelie took her through to the spa and explained her itinerary for the rest of the day. Seaweed body wrap, waxing, full body massage, facial, manicure, pedicure, makeup and hair.

She had never known such pampering.

She had never known such pain either.

She didn't even know what a bikini wax was when she went in, but she certainly did by the time she came out. And she'd always been perfectly happy with one long eyebrow but Amelie insisted she should have two of them, and those little hairs underneath were absolute agony when they were tweaked out.

The seaweed body wrap felt very odd indeed, and she wasn't at all sure what to make of the sensation of, once thickly coated in green gunge, being wrapped in cling film like a mammoth portion of sushi and then in towels to ferment for what seemed like hours, and she was very glad to wash it all off under the shower and fully expected to be covered in blotches.

But after she had washed it all off she couldn't believe how great her skin felt. It glowed and tingled and felt like new, and no blotches, thankfully.

The facial was paradise itself; Amelie's gentle fingers performing soft sweeping upward strokes around her face and neck, and she actually fell asleep on the couch during her full body massage, until Amelie got to her knotted shoulders and underarms, which nearly sent her through the ceiling.

Next, she had her pedicure and manicure. More heaven, she decided; having your feet massaged after they'd been bubbling in blue stuff in a foot spa for ages was simply wonderful.

Her finger nails, it was decided, were beyond redemption, so she had extensions attached by a tiny Chinese girl with jet black hair and hypnotic eyes, and then a hard gel coating and a deep rich plum colour were applied. They looked completely natural and, Tai Tai assured her, would probably withstand the weight of an elephant treading on them for weeks and they still wouldn't break!

Her final treatment was her makeup and hair, and Amelie took her through to the salon and introduced her to her stylist, Carmel. A petite, winsome girl with very short wispy hair and a beautiful translucent complexion almost devoid of makeup, it struck Jules that she looked just like Peter Pan, and she half expected to hear her crow *cock-a-doodle-do* as she considered her tangle of curls; playing with it for a few minutes while she had a think.

'She's going to take years off you!' Amelie smiled at her obvious nervousness, 'Trust her, she's a total genius!'

Jules looked at Carmel in the mirror's reflection doubtfully, and tried to read her expression.

'We'll take out the grey,' Carmel announced, and whisked Jules' wheelie chair around to the sink. 'Then we will give you a colour to bring out your lovely face... we won't cut much off, it suits you long... just the ends to tidy it up, and we need to tame those curls a bit!'

Three hours later it was almost 7pm and Jules was finally done. Her hair, now a rich brunette and shiny as a fresh conker after being highly conditioned with hot wax, now fell in a cascade of individually defined curls around her shoulders and lifted and fell in an elegant bounce as she walked towards the changing rooms. Amelie had been busy removing all the labels and assisted her in dressing in her new and fabulous clothes.

Michel was right about the underwear. Jules felt like a million dollars plus interest, thinking that the whole day probably cost that much too.

As she was leaving the hotel Amelie called her back.

'You'll need these too!' she smiled, handing her a pair of very large Chanel sunglasses. Michel came back to leave these for you, he said to say you look like a film star now so you can hide behind these when everyone is staring at you in wonder!'

Jules smiled at that as she took them and put them on, and thanked all the girls, who had come out to see her completed transformation and wave her off.

Once outside, she adjusted her hold on her bags and scanned the car park for a taxi to take her back to the marina. At the front of the hotel there were some very impressive cars as well as one or two taxis. One of the impressives was a patent leather-shiny black limousine, and its driver was leaning against it with one foot on the kerb of a flower bed, waiting patiently with the rear door slightly ajar. He was talking to the doorman and had his back to her, and the doorman said something that made him turn around quickly.

'Mrs. Taylor?' he asked, in a broad Irish accent, and walking across to her.

'um, yes...?' she replied, looking at him.

'I am to take you to the marina,' he smiled, opening the door a little wider, and motioning for her to climb inside. She handed him her bags in a bit of a daze and climbed in to the back seat, watching his face in puzzlement in the rear view mirror the whole time.

As the car moved slowly towards the exit, Jules looked back and saw Carmel waving to her through the window of the salon, smiling broadly, looking even more like Peter Pan than before, and for all the world as if she was saying; *'Second star to the right and straight on till morning!'*

# Chapter twenty five

The evening sun was still blazing and there were people everywhere, either meandering aimlessly or heading purposefully out to eat, but all eyes followed the discreetly glamorous car as it glided almost soundlessly down the slope and into the marina. Stopping, the driver got out and opened the rear door, and Jules stepped out onto the quayside nervously, and very, very glad of her sunglasses. He opened the boot of the car by pressing something on the dashboard, and took out her bags. She held out an arm to take them from him, but he shook his head. 'No madam, I'll carry them for you...' and locking the car behind him he set off in front of her, clearing the way like Moses parting the Dead Sea while she tried really hard not to scuttle to keep up with him, or march in time to his wide stride so they looked as if they were changing the guard at Buckingham Palace.

She was wearing white cropped pants of the finest cotton, pocket-less and tailored and zipped at the side to flatter the hips beautifully. A primrose yellow silk camisole under a matching white blazer with enormous gold buttons, and her gold Gucci pumps and tote bag finished the look. Her hair bounced and played joyfully around her shoulders as she walked, and Amelie had tied the Hermes scarf around her throat and pulled the knot to one side for a flash of colour, in what was otherwise an ensemble of classic and understated French *chic*.

As they made their way along the jetty, the tourists clearing the way before them as if she really were a film star, a deeply bronzed and confident young man wearing nothing but his frayed shorts and engaged in washing the decks of the yacht he was working on, watched her pass below him. He let out a long and appreciative wolf whistle, and she halted suddenly, turned at the sound, and looked up. He smiled lazily down as the hose in his hand continued to trickle water, and he winked at her.

Hiding behind her glasses, the new Jules bit her tongue hard and resisted the old Jules' urge to shout *'Thank You!'*

As she approached *Gi Gi's* mooring she could see Michel was there and talking to another man on the jetty, and with his back to her as she approached. The other man saw her and said something quietly to Michel, who turned around. His face broke into a huge smile as she removed her sunglasses, and he walked towards her and said, '...there you are!'

'I'm sorry I took so long it...'

'No,' he interrupted, taking her by the arms and looking her up and down appreciatively. Taking her face in his hands and looking deep into her eyes he whispered 'I mean, *there* you are!'

Having relieved the driver of her bags, and tipping him generously with a *Merci beaucoup,* he took her arm in his and escorted her up the gangplank and onto the boat.

He was so visibly thrilled with her she couldn't help but laugh; running his fingers through her hair, all the way to the ends without getting stuck once, and twirling her around to see her properly.

Then he went across the cabin to his jacket that was hanging across the back of a chair. Removing a small box from his pocket he opened it as he came back towards her. Inside was a pair of earrings, with diamonds somewhat shockingly the size of frozen peas in them. And the Birds Eye ones, not the little French ones...

She looked at him and smiled. 'Michel...I'

'Shh' he said, 'put them on. I want you to see them every time you look in the mirror... to remind you that you are a diamond.'

✯

All too soon Jules' holiday was over save a final weekend in London with Marcus and Sam before braving Clearwater House again, but standing in the airport lounge at Nice with Michel, sad as it was, it felt like the right time to say goodbye. She felt relaxed, she felt strong, she felt confident; she felt new.

And she couldn't wait to show off.

Then, taking her ticket from her hand, and looking at it as she was talking, he shook her totally by tearing it slowly in half.

'Michel! What on earth...' and for a brief moment when he looked at her she thought he was about to say *'stay'*, but instead he took her hand and led her towards the window. On the hardstand just below the window stood a sleek white private jet, and her eyes almost popped out of her head, too used to his surprises now to be doubtful of his intent.

'It belongs to a business friend of mine who's here from Barcelona for a series of meetings. It's going to the London City airport collect his wife this evening... so I had a word with him, because I thought that as you are going to see your son anyway you might like to go home in style...'

Taking her across the tarmac and up the steps of the plane, he settled her into an extremely plush cream leather seat.

'Michel I just don't know how to thank you for all this...'

He put his index finger onto her lips and shook his head.

Kissing her for the last time he took her face in his hands and looked deep into her eyes.

'Jules,' he said. 'You told me once that Paul said you were the worst mistake he ever made...'

She pulled away and looked dumbstruck at those words that Catherine had thrown at her back in February, but he smiled at her and ran one finger slowly down her cheek.

'Now go home and prove it to him...' he said.

# Chapter twenty six

Catherine had reckoned she could leave a day early for Edinburgh as Paul was still in America getting inspired by dust and mountains, so had stopped off in Manchester en route, and was in fact in a plush hotel bedroom with the other odds on favourite for love of her life, Daniel Makepeace. Daniel, according to his Google diary that Sabrina was checking at home at that precise moment, was allegedly chairing a meeting of a different kind altogether, before they had a dinner engagement with friends in a local restaurant at eight.

Catherine was rattled. Paul had been grumpy and tetchy ever since that day in Frincham when Jules had been so poisonous, and then came the divorce, and now he had gone off to The States barely asking her what her plans were before he left.

She had been almost dizzy with excitement at the prospect of a whole afternoon and evening of unbridled sex with Daniel. She had been so put out with Paul's mood she'd almost told him and got it over with too, and Daniel had told her he'd told his wife about them so she could have done; she'd have to soon if they were going to be together....

But it hadn't been quite as idyllic as she had expected. Daniel had met her in the hotel lobby as arranged, but almost an hour late and obviously post boozy lunch somewhere, and had whisked her up to the room at the speed of light. Clothes off, into bed and into her as if on some kind of speed trial, he hadn't even had his usual simultaneous grope in the inside pocket of his suit jacket for a condom. The final insult happened when she turned to him, ready for a slightly more loving version of why they were there together, and he'd leapt out of the bed wordlessly and into the shower, scrubbing himself vigorously to remove every trace of her as if she'd been ordered with a credit card. He may have been fantastic lover, well, normally... but sex wasn't everything; he was being a bit of a pig today. Paul might be a bit on the erratic side just lately and a bit too old for her, but at least he knew how to treat a girl.

She sat there in the bed with one foot twitching in ill concealed irritation and examined her fingernails, as his mobile then proceeded with its annoying *'simply the best'* ring tone, again. For several minutes he was involved in a long conversation with someone at the paper as, inside her brain, her temper setting knob notched itself up from irritated to seething. Hanging up, he threw the phone onto the bed as he continued to do his tie, and noticed her look of impatience.

'Sorry darling that was Peter at the paper...'

'Peter who?'

'Peter... the new News Editor... you know? You met him last summer at the Wilson's in Alderley Edge... he liked your new haircut?' He turned to the desk and picked up his watch and cufflinks.

A tell tale glint of anger came into her eyes as she cast them downwards and she spoke very slowly. 'I haven't been to the Wilson's in Alderley Edge, or anywhere else, Daniel... and I haven't done anything to my hair...'

He turned back to face her, a slight flush of realisation on his face at the slip as he clipped his watch in place.

'That must have been your wife!'

He swallowed hard and had the decency to look uncomfortable.

Throwing back the bedclothes she stalked to the bathroom with as much dignity as she could muster but was burning with humiliation, disappointment, and frustration. Daniel reached the door in one long bound and forced it open, pushing his way in.

'Catherine... darling... I'm sorry...'

She burst into greatly increased tears and fell into his arms. 'I've been so looking forward to seeing you Daniel...' she sobbed, 'I could barely wait... it's awful at home... I almost told Paul about us and got it over with... I so nearly did....'

He pushed her away from him suddenly. 'Tell Paul?' he said incredulously, 'Why? I mean... why on earth would you do that?' his head began to shake slightly from side to side as if he couldn't believe what he was hearing, 'I... we're just having a bit of fun today aren't we...? A last hoorah... you know....' He looked totally shocked. Paul Taylor? The last thing he needed was his name splashed all over the papers getting mixed up in a celebrity cat fight with him. His father in law would have him for an after dinner cigar.

'But... I... I don't understand... Daniel...I.... ' She tried to put her arms around his neck, but he stopped her.

'I thought we understood eachother.... I can't risk losing Sabrina, Catherine... her father would absolutely crucify me! He'd sack me tomorrow and my name in the industry would be mud... he *owns* most of it for Christ's sake! And besides... when she found out about us I promised her we weren't seeing each other anymore! Or... or she'll tell him I'm still... and...'

'You did what?'

'I promised her...'

'But you said you'd told her... you told me you'd told her... about us...'

'I didn't, I said she knew. She found out...'

'She... how?'

'An anonymous phone call... someone saw us and... and called her at the house. Her father was round like a shot and pinned me against the wall.'

'But you came here today... you said... you... couldn't wait to see me... I... thought...'

'I know darling... but I thought you knew what I meant.... I just wanted to see you one last time.... You said you were on your way to Edinburgh on a job and I thought you'd come to say goodbye....'

'G...goodbye?'

'Yes, goodbye... you must see that! We can't see each other anymore Catherine... I said. I thought we understood eachother. I can't risk losing my job... my wife and... and my children for something as...' he stopped talking.

Her head was spinning and she began to shake as he reached down and picked up his phone, putting it calmly in his jacket pocket.

'I have to be somewhere...' he checked his watch awkwardly. 'Sabrina and I have plans...'

She stopped shaking abruptly and glared at him. 'Save your breath Daniel!' she spat. 'Go on, get out! Go and spend the evening with your wife then... go on... run home to Sabrina and your precious brats.... Snap to it! Mustn't upset your father-in-law now! Don't be late!'

She turned and marched back towards the bed, half expecting him to run after her, but the door closed behind him, and he was gone.

# Chapter twenty seven

London City Airport was, as usual, full of businessmen and women in dark suits that all looked as if they were going to a funeral, but carrying laptop bags instead of flowers. Paul was sitting at a table by a window in arrivals with a fairly disgusting bucketful of coffee that was deeper than its little wooden stick that passed for a spoon, and therefore didn't reach the sugar, whilst impatiently waiting for Catherine's flight to come in from Edinburgh.

Aimlessly watching the planes coming and going, he watched as a Lear jet landed and then taxied onto a hardstand just below his window vantage point. The cabin door opened and the steps came down in one fluid movement, and a liveried steward stood patiently at the bottom of them, having just trotted lightly down from inside the plane. The weather was sunny but windy, as airports always are, and as the single passenger appeared from the cabin she held onto her hat as the wind caught it. She was very elegant, and he found his gaze captured as he watched her shake hands with the steward, laughing, and head for the building. He could not see her face, but he knew that she would be beautiful. Her appearance and her grace had declared it so.

A few minutes later and still watching out for her in the constant stream of passengers making their way through Arrivals, he saw her, pushing a trolley of cases that he recognised as identical to a set he owned himself.

Her hat and sunglasses still on, and striding confidently towards the exit he still could not see her face properly but continued to watch as she stopped momentarily to look at a dress displayed in a shop unit window.

Looking at the dress on display Jules suddenly saw him watching her in the reflection of the glass and froze. Did he know she was coming in? How did he find out? She hadn't even known…. Had he come to meet her?

Through the anonymity of her sunglasses she watched him for a moment as he watched her, his eyes scanning her up and down lazily, then his gaze left her and returned to the arrivals board above him, and then he stood up and checked his watch. As he did so the reason for his being there then became apparent, and Catherine appeared at his table pulling a classic Louis Vuitton trolley bag. She continued to watch the reflection as he greeted her, she looking flustered and very rattled and complaining audibly about a delay with her flight making her late back to file her copy.

Now realising that he hadn't actually recognised her as he had watched her, and feeling a just a little bit confused as to whether she was smug or disappointed, she let out a slow breath of relief and headed for the exit.

Paul's eyes followed her over Catherine's shoulder, all the way to the exit, and leave.

※

Arriving at Marcus and Sam's apartment building slightly less relaxed having been stuck in the traffic for ages in a black cab, Jules stood at their door and rang the bell. Straightening her jacket and hair and removing her hat and sunglasses as she did so, she prepared herself for her Extreme Makeover reveal moment. Waiting for a couple of minutes, and becoming a bit puzzled, she tried ringing again, but the bell rang an unanswered echo inside. That's odd, she thought, I told them what time I'd be here...

Reaching into her bag she was just about to ring him when her phone burst into life with a quick burst of Rebel Yell that Michel had downloaded, and she smiled at it, but the smile was whipped off as soon as she realised it was Marcus on the other end, breathlessly telling her that Sam had been rushed into hospital.

She was to find the spare front door key under the fire extinguisher, dump her bags inside their apartment, and head straight there. She did a quick calculation in her head. The baby wasn't due until August... She was barely twenty weeks pregnant. This was far too soon.

Coming out of the lift at the hospital maternity wing Jules came to an abrupt halt just as the, 'doors closing' announcement sounded behind her. Paul was there, and talking to a nurse.

So Marcus must have called him too.

He looked up momentarily and saw her standing there, and did a visible double take as the woman from the airport was now tentatively walking towards him... and the woman from the airport was Jules.

✯

'Jules! What?... Jules how?... you look... I saw...' he blustered, shaking his head in disbelief.

'What's happening?' she said, now visibly shaking from head to foot. 'How's Sam? Where's Marcus?' Then he pulled her into his arms without even thinking about it, and held her.

'She's lost it Jules... they've lost their baby... I'm so sorry...' and she cried as he held her, both of them in pieces, and he holding one hand against the back of her neck, pulling her into his chest. Then Marcus appeared around the corner moving as if on autopilot, and when he saw them both there, like that, and totally oblivious to the miraculous change in his mother's appearance, he let it go with a wail of despair.

They ran to him, and together they held their son as he sobbed uncontrollably, incoherently telling them that the tiny existence that had so tested their relationship and judged him completely as a grown man was no more. He'd never get to see or hold him now, never get to see Sam be a mother to him... and he'd never wanted to be a father more in his life.

# Chapter twenty eight

Catherine had gone into the office to file her copy when Paul had dropped her off at the paper and, having received a text from him saying where he had gone now, she walked out of the lift at the maternity wing to see this tender tableau happening in front of her. Watching the three of them, and taking in the vision that was Jules with her eyes opened wide in surprise, even if she was in bits at this point, and all of them completely unaware that she had arrived, or even existed at that moment in time, she went swiftly into reverse and stepped back in the lift.

So Sam must have lost it, and just look how something as insignificant as that had pulled Paul and Jules back together. What a fuss about a baby Marcus never even wanted to start with! He should be relieved. Anyway, they were still young... they could soon have another one.

...And as for that Jules....

She was suddenly struck with the answer to the mystery; *she* must have been the anonymous caller that had rung Sabrina Makepeace! …she was the one that told Paul about them back in February. And now look at her looking fantastic… no longer the frizzy frump, and fawning all over him… It had to have been her. Well after what she'd done to ruin her relationship with Daniel, if she thought she was going to get Paul back now and leave her with nobody she had another think coming!

✷

Paul rang Catherine later to say he was going back to Marcus' apartment to look after Jules while Marcus stayed with Sam at the hospital, and she feigned compassion, but she was scared. She wasn't going to lose him back to that Jules. She wasn't prepared to face that humiliation, not twice in two weeks. She paced their apartment indignantly, slopping wine all over the floor as she poured herself another glass.

# Chapter twenty nine

Back at Marcus and Sam's, Paul was rummaging around in their kitchen drawers trying to find a foil cutter, having stopped off at Threshers on the way back to buy a bottle of medicinal brandy. Not that when he was getting it he was sure whether it was for Jules or for himself though, because apart from the obvious, he'd had quite a jolt when he'd seen her at the hospital. The apartment was open plan and he could see her now, sitting on the edge of the sofa with her head down, and she was still weeping as he passed her a glass. Taking it with her left hand that he noticed with a jolt was still wearing a wedding ring. She mumbled a thank you and took a tiny sip, pulling a face at the fierceness of it as she did so.

Paul chose to sit in an armchair after a moment's hesitation rather than next to her, and swirled the drink around the bowl of his brandy glass, waiting to see if she would speak first.

'So... does Catherine know where you are?' She said it quietly and totally without sarcasm. 'She must be worried... it's getting late.'

'I sent her a text,' he said. She just got back from Edinburgh this afternoon and she had to go in and file some copy at the paper....' He took a sip of his drink and looked down into his glass. 'I saw you...' he said, 'at the airport this afternoon...'

'Really?' she lied, convincingly. 'Yes... that's right I was there,' she said absently, wiping her eyes with a tissue. 'I just got back from a lovely holiday....'

'In a private jet?' he asked incredulously, and slightly too loudly. 'Whatever did you get for that painting at auction?' as if he didn't know.

'Don't flatter yourself Paul,' she said shortly, knowing he'd want to get his four pennyworth in about the sale ever since he'd heard about it. 'It didn't fetch enough to get me one of those... you'd have to be dead to fetch those kinds of prices. That plane belonged to a friend of a friend that I met in France.'

'A friend of a friend?' he asked, placing his glass on the coffee table and looking at her. 'Does your friend have a name?'

'Michel... not that you have any right to ask me now, in any case...'

Picking up his glass again he sighed. 'No of course not. I...didn't mean...' then he took a very deep breath. 'Please can we not do this tonight Jules?'

She looked at him and then looked away in silent agreement: now was not the time for another row.

They sat quietly for a few hours of minutes, until Paul stood up and walked across to the window. Standing with his back to her and relieved beyond words that her friend had been a woman, he almost whispered; 'Can I just say though... you look fantastic Jules... you're holiday certainly did you a power of good...'

'Yes,' she said. 'It did.'

Sitting back down again he noticed her earrings, which were easily twice the size of the one's he'd bought for her but gave Catherine on Christmas Day.

'Beautiful earrings too...'

'Yes, they were a present from Michel too...' she said, standing up. 'Are you hungry Paul? Shall I get us something to eat?'

Refusing to be put off he mumbled, 'how did all this happen to us Jules? It's like a bad dream... not my life at all...'

'Oh it's yours alright...' she said, heading for the kitchen and opening a cupboard. 'But right now I'm more concerned with what's happening in our son's. Is beans on toast ok?'

✶

Jules slept in Marcus and Sam's bed, and Paul took the spare room futon, and in any other circumstances it would have been amusing to see him trying to sleep on something almost two feet shorter than he was, but he'd insisted.

The following morning, Marcus arrived home early to shower and change and then to arrange emergency cover for his patients. Sam had slept fitfully, and Marcus had spent the night in what passed for a hospital armchair by her bed, with a blanket that sparked static every time he moved, so consequently he didn't, and now ached all over: inside and out.

Jules hugged him as tightly to herself as she possibly could; gently caressing his hair in her fingers, just as she had always done, and she would have sacrificed anything, anything to make things alright again for him. He'd just said that Sam was in the operating theatre having a small operation to make sure everything had gone, and the nurse had sent him home to have a break and a shower.

She was devastated and had hardly spoken to Marcus all the time he'd been there; merely lying on her side, and staring blankly into space as her tears had progressed slowly across the top of her nose and down her other cheek, onto her pillow. The doctor that had helped her through her miscarriage had assured her that she would still be able to conceive; even suggesting they try again immediately, but first she had to grieve: they both did, and nothing was going to help them to get over something so emotionally wrenching, but time.

Jules knew this was something they were going to have to face together.

And it would either make, or break, their relationship.

After Jules had fixed some breakfast that she practically forced down his throat, she and Marcus were washing up at the kitchen sink. Marcus was still very distracted and quiet, but turned to say something to her and then stopped mid sentence, his eyes widening in surprise as if only just opened and suddenly aware of the change in her, blinked in disbelief. Exclaiming in surprise, he hugged her to him just as his father entered the kitchen carrying his empty cereal bowl. Marcus turned to him and smiled incredulously.

'Yes, she does look fantastic... really fantastic...' Paul said, handing her the bowl with a little smile.

✯

After a couple of days Jules was dispatched back to Frincham, under protest but understanding that Sam needed Marcus, and not a whole lot of fuss. So it was Paul who had come over to help Marcus box up all the baby things that they had been collecting so that Sam would not see them, and as much as he had tried to be a man and be strong about it, it was Paul who had held him in an uninhibited and solid embrace each time his heart broke again. It had been a time of healing and reconciliation for them both in the most desperate circumstances imaginable. Marcus realised just how much he still loved and needed his dad, and Paul realised how much he had missed being a father.

When they'd finished clearing everything away Paul had stacked the boxes into his car having absolutely no idea what to do with them. There were only five boxes. Five boxes; filled with preparations made with joy and excitement for the arrival of their little boy; for they had known they were having a son. A son so resented by his daddy at first, and now no more; and before he'd even had a chance to say sorry. A son who would not grasp or seek comfort from the little Harrods teddy bear; never follow the clowns mobile with his little eyes; never cry for attention through those monitors, never sleep in that cot.

Paul doubted they would ever want to see these particular things again, even if they had another baby, and pulled over onto the pavement outside the first charity shop he saw.

# Chapter thirty

Marcus brought Sam home; still very pale, but glad to be out of the hospital. In her bag was a pile of helpful leaflets, all packed full of information about how to *Manage a Miscarriage*. She now knew that she had suffered something called an *Incomplete* Miscarriage. That meant the baby had gone but she had had to have an operation to remove what the doctor had called, somewhat briskly, 'everything else.'

So now she was all flushed out and clean again, which was good, he'd said; excellent, he'd said.

And empty.

So very empty.

Because he had been born under twenty four weeks there had been no legal requirement to have a burial or a cremation; it was like he hadn't actually existed ... to anyone else but her. But he had looked like a baby. She'd seen him. They'd tried to take him swiftly away but she'd seen him.

She became afraid to sleep because whenever she did she relived it all each time. Each time she slept she heard him crying out for her; calling out to her from the inside of a blood splattered surgical waste bin. The Doctors and nurses in the delivery room all had grotesquely distorted faces, and the screams of her baby became her own as she awoke in darkness and terror again and again. As the days went by with little difference between night and day she became more and more quiet and withdrawn. Marcus was running ragged trying to get her to shower and dress; to eat; to get some fresh air; to let him hold her. And he tried everything he could just to be there for her, following his mother's advice to just be patient, but she seemed to be increasingly lost in a world where nothing and nobody mattered.

One Saturday morning as he carried a pile of clean clothes into the bedroom he found her sitting on the floor, propped against the bed, and sobbing. On the floor beside her lay the little red leather box that he recognised as having been the one her Christmas bracelet had been inside. The box was open and for a moment he thought she might be upset because she'd lost it. Dropping the pile of clothes onto the bed he sank down onto the floor beside her and pulled her into his arms whether she wanted him to or not, and held on tight. In her hand was a little black and white scan photo, a misty grey blur of indeterminate content, but nevertheless her only physical reminder of a life that had truly existed, however briefly. Inside the box was her anti-natal clinic appointment card folded in half, and the plastic identity bracelet that she'd had on her wrist at the hospital. Seeing this sad little box of treasures and unable to be strong and hold it in and be strong for her any more, Marcus let go and wept, great heaving sobs, and pulled her closer towards him, and it was as if her eyes had finally opened. This wasn't her private tragedy; Marcus had lost his son too, and her hand slowly took his, and kissed it tenderly.

✯

Jules was having coffee with Dizzy up at the rectory. It was Hector's day for a visit from his good friend Phillip, the Rural Dean, and they'd taken the girls, and Phillip's chocolate Labrador Leo, on a nature ramble. So making use of the unusual peace and quiet, they were discussing Sam and Marcus in two very shabby but comfortable padded chairs in the garden.

'Marcus says Sam feels a complete failure and angry because they've been robbed of their relationship with their son before it even started, and Sam says Marcus thinks it's his fault… that he's being punished by God for reacting so badly at the start…'

'They're going to feel all these things Jules, and more; that's called grieving and it's a journey they have to make. But the way I see it is, and I really hate this expression, but it's true in this case: they have no closure. He was real to them and they didn't get to say goodbye to him, so how can they be expected to move on? They're in limbo.

You know, a funeral service helps so much when somebody dies…. It's as much a chance to draw a line as it is to say goodbye.'

'So what are you saying? They need a funeral? How? There's no…'

'We can have a service without a coffin Jules. If you think it would help them, get them here and we'll do it.'

# Chapter thirty one

Marcus and Sam had barely needed to discuss it. They'd jumped at the idea, so went down to spend the following weekend, and on the Saturday morning they dressed up bravely, and arrived at the church to meet their family and friends, and say goodbye to their son.

Walking into the church, it was almost too much for them when they saw the amount of trouble that had been taken: the church was filled with white Lillies, courtesy of the ladies of the Mothers Union. But that wasn't all. Sitting half way down the church on the left hand side were two of the last people they had expected to see there, and Tom and Patsy Williamson stood up nervously to greet them. Tom put out his hand in a totally genuine gesture of love and compassion, despite Marcus' treatment of them both at that terrible Christmas party, when they had brought along their fractious son and Marcus had behaved so badly. Marcus took Tom's hand wordlessly but spoke volumes.

Sam took Patsy in her arms and whispered, 'thank you for coming' through her tears.

Patsy kissed her lightly on the cheek. 'We wanted to come,' she said gently, and then looked into her eyes. 'Sam... can we meet up some time?'

Sam nodded, and tried her best to smile, then walked on and joined Marcus, taking his hand, to sit in the front pew.

Hector was always brilliant, but Dizzy found that she loved him even more every time he showed his true gift for his calling in situations like these. The first thing he had suggested when he had discussed the service with Marcus and Sam at the Rectory, was that they gave him a proper identity and named their son, so they had; they called him Henry. All the way through the service Hector referred to him by his name, and by the end of it they both felt at peace; Henry had existed, was real, made a difference; and he'd mattered.

Hector had also suggested that they make an area in the garden so that they could always sit and spend time in peace with their son. So when the service was finished, the family returned to Clearwater House, and to the garden where a wrought iron bench had been placed by the crumbling old brick wall; and a little memorial plaque marked the planting of a pure white rose tree that was already showing its promise for years to come. And Hector had blessed it, and brought to their attention that the rose was surrounded by both buddleia and lavender, that would attract the butterflies, as perfect and vibrant proof of how when one life ends, another, much richer one begins.

# Chapter thirty two

And so Marcus and Sam returned to London, and to work, and slowly but surely, life resumed and Marcus, and eventually Sam also, began to smile again. They had found genuine friendship in Tom and Patsy Williamson, and Sam and Patsy began to swim together on Saturday mornings while Marcus joined Tom with his Saturday morning daddy-bonding sessions taking Matthew, their totally normal and not in the least demonic son, to feed the ducks and play on the swings in the park.

As they lived quite close to each other, and as a ruse to build up their confidence, they had also suggested that Sam and Marcus might baby sit Matthew sometimes, so that they could start going to the gym together as well. So that had become a regular Tuesday evening event too; Patsy and Tom to the gym, and Sam and Marcus revelling in bath times, giggles, snuggles and bedtime stories.

Tom and Patsy provided their shoulders to either cry or laugh on as appropriate, and had not only given them unconditional friendship at the most difficult time they had ever faced as a couple; they had intentionally given them healing in their own son, and hope for the future.

As if to seal this pact, whilst enjoying a meal on an anonymous Sunday lunchtime at the pub and as Matthew sat in a highchair and sucked on a chicken nugget, they were completely taken aback when Tom asked them both to be Godparents to Matthew at his Baptism planned for the following month. They accepted without hesitation and on the day, as well as promising to help him *fight valiantly, against sin, the world and the devil,* promised to always provide toothpaste... and a gum shield when he was old enough to take up rugby like his dad.

## Chapter thirty three

Jules had gone back to work after her holiday to a rapturous welcome and a few wolf whistles from both staff and children regarding her new look, and at the end of her first week back she was given a card signed by all the infants. On it was a very approximate likeness of herself in her new clothes and with her new hairstyle, drawn in pastels in slightly more vibrant colours than the real thing. The card took up pride of place on the kitchen wall at Clearwater house, just to the right of the clay footprints and just below Jemmie's pasta sunflower.

School was her bolt hole, her safe haven from all the stuff. Her friendships with Christine and Gill were genuine and sincere, Peter was the perfect head teacher who had the children wrapped around his little finger in their desire to please him, and she adored all of the children. Leaving home each morning with her head bursting with worries and confused feelings and horrors over the last few months; she hardly knew how she would have coped without the work, and the anonymity, of the school.

The blissful anonymity didn't last though. Soon after her return to work after her holiday one of the parents had made the connection after seeing Jules' picture with Paul in an old newspaper she'd found at the bottom of a pile in her shed, and with the speed of light that gossip always has, her secret was out, and all over the school. Mrs. Taylor was married to PAUL Taylor the artist, and he'd left her for a younger woman... and so Mrs. Taylor had had to get a job so she wouldn't starve; or words to that effect.

The Chinese whispers became more and more inaccurate and ridiculous and the children's questions more and more bold and intrusive.

So, decision time: did she ride it out or leave?

Then she had a memo from Peter, asking her to see him after school one deceivingly bright and sunny afternoon, and she thought the decision had been made for her. She was bringing tabloid scandal into school and he wanted her to leave.

Spreading the dishcloth to dry over the taps after she'd finished washing up the glue pots in the Infant's classroom, she sighed deeply, unable to put it off any longer. So she stretched her back from bending over the low sink for too long, removed her rubber gloves and her apron, and made her way tentatively through the hall and up the stairs, to his office. She passed nobody on the way, and surmised that he had asked the rest of the staff to leave promptly so that he could talk to her, and then presumably so she'd leave without any further discussion with them.

Knocking softly at the door, she was reminded of the day just seven months ago when she'd come here for her interview; so excited, so full of hope, and considering how hard or soft to knock at the door to create the right impression.

She should have guessed it couldn't last.

Peter opened the door and motioned her inside with a sweep of his arm.

'Well Jules....' He came straight to the point as always. 'How are you doing with all this?'

'I...' she was surprised, it wasn't the question she expected, and he sounded full of concern. She shook her head slightly. 'Well, you know... I thought it had all blown over now we're actually divorced... that nobody would be interested anymore... but it doesn't seem to get any easier after all.'

'I wish we could have been more help to you when it all came out.... But the thing is Jules... you never mentioned him when you came for your interview and it was as much of a shock to us as it was to everyone else.... It would have been so much easier for us if...'

'I know... I know.... I'm so sorry... I should have told you but... but I was... I was just trying get a bit of a grip. To get on with *my* life... I wanted... I didn't want to... mention...'

'I understand,' he said, putting his hand on her shoulder. 'It will all blow over you know... these things always do... once someone else makes a blunder you'll be old news and...'

'I know, I know...' she fumbled in her pocket for a tissue and wiped at her eyes as they started to betray her yet again.

'Would it help if you took a few days off Jules?'

She looked at him, searching his face for the words between the words; '*We would prefer it if you leave us Jules... we can't afford the upset in the school... we have our reputation to consider...etc. etc...*' but it wasn't there.

'It would give us a chance to sort this out; talk to all the children while you're not around... maybe get a letter out to parents that puts them all straight and stops all this ridiculous gossiping...'

She smiled at him, maybe he was right.

'We value your commitment to this school Jules... and your role in our team. We love working with you... we wouldn't want you to leave, and certainly not because of this. And besides,' his head tilted to one side, 'you certainly brighten the place up these days...' he took a strand of her hair in his fingers and let it go again, and she laughed. He was right, as always.

So she agreed to take a few days off, and left him feeling very much calmer than she had been all week.

Gill and Christine had miraculously reappeared and were sitting on the library chairs by the front door, waiting for her. They stood as she approached.

'Don't get too used to sitting around at home Jules… we want you back here!' Gill wrapped her in a hug and squeezed her tight.

'And we'll miss you…' said Christine, kissing the top of her head. 'Don't worry about it. We'll sort this out and then when you come back it will all be ok again… we promise…'

※

Whoever had been on Barney duty had put the day's post on the dresser in the kitchen when she arrived home that afternoon and, rummaging listlessly though it all as Barney danced around her legs in his usual rapturous welcome, she found a letter that actually didn't have a window in the front for a change, and looked at it more closely.

It had a Spanish postmark…

Puzzled, she ripped it open, and inside was a letter, albeit a short one, from Michel.

*Ma Cherie diamond Jules*

*Bonjour ma petite rebel! How is the yell? Can Paul hear it yet?*

*I'm in Spain and now I find I must come over to England for a few days next week and I would love to see you and catch up on your news- any chance we could meet?*

*You could maybe take me out for roast beef!*

*Call me to let me know if this is possible.*

*Until we meet Cherie, and you can show me the beautiful lake I only see in my head*

*Michel*

At the bottom of the letter was a telephone number so, ignoring Barney's protests, she picked up the telephone and dialled it.

Three short days later she was standing nervously at the windows in Stansted airport and waiting for his flight to land. She saw him straight away of course, skipping lightly down the steps from the plane and heading for the doors into Arrivals. He looked unmistakably French as usual; sporting a pair of glamorous sunglasses perched on the top of his head. He was wearing faded jeans and loafers with a pale pink shirt, and carried a bulging black flight bag on one shoulder. There wasn't a crease on him. He looked as if he'd just been steamed from head to toe before he left the plane.

She was about to turn and walk away from the windows to meet him when she suddenly caught sight of someone else following him down the steps. Victor Allen Frobisher was on his way home from a few weeks at his holiday villa in Spain. In complete contrast to Michel, he looked sunburned and frazzled, and he had the crumpled, lived in look of the English traveller. He was doing his best to get his jacket back on as he negotiated the steps and despite her surprise at seeing him there, she smiled. Only Victor would travel home from his holidays in a suit.

Michel made it through Arrivals in record time, dropped his bag with an impetuous thud and swept her into a great bear hug, kissing her enthusiastically on the lips before she even had the chance to say hello. Behind him, Victor had recognised her with a smile and a wave and was just about to greet her, when the rather gorgeous man he'd sat next to all the way from Barcelona suddenly got there first, completely taking his breath away by taking her in his arms and swinging her around, and then going in for a full on snog.

On the journey, once Victor had taken advantage of being 35,000 feet closer to God to close his eyes and proclaim *well done!* He'd asked Michel the reason for his trip, in order to practice his already flawless French. Michel had said he was coming over to the UK on business, but mentioned that he intended to combine business with pleasure, and stay with a very good friend. Some friend!

Seeing him over Michel's shoulder, Jules blushed and gently pushed Michel away.

'Victor! What a surprise! How lovely...'

'Jules...' he nodded, and looked from her to Michel and back again.

'Ah, so you know Jules then Victor?' Michel laughed, completely without embarrassment, and slipped his arm around her waist.

Jules cleared her throat. 'Yes... er... Paul used to work at Victor's gallery.... So... you know Michel then Victor? We met... um... when I was on holiday in France at Easter...'

'Ah yes,' Victor nodded, 'Paul mentioned you'd been away.... You look very well Jules....Your... er... holiday... um obviously... did you good...' but he was looking at Michel. Looking back towards her he continued. 'Paul... um... mentioned to me that you had met a new friend on your holiday... but he seemed to think your Michel was... a woman...?'

Jules bit her lip at this and tried not to laugh. No wonder Paul hadn't asked her any more questions about him back at Marcus' flat. 'Yes... well... I suppose if you only hear it said instead of seeing it written down... it would be easy to mistake...'

'I was so sorry to hear about your div... I mean... I was very sorry to hear... about you and Paul...' he interrupted. Poor Victor looked stunned, and very disapproving. He'd been not very secretly in love with Paul for years and couldn't bear to see him hurt or humiliated.

Jules looked to Michel for help with pleading eyes.

'Come on my darling, we must go, we'll be late.' Michel took her hand firmly and began to turn away from him. 'Goodbye Victor... it was very nice to meet you.' Then just as it looked as if he'd finished his farewell, Michel turned back again to face him. 'Oh... and I'm sure you'll be speaking to Paul again very soon so please give him my regards.... I am most grateful to him for running away with a woman half his age... so Jules had the courage to divorce him and is free to be mine now...!' He nodded at Victor by way of a visible exclamation mark and turned away so that Victor could not see the mischievous twinkle in his eyes. They managed to get most of the way back to the car park before he burst into hysterics. 'That should, how you say... set the cat after the birds!'

'Oh Michel!' she laughed, 'this isn't funny! He'll go straight back and tell Paul now!'

'Isn't that a good thing...?' He stopped laughing but was still smiling as he looked at her.

'You're a wicked... wicked man...' she smiled.

# Chapter thirty four

Jemmie had managed to get five precious days off and had spent three of them on her birthday trip to Paris with Martin, and was now staying at the cottage. Intending to surprise her mother with an impromptu visit, they set off with Dipstick to walk along the lakeside to the house, but were surprised to see her walking Barney and heading straight towards them; and even more surprised to see that she was arm in arm and chatting very animatedly to an extremely handsome man.

On the phone to Marcus later that evening, she asked him if he'd known anything about Jules having somebody French staying with her, called Michel.

'Michelle?' he said, 'Isn't that the friend she met in France on holiday? Dad mentioned it... I'm sure he said she'd met a woman called Michelle... they'd become really good friends, he said...'

'Close is right...' she said quietly. 'But a woman he certainly isn't, that's for sure! He's tall, dark, and a dead ringer for David Ginola!'

'No!' he gasped...'Oh my God! Dad thinks...oh Jems! He said she'd met someone called Michel and he must have automatically thought she meant.... Oh my God... Michel is the French for Michael isn't it? So that must be how she got the makeover! Who's going to tell him...you or me...?'

'Why should we tell him anything? They're divorced remember? She's a free agent...'

'Oh, open your eyes Jem! That's rubbish. He still loves her and she still loves him...'

'What?'

'Honestly! ...you should have seen him when they were here together.... He couldn't take his eyes off her!'

'Oh Marcus! You've had rose tinted glasses on since you and Sam set the date! And if that's true... what about this Michel then?'

'No I have not! You should have seen him... and I don't know what we should do Jem. It beats me! When they were here a few weeks back, right after her holiday makeover, she looked just as smitten as he did... and have you noticed? She still wears her wedding ring?'

'Yes, I noticed that. So what do we do then?'

'Nothing Jem.... We do nothing. They're big people. Let them figure it out.'

✷

Paul put down the phone and swallowed hard. Catherine was chattering away about something in the background but all he could hear were Victor's words. 'Jules seems to be getting over the divorce very quickly Paul...' and what on earth had he said about a Frenchman called Michel he'd seen her with? She'd said Michelle was a woman... hadn't she? He cast his mind back and tried to remember what she'd actually said, and felt suddenly foolish. Of course he was a man. What woman would buy another woman diamonds? His heart gave a painful lurch and he reached for his whisky glass, and gulped.

'Steady Paul!' Catherine said. 'That isn't lemonade!'

'Sorry' he muttered.

# Chapter Thirty Five

'Come on darling we'll be late...!' It was June the tenth, and Catherine came out of the bedroom fiddling with one of her diamond earrings and simultaneously slipping her feet into some strappy shoes, and she looked absolutely stunning. She had booked a table at his favourite restaurant and time was running short. It had taken her ages to get him motivated into getting ready, and even now he looked moody and withdrawn. Being with Paul was becoming very hard work lately. She'd tried nearly every trick in the book and she was still treading on eggshells with him, so this was her last ditch effort towards getting him back on track.

He'd been divorced almost three months now and it was way past time he popped the question, and time was running out. So she was setting the scene for him, and this was going to be perfect.

Arriving at the restaurant, he had been momentarily distracted by a couple of actors he knew, that were also eating there, and spoke to them for a few minutes before joining her at their table.

'What's with the champagne?' He indicated the bucket on the little stand beside the table with a jerk of his head as he sat down.

'We're celebrating darling,' she smiled.

'Celebrating what?' He was puzzled.

'Celebrating our one year anniversary of course...'

'Our... what?'

'It's June the tenth Paul. It was exactly one year ago this very night that we met... don't you remember?' She slowly ran her foot up the inside of his calf under the table, and reached over to take his hand in hers.

He had the decency to look embarrassed. 'Oh... yes of course.' He took the bottle out of the bucket and gently wrapped it in the white cloth that was draped over the stand. Popping it expertly and without spilling a drop he reached across to pour her a glass, and then poured one for himself. She lifted her glass and waited for him to do the same, they clinked glasses in salute and he sipped. Catherine though, was too busy watching him closely.

'So darling... where do we go from here?' She put down her untouched glass. It was bold question, and he looked nervous.

'Catherine.... I need to talk to you... I think I...'

'Shh darling,' she patted the back of his hand as the waiter approached to take their orders. Her brain was working overtime.

After the waiter had moved away, she said, 'I heard Jules has got herself a new man Paul...'

He looked up into her face from his previous focus on the tablecloth. 'Where did you hear that?'

'Oh good news travels fast.... Victor.'

'Apparently so...' he said quietly.

'So... now that she's sorted... there's no reason why we can't... you know...'

'What?'

She sighed impatiently. 'Get married Paul.... You said as soon as your divorce was finalised... we'd get married....'

'Married?' It felt as if she was talking in a foreign language.

'Married Paul... that's what people do when they fall in love... isn't it?' She picked up her glass of champagne and went to sip it, but put it down again.

'Well yes... but I...'

'And you know how much I love you Paul.... We're committed already, I know that but... I need something more permanent... I'll never want anyone but you... let's drink to it.' She lifted up her champagne glass once more.

As if in a trance, he lifted his glass and sipped, but she put down her glass without drinking anything again and he frowned.

'You're not drinking...' he said.

'That's something else I need to tell you...' she smiled. 'Paul... I really love you and want us to get married... but it will have to be soon... I wouldn't want to look fat in the photographs...' She tried to laugh. 'Wake up darling! Can't you guess? I can hardly believe it myself but... We're going to have baby!' She exclaimed it, and Paul's friends on the table behind them stopped eating and began to whoop and cheer as they heard. Their table instantly became surrounded by people, all hugging her and slapping him on the back in congratulation, and out of nowhere three musicians in ridiculously large sombreros arrived at their table, playing Spanish guitars and serenading them noisily. But Paul's face was ashen, and it was as if there was no sound in the room. She was lying, and he knew it. And if she wasn't lying about being pregnant, she was certainly lying about how she got to be.

# Chapter thirty six

School had been so much better. Peter had been so right; a few days to get some ground rules in place had worked wonders. And then this morning when she arrived, there were all the parents with their whispers and their stares as she walked across the playground. Whatever now?

In the staffroom, Jules stared open mouthed at the newspaper photograph showing the two of them announcing their engagement, with him giving absolutely nothing away with his eyes as usual, and her smiling smugly up at her, flashing the rock of Gibraltar on her finger. She shut the paper with a loud rustle of disgust, and as Peter walked into the staffroom he saw her fold it in half and then throw it, with some velocity, into the bin. Would poor Jules ever be able to pick up a newspaper without seeing her ex husband and his public love life splashed all over it, he wondered?

Hugo and Paul meanwhile, were sitting in his apartment and having their regular weekly meeting to discuss his calendar of diary engagements and proposed events. On the desk in front of them sat a pile of invitations, all presented on thick white card, and colloquially known as 'stiffs.' Half heartedly leafing through them and wishing he could get back to his latest project, Paul's eye caught an invitation from the Guildhall Gallery in Manchester to attend an exhibition and reception for a familiar name the following month; his best man when he'd married Jules in 1980, David Walton.

'Hugo... how's my diary looking for August 11$^{th}$?' he asked casually.

Hugo looked up from his laptop screen. 'Clear as far as I can see.... You don't like me booking you up in August usually... and you still haven't set a date for the wedding.... How am I supposed to work around it if I don't know when it is?'

Paul didn't answer, tossing the invitation over to him. 'This one is for a friend of mine.... RSVP me as a yes to this Hugo please...' he said.

'And shall I say Catherine too?'

'Oh yes, Catherine too.... In fact... better still; make it for all of us. David is a family friend. We'll all go.

Hugo blinked and pulled a face. 'Are you sure that's wise?' he asked quietly.

'Let me be the judge of that...' said Paul evenly.

Picking up his phone from the desk in front of him he dialled Jemmie's number, and was a little taken aback when she wasn't the one who answered it.

'Martin? Oh... It's um... Paul.... Is... is Jemmie there with you?'

'Yes she is...' Martin said stiffly, handing the phone to her as she walked into his kitchen, hair still wet from the shower.

There was the sound of whispering as he passed it.

'Dad?'

'Hello darling, sorry to disturb you... both; listen. I'll be going to the reception at the exhibition you said Martin is working on for David Walton in August... up in Manchester. I know I'm the only one who has really seen Uncle David for years and... I just wondered if you'd like to come with me...'

'Martin too?'

'Everyone; Martin, Marcus, Sam... your mum... and a guest if she has...'

'She hasn't Dad. Michel went back to France... and she told me he was just a friend.... Anyway, I'm not sure about this.... Is Catherine going with you?'

'Possibly... I'm not too sure yet.... She hasn't been too well lately...'

He heard her sigh impatiently. 'We all know she's pregnant Dad... you don't need to be so cloak and dagger.'

'Yes... well, anyway....' He sounded uncomfortable.

'Oh ask her to come, Dad... we could all do with some fun watching her waddle about...'

'She's not waddling about Jemmie... don't be ridiculous.'

'Sorry Dad. Bring her. She'll only think we made you leave her out if you don't.'

As he finished the call he smiled to himself, this was going to be perfect.

※

'But why do I have to come, Paul... and with all of *them* for pity's sake? I hate those kinds of evenings... you always leave me by myself to talk to a load of stuck up old bores that make my skin crawl... and I feel so fat already and they'll all want to put their creepy hands on my bump. Your family will all glare at me like the spectre at the feast too, and there's bounds to be loads of...'

'They won't glare at you.... It was Jemmie's suggestion that you come along. If you and I are to be married we all need to learn to accept eachother and this is the ideal way to start.'

'By leaving me in a room full of people I've written bad reviews for, that all want their four penny worth out of me for hours while you work the room?... and Jules might have been happy chattering away with the bores all evening Paul, but I am not Jules...'

'No, you're not...' he said quietly, then recovering speedily he said briskly; 'It will be fine you'll see... and anyway, you don't look fat... not in the slightest. We do all have to get along sometime.... Oh come with me... I want you to.' He put his arm a round her shoulder and kissed her lightly on the mouth. 'Please?'

She was in a corner and she knew it. Daniel would be bound to be there and she didn't want to face him after making such a fool of herself the last time... and in front of Paul's whole family? It didn't bear thinking about.

She sat down and thought about it for a few minutes. She knew perfectly well she didn't have much of a bump yet... and she could always wear those hideous Bridget Jones hold-everything-in-pants... and if she arrived looking a million dollars and on the arm of one of the country's best known artists... and everyone knew they were actually engaged and that she was having his baby now... that might be enjoyable.

...To see Daniel's face when he saw her looking radiant, instead of falling apart like he probably expected her to after he dumped her like that, and for that sloaney Sabrina and his precious kids...

...And to see Jules looking redundant and with no man on her arm despite her French fling and her miraculous makeover... she was still too fat to get a man.

'I'll come.' She said, with her best smile.

※

Down in Frincham, Jules put down the phone after speaking to Paul. She had agreed to go: seeing David was going to be a treat after so long, and he and Paul had been such good friends. David had been Paul's best man at their wedding and it would be good to see him again. It was somewhat ironic though that Paul never offered to take her on any of his engagements while they were married, and now he had invited her; and his mistress too. Or maybe Catherine couldn't be called his mistress anymore… not now they were engaged.

She raised her eyebrows slightly and pulled a face.

Well, she'd go. There was safety in numbers and Paul said that everyone was going, but she bit her lip and wondered if David knew they'd divorced… she hoped so, or this could be embarrassing.

This needed some serious thought.

※

'Mum! that looks absolutely great on you!'

Jemmie was lounging on the bed in Jules' room watching her mother as she twirled in front of Paul's full length dressing room mirror. She was wearing a full length jade green satin evening gown with its label still hanging down the back and some perfectly matching shoes she'd just bought at dizzying expense to wear to David's launch party. Now decided, she intended pulling out all the stops to look fantastic knowing full well that Paul would be taking Catherine along. Also, knowing that the press would be there as well, harbouring a strong determination not to be photographed as the frumpy ex wife, ever again.

'Thank you darling!' Jules said gratefully. 'What are you planning on wearing Jems?'

'Absolutely no idea!' she replied. 'I don't have anything remotely suitable for a do as high brow as this and when I went shopping last weekend, even in Paris I couldn't find a thing that I liked. I was thinking I might hire...'

'Just a minute!' Jules had swung round to look at her and, dress label flapping, headed across the room, moved the chair from the wow end of her wardrobe and threw open the door. 'I think I might have just the...'

'Oh *Mum!*' exclaimed Jemmie, as the Gianni Versace dress came back out into the daylight once more.

'You like it?'

'I... *Mum!*'

'I'll take that as a yes then!' she laughed.

'Are you sure about this...?' Jemmie's fingers were running through the folds of the fabric in awe.

'You're welcome to it darling. I must admit I did have a bit of a dream I'd fit into it again one day and I have lost a little bit of weight but I think my size ten days are long gone... and anyway it's far too young a style for me with that great sweep down the back and... well, I don't need impossible dreams anymore. They just make you weaker...'

'Can I try it on please?' Jemmie's eyes were dancing and Jules knew she'd made the right decision. It was time that dress worked its magic again, and Jemmie was going to look fabulous in it, she knew.

# Chapter thirty seven

August 11th arrived, and up in Manchester the gallery reception was in noisy full swing when Paul made his usual late but conspicuous arrival with Catherine on his arm looking absolutely stunning in what Jules whispered to David was best described as a gownless evening strap; much to his delight.

Paul was resplendent in an immaculately cut suit, but looked uncharacteristically nervous. Catherine looked outwardly excited, but on closer inspection her smile was brittle, and her eyes were all over the room, seeking Daniel Makepeace, and his plummy wife.

After greeting his old friend David and kissing Jules on the cheek and admiring her gown that brought out the colour of her eyes, Paul and Catherine soon became separated. Paul was whisked off to meet and greet, and so Catherine began to work the room with her teeth gritted in her usual professional manner in order to avoid the stuck up bores, and also whilst studiously avoiding Jules who seemed to be hogging the host, which had been her own Plan A.

The rest of the family were sipping champagne and looking at David's paintings on display, and Jemmie and Martin, slightly separated from the rest of them, were discussing how David and her parents' had been friends for many years; he was gay and had been having a relationship with Victor for a while until his career, like her father's, had taken off and he'd found bigger fish to fry; also like her father. Martin had been absolutely blown away at the sight of Jemmie in the red Versace dress, and Jules had been quite right. Jemmie did look better in it than she ever had. It was as if it had been made for her. With her hair worn loose and her lips slashed with scarlet, she looked absolutely amazing. Martin was just telling her so for the umpteenth time when, out of nowhere Paul suddenly appeared and spoke urgently to him.

'Come with me...' he said.

'Where?'

'I don't care!' he said, 'anywhere! Just come with me!' then, as Jemmie started to move too, added; 'Sorry, not you darling... and don't you look beautiful? I just need Martin.'

Martin looked puzzled, and shaking his head towards her, shrugged slightly and followed Paul through a side door and into the corridor that led primarily to the toilets.

'What is it Paul? I...'

'I need you to show me who Daniel Makepeace is...' he said hurriedly. 'I know you can Martin.... He is here, I take it?'

'Yes, he's here, he just arrived... with his wife... I don't quite understand Paul... Why?'

'Just say I need to know.' He said firmly.

Together they walked back into the gallery, though slightly apart, and Martin surreptitiously jerked his head towards Daniel to show Paul where he was. Daniel was standing with his back to the rest of the room; alongside the woman that was presumably his wife, and was talking to a large group of people; he was laughing and obviously the centre of attention.

Catherine was nowhere to be seen; he noticed.

One of his assembled group saw Paul standing there and quickly pulled him into the conversation, neatly introducing him to Daniel in the process, and though outwardly joining in the discussion, Paul's eyes were telling a different story; scanning his love rival critically from head to foot, and wondering if he'd known she was living with someone else while he was with her. He had certainly known that Daniel existed in her life, even if not actually by name at first. It was Jules who had named the faceless man he'd suspected, but had chosen to ignore, back in February.

After a few moments of falsehood Paul noticed that Catherine had reappeared, and was standing some way off, watching him. She was as white as a sheet as she pretended to talk to some people by a food table; her hand on her glass of fruit juice shaking visibly.

Stopping Daniel in full conversational flow with one hand on his arm, Paul beckoned across to her, asking her to come over to them. She crept forward nervously, visibly quivering, but trying her best to look calm.

A few feet away and watching intently, Martin had returned to Jemmie's side. Marcus, Sam and Jules were now with them, as was their host.

'What's going on Martin? What was all that about?' Jemmie whispered.

'I've absolutely no idea darling… but one thing is for sure… he knows. He knows about Daniel Makepeace and Catherine… and seeing this now, I think the poop might be about to hit the fan…!'

'Oh my God Martin it was me! I told him!' said Jules in horror. 'They both turned up at the house just after you and Jemmie told me you'd seen her with Daniel Makepeace in Manchester… and he was being so… so I threw it at him! I couldn't help myself!'

They crept as fast as was possible whilst still remaining unnoticed, towards the group so that they could hear what was going on, but Jules stayed put, watching silently and frozen to the spot beside David, who was now holding her hand tightly.

Paul hadn't said a word about Catherine and Daniel after she'd told him about it back in February, not one. So what on earth was this about?

'Daniel... I believe we have mutual friend here...' said Paul loudly, taking Catherine's arm and reeling her in the last foot or so.

Daniel had his back to her, but the smile vanished as he turned and saw her standing there. 'Oh really Paul I... Catherine!' he said, visibly startled.

'That's right Daniel... and Catherine, this is Daniel... but then you already know that don't you?' he said innocently.

'Yes, we have met...' she said quietly.

'Yes...I... er... we....' Daniel blustered.

'Spit it out man.... What you're trying to say is that you were screwing her while she was with me... that's right isn't it?'

'Paul!' she said, horrified, 'I... Paul... how could you?'

'How could you more's the point darling?' he said, plainly enjoying their discomfort.

Daniel lowered his voice almost to a whisper and hissed at him. 'Not here Taylor... everyone's watching! Let's go outside....' He put down his glass and began to make for the door.

'By all means Makepeace...you certainly don't live up to your name do you? But Catherine here is almost four months pregnant, so she'd better stay inside... I don't want her getting stressed unnecessarily.' He pushed her down into a chair heavily. More and more of the other guests were beginning to stop talking and enjoy the spectacle, with journalist after journalist transferring their attentions from David, to grasping for a new page in their notebooks; all sensing the gift of a free scandal to boost the morning editions. And then a camera flashed from somewhere.

Paul spoke to the back of the retreating Daniel's head. 'Oh but forgive me... that's not for me to say is it Makepeace? Do you want her to come outside and watch? Bearing in mind her condition?'

Daniel stopped dead in his tracks and his head shot back round in surprise. 'What on earth do you mean, do I want her to...?'

'Well after all it is your baby she's having... I assume, unless of course she's been stringing us both along and there's yet another poor sop somewhere...'

Martin's eyes were wide open, Jemmie's hand was over her mouth, and Jules closed her eyes, ineffectively.

Sam grasped Marcus' hand and held on tight, her engagement ring pinching him and making him wince.

There was an audible gasp from the entire room but after that you could have heard a sold sticker drop as everyone waited, with all eyes on Catherine.

'Is there another man Catherine?' said Paul evenly.

She was dumbstruck and shaking, and did not answer him.

'Catherine?' said Daniel, is this true? Is it mine? You told me you were on the...'

'Of course it isn't yours!' she snapped suddenly. But that last time they'd made love so speedily at Easter... when they'd been too past caring to use a condom.... She paled. She wouldn't give him the satisfaction. Of course it was Paul's! But she was breathing fast and despite the air conditioning her dress was beginning to stick to her back uncomfortably. 'Paul how could you do this to me? I'm having your baby, our baby... Daniel and I never...'

'Oh spare me do!' Paul laughed mirthlessly. 'Give up! It's his and you know it, and when he dumped you, you tried to palm it off on me...'

'What do you mean? Of course I didn't... I didn't know...'

'What?' said Sabrina suddenly butting in, 'You didn't know which one of them was the father because you're such a whore you were doing the horizontal hoopla with both of them at the same time? So you tried accusing both of them to see which one bit? Daniel spoiled that one though didn't he? When he saw through you and came back to me...'

'You only found out because SHE told you!' Catherine shrieked at her and pointed across the room at Jules, who looked as if she might faint.

'Jules never told her...' said Paul quietly, 'I did. Way back in February. Valentine's Day if I remember rightly... wasn't it Sabrina?'

Daniel caught hold of Sabrina's arm gently as she nodded at Catherine to confirm it had been a man's voice in that anonymous call, not a woman's, and she slipped her arm though her husband's, possessively; but her heart was beating visibly, indicating that there would certainly be tears before bedtime at the Makepeace house.

Tears now began to fall unchecked as Catherine turned back to plead, 'It is your baby Paul! I don't know how you can say it isn't!'

Then Paul's face came down hard against hers and his eyes were like daggers. 'Shall I tell you how I know it's not mine?' he stood back up and turned to face the room, ensuring that everyone could hear him, and that the journalists were all scribbling frantically. 'It's because I had the snip Catherine! I had the snip back in March, at the first opportunity after Jules told me about you and him … When I told you I was going to America I was holed up in a hotel not two miles away from you! And where did you shoot off to the minute you thought I'd gone eh? Don't shake your head Catherine, I had you followed, and that room service bottle of champagne you ordered to room 247 at the Metropole hotel didn't get delivered by a hotel employee, he was mine! Didn't you think it was a bit odd that you signed for it on a blank sheet of hotel note paper? He gave it to me as proof you were there! Here!' he pulled a screwed up piece of paper from his pocket and showed it to her. 'I knew you wanted a baby as soon as I found the torn up prescription for your contraceptive pills in the bedroom waste bin that *I* had to empty when it was full to overflowing. But after Jules told me about you and him I couldn't bear the thought of being tied to you that way forever with a child that might not even be mine.' He paused briefly to look across at Jules, and smiled slightly. 'And besides... I have the only two children I ever wanted... and I had them with the only woman I ever wanted to have children with.... I had them with my wife.'

# Chapter thirty eight

The following morning every newspaper in the north, with one notable exception, had splashed the scandal all over the front page, and the only plus side of it was that all the free publicity meant David's exhibition was extended by an extra week.

By the following day it had all been picked up, and greatly embellished in some cases, by the nationals, and included some very graphic *snot and tears* shots, taken by the freelance photographer who had struck lucky that night.

There were journalists gathering like wasps around a fizzy drink outside the apartment building in Eaton Square, and at Clearwater House, and after Jules and the rest of the family had fled the exhibition as soon as the journalist frenzy started, Paul had apparently gone to ground somewhere, presumably until the fuss died down.

Catherine had left the gallery with her head held high, but her heart was broken. Humiliated beyond redemption, to cap it all, Jules had won Paul back without even trying, and ironically, by the look on her face as she'd left so suddenly at the discovery of yet another secret, she didn't even want him. The whole gallery, mostly filled with artists that she had dissed cruelly over the years, had slow clapped her as she'd left, and once the gory details hit the tabloids, she was suspended from her job for gross misconduct, giving her ample time to decide about her future. A strict Catholic upbringing had given her principles she had largely chosen to ignore, but even after everything that had happened she could not bring herself to have a termination. If she couldn't have Daniel she'd have his baby, and he'd pay for it.

Daniel, she heard later, had resigned his position before his father in law could sack him, and left to 'spend more time with his family.'

※

After a three week absence, Marcus put aside his *'to do before the wedding'* list and set about finding his father, because even Hugo had no idea where he'd gone and was becoming uncharacteristically flustered. After almost month, and less than a week before the wedding with still no word of him, Martin and Jemmie had found Paul's blackberry under a pile of paint soaked rags at his London studio, on a table next to an easel that held a half finished portrait of the most beautiful picture of Jules they'd ever seen. They'd called everyone in his address book, but nobody in it knew where he was either. Jules was at a complete loss; he had either disappeared off the face of the earth, or someone was hiding him.

She went back to school at the start of the autumn term and spent her evenings at home on autopilot, making cups of tea for the three stalwart journalists still camped out by her front gate in anticipation of the romantic homecoming scene, until one night, as she picked up a bottle of wine and looked at the label, the penny finally dropped with a clatter. Grabbing the phone in the sitting room she simultaneously picked up the phone pad and looked up a number. Checking her watch; it was 7.45pm, so it would be 8.45pm there; she dialled.

The telephone rang a few times before he picked it up and when he did, he sounded a little impatient and she could hear muted voices in the background.

'Michel?' she said, 'is that you? This is Jules... I'm sorry to disturb you but...'

'Darling!' he said delightedly, 'what's up? I'm afraid I'm in the middle of a dinner meeting...'

'Where are you?' she said, praying he was about to say what she was hoping.

'I'm in Barcelona... why?'

'I need your help… if I fly out tomorrow can you meet me at the airport?'

'Of course *cherie*… what is it? Are you in some kind of trouble?'

'I think I know where Paul is…' she said.

※

Jules managed to get a flight from Luton airport to Barcelona at 11.30 the following morning. Michel met her in Arrivals and kissed her on both cheeks in the classic French manner, she no longer the lover but the friend in need. Heading straight for his car and climbing in, Jules brought him up to speed with her theory.

'I think Paul is holed up in Victor's villa,' she said breathlessly. 'He must be. We've tried everything else and when I thought about it, it was so obvious. Of course Victor would help him! I've been there before but not for years. Not since the children were small and I know I'd never find it now so that's why I called you. I need you to help me find a town called Calonge, it's about an hour and a half from here… out past Girona. I thought with your business interests here you must speak Spanish Michel so I may need your help if we get lost….'

'Spanish will not be too much use here Jules we're in Catalan territory! Look. See the flags on the houses are different and all the cars have a little donkey logo on the back, instead of a Spanish bull.'

She looked worried.

'It's no problem Jules I speak Catalan too… I need to, to be able to run my business… they can be very cunning these Catalans!' He negotiated the exit road from the airport and headed north.

'What *is* your business in Barcelona?' Jules asked as they joined the motorway.

'I'm in real estate, the same as I was in France until a couple of years ago. Cataluña is the new Provence so they say. I look out pockets of land for redevelopment and negotiate the deals between the land owners and the developers. This area is so stunningly beautiful and is becoming more and more popular with the second home seekers…. Anyway what I *don't* get is if Victor speaks such flawless French and not a word of Catalan as he told me on the plane, why he chose to have a villa here and not in France? If he can't communicate he must struggle….'

'Paul said Victor told him it was because he loves beautiful things and Gaudi's Cathedral in Barcelona has it hands over fist with anything else in the world he's seen so far, and that he didn't need to speak a word of the lingo to stand in Barcelona with his mouth open and his eyes popped in wonder at it…' she said quietly.

'Not much use though if it takes you more than two hours on this road every time you feel the need to gasp...' he smiled. 'It must be a lovely place he has....'

'Oh it is...' she said.

A couple of hours later they left the motorway and were following the road signs for Calonge.

'There! There! Look!' Jules said suddenly. 'That's the Petronas garage where we had to pump up a slow puncture in our hire car every day the first time we came here!' Jules had found her land mark. 'And look! That's the supermarket... go down here! There should be a huge metal globe sculpture on the roundabout... There! There it is! Oh Michel I know where I am! It hasn't changed!'

'What's the name of the villa Jules, do you remember? These villas are all in little developments...'

'It was called *Villa Bonita* and it's on a road called Edinburgh, I remember that... it seemed so funny at the time...'

'Well there's a road called Manchester I think we must be close!'

'There! There it is! *Villa Bonita!*' Jules put her hand on his arm to make him pull over. 'I remember the garden fence... look Michel! It's the style round here... In between the metal fences it's done with frosty artificial fir... it reminds me of fake Christmas trees... this is it! Stop!'

Victor's villa stood in small development of what were predominantly second homes. Surrounded by tall and elegant pines and built in the Catalan style, it had a terracotta tiled roof, was painted all in white, with dark wood windows and had a gated veranda running right around the back, overlooking the swimming pool. The veranda fence itself was completely curtained in trailing pink bougainvillea, but apart from *Villa Bonita's* tempting exterior, the villa itself looked totally deserted, and Jules' heart sank. The shutters were all closed, and Victor's little runaround red Seat sat on the gravel driveway with pine needles all over the bonnet and obviously hadn't moved in a long time.

Michel pulled a face. 'It doesn't look promising Jules...'

'Let's just take a look,' she said, unfastening her seat belt and opening the car door.

Standing at the front door Jules began to shake as her right hand tried to decide whether to pull the bell chain or try the handle in the paneled dark wood door. The door's wrought iron security gate stood clipped back against the wall, so someone was obviously around.

Pushing down the door handle tentatively Jules held her breath as the door opened easily, and the smell of body odour and stale wine hit her full in the face.

Paul was fast asleep and snoring on one side of a long pale blue corner sofa in the sitting room that was just to the right of the front door. Four empty Rioja wine bottles were lying next to him, one of them having spilled the remnants of its contents onto the ceramic tiled floor that he had once joked was the colour of Marcus' nappy after they'd given him some of their take away Paella when he'd pestered for some. The room stank for want of fresh air and personal hygiene, and the floor was littered with pizza boxes; well at least he was eating.

Heading straight for the kitchen she threw open the window shutters, and Michel opened a drawer and tore a bin bag from a roll and proceeded to collect up the rubbish that was piled on every available surface.

The noise woke Paul from what was very obviously a drunken slumber, and Jules was shocked at his appearance, but not nearly as shocked as he was to see her... and with a man.

Paul looked absolutely appalling: wearing his blue fleece that was covered in stains, and a pair of grey joggers with saggy knees from over wear. His face was obscured by at least three weeks growth of stubble and his hair was a flaky mess and almost down to his collar. He looked like he'd just got home from Glastonbury, still stoned.

'What are you doing here?' he mumbled, sitting up and holding onto his head as a hangover hit him with its boost on. 'And who's this?' he indicated Michel. Not waiting for a reply he mumbled, 'I... I think I'm losing it Jules...' pathetically, and she snapped.

'This is my friend Michel, Paul! And rather than look at him like that you should be grateful to him because you of all people should know I'd never have found this place without him! Have you any idea how worried I was... we all were, about you? Selfish as usual... and you are aware that Marcus and Sam are getting married in five days I suppose? Or don't you care?'

'Of course I care! Jules... I... what I mean is... oh it's so good to see you Jules.' He tried to stand up and his hand shot to his head again as the hammer blow hit. 'Let me help you...'

'Stay where you are Paul we can manage.' She took the bag from Michel and resumed her rubbish clearance noisily.

'I want to help.... What can I do?' He was shaking and shivering as if he'd just woken up in a freezer, despite the fact the villa was stifling, having had all its windows closed up tightly for goodness knows how many days.

'Shower,' she said. 'You stink to high heaven. And for goodness sake change your clothes. Then we'll talk.... While I see if I can find a half decent pair of scissors so I can cut your ridiculous hair....'

✮

Half an hour later Paul padded sheepishly back into the kitchen barefoot, having had his first shower for over a week and wearing a clean cotton short sleeved shirt and some faded blue jeans, neither of which she recognised and found herself wondering where he'd got them from. And the gaping hole in time since he'd left her hit home with a jolt once again; one whole year of his existence that she had had no part in. It was a hole that each time she saw something like this she could feel it like a physical void that ached inside her body, and one that actually made her draw breath deeply to try to ease it.

She had finished tidying up and was now waiting by a chair placed in the middle of the kitchen floor with a small but suitably sharp pair of scissors and a comb in her hand.

'Where is he?' he asked, looking around.

'He's gone.... He has an important meeting this afternoon, back in Barcelona. Anyway I see you have Victor's little red car outside so said I could manage now, as long as I can get it out through that front gate that is only about half an inch wider than the car on each side, as I recall...' she said.

Indicating that he should sit in the chair she had placed ready, as he sat she noticed that his wrists were both very bruised and had a feeling of foreboding as to what he'd tried to do to himself in his isolation here in the Catalonian hills. 'Those bruises Paul... what happened to you?' she asked gently.

'It was the toadstools!' he muttered pathetically. 'They still get me every time... they used to get you too, remember?'

She heaved a quiet sigh of relief behind him. All of the door handles in the villa were made of unforgiving wrought iron and the knobs were shaped as toadstools. On the two occasions they had stayed there when the children were small they both went home covered in bruises; Paul on his wrists and Jules higher, being so much shorter than he, on the fleshy skin just below her elbows. It had been a joke to them, back then, the constant thud, *ouch!* around the unfamiliar doorways.

'Toadstools... yes I remember those,' she smiled, 'and the heavy creaky doors... we had to buy door wedges remember? To prop them open, so they wouldn't creak in the night and scare the children rigid after you told them they sounded like haunted house doors... remember?'

'I do... they're still here... look,' he pointed to a rubber door wedge propping open the kitchen door.

Smiling at the recollection she placed a tea towel around his shoulders.

He sat back and closed his eyes and allowed himself the sensuous feel of her fingers against his scalp as she gently combed up small sections of his hair and began to cut. He found himself swept back in time to the days when they were young and in love, and delighting in and sharing each others experiences: back to when she loved to cut his hair just like this, and he remembered how she'd had this way of blowing the tiny strands of cut hair gently off his face and neck that had made his senses reel, back then. In fact she'd always cut his hair before... but he could not remember when or why she had stopped.

When she moved around to the front of him to begin cutting above his forehead he opened his eyes and sought hers.

'You know, I love it when you cut my hair Jules... I always did,' and then looking at her face more closely he smiled tentatively as he remarked; 'You look so beautiful in the light from outside coming in that window... half of your face is in shadow and half in light... and your eyes are... glowing....' He closed his eyes again and then sighed a little. Opening them once more he looked at her face searchingly. 'Did you know that to an artist Jules, the shadows are just as important as the light...?'

She still didn't answer him, but continued to snip quietly as she made way back behind him. 'So can't we please put all this behind us and... and...'

'All done,' she said suddenly, removing the tea towel and beginning to brush the hair from his back, but when she pursed her lips and breathed her customary gentle blow to the nape of his neck, and then his face to remove the hair from the tender skin below his eyes he almost fainted with longing.

'Jules I...'

'Stay there,' she said briskly, swallowing hard and to stop him before he said anymore. 'I'll see if I can find a razor and we'll get you shaved as well.'

Back in the kitchen a few minutes later with a tin of shaving cream and a fresh disposable razor she'd found in a packet in the bathroom, she draped the tea towel across the front of his neck this time, and began to apply the cream in gentle swirling movements with her hands, and his eyes closed once more, relishing each touch of her fingers.

'Up or down?' she asked as, as if startled by the sound of her voice, he opened his eyes suddenly.

'What?' he said, looking at her with a slight shake of his head.

'The razor... do I shave up or down with it?'

'Oh... up... please... or do you want me to...'

'Not in the state you're in Paul, shaking like this, you'll cut yourself to ribbons!' She still sounded brisk, but at least she smiled slightly.

She began then to shave him in smooth upward strokes, against the hair growth, only breaking the silence in the villa with the sound of her sandals on the tiled floor, and the razor being rinsed in the sink full of water beside her. He felt the brush of her body against him as she worked and he felt her breath as she leaned in closely to shave the area above his mouth, but when he opened his eyes just a fraction, he felt perfectly sure that she had absolutely no idea of the effect she was having on him as she continued her task, despite the fact he could feel the tea towel across his chest moving in rhythm to the beating of his own heart.

Finished, and handing him the towel to wipe his face she looked at her handiwork quizzically. 'Not bad for a beginner...' she smiled.

He ran his hands over each side of his face and nodded wordlessly.

'Have you eaten?' she asked, turning away to open the fridge and pulling a face.

'Not recently.'

'I can see that...' she had closed the fridge and opened a cupboard, closing that in some disgust also. 'Come on... let's go and get some lunch somewhere, I'm starving!' she picked up her handbag from the dresser where she had left it on her arrival and turned to him expectantly. He stood up and led the way out of the kitchen, passing her Victor's car keys from a hook by the front door.

※

Lunch, turned out to involve a trip to the supermarket, having found themselves reminded that the lunchtime siesta in this part of the world included all the restaurants too. Back at the villa again, she laid a cloth on the veranda table and set out bread, sausage, cold chicken, tomatoes and cheese, and a bottle of apple juice, deciding that Paul had drunk more than his fare share of wine. They sat quietly as they ate, Paul listlessly and Jules watchfully, searching his face for some signs of his state of mind. He hadn't said a word in the car. He looked lost, broken, and was still shaking as if suffering some kind of withdrawal symptoms.

Breaking the silence she looked at the two villas whose roofs were visible from the veranda and touched his arm. 'Do you remember what Jemmie said about those?' she said quietly, indicating their pitched roof chimney pots, trying to get him to speak. He shook his head slightly and turned to look at her.

'She asked who lived in the little houses on the roofs... remember?'

'The little windows in them for the chimney smoke...' he said quietly. 'I remember...' his voice trailed off as he continued to look at them.

'You need to get home Paul... you can't stay here... people are worried about you....' She began.

He nodded. 'I know Jules... I know why you've come... Marcus is getting married...'

'Yes he is...' she said gently. 'I've come to get you for the wedding... let's get you back and then you start to get yourself well again... back to normal...'

He turned to her and looked right into her eyes. 'Normal...? What's that anymore?' he asked, running his hands through his freshly cut hair.

※

Arriving back at Clearwater House with Paul fast asleep in the hire car beside her she said a silent prayer of thanks that the three resident journalists had finally given up and gone, and as she drove through the gates the sound of the tyres on the gravel woke him. He looked disorientated and very surprised and looked at her incredulously. 'Jules! You've brought me home... here... I never expected... I thought you meant Eaton Square!'

'Don't get your hopes up Paul I'm really not too sure about this and I changed my mind at least three times while you were asleep.... I just want to keep a close eye on you so you don't disappear again so and that you'll bear some resemblance to his father when Marcus gets married on Friday.'

She opened the car door and got out, slamming it behind her and he winced before letting himself out of the car and following her meekly towards the house.

This was going to be tough.

Barney was ecstatic to see his dad and sang with joy as his tail thumped painfully against Paul's legs when they entered the house by the back door.

Following her up the stairs, with Barney close at his heels, Jules put Paul's bag in their old room, explaining that she no longer used it, but not having to explain why, and left him to go back to bed and sleep off his weeks of degeneracy properly.

It was early evening when he appeared at the kitchen archway, tempted by the smell of a vitamin rich liver and bacon casserole that had entered his sleeping subconscious with a tantalizing dream of home, and found he had woken with tears on his face. When he'd realised he really was home he had cried even more, before washing his face hurriedly at the sink in the ensuite and going downstairs to find her.

Jules had her back to the doorway and was vigorously whipping cream into mashed potatoes as he entered, and he watched unnoticed as she continued to busy herself with preparing the meal, wondering how on earth he had ever not savoured the very sight of her.

Bending down to open the oven door and humming along to a song on her old radio, she removed the casserole dish, and as she turned and saw him there, smiled nervously. 'Where would you like to eat this?' she said. 'Dining room... on a tray in front of the TV, or in here with me?'

'Oh in here, with you...' he said, pulling open a drawer to extract another set of cutlery and placing them down opposite hers. Then he sat down before she could protest.

'Let me....' He leapt up as she went to get the plates from the oven and, taking the oven gloves from her, took the plates out and laid them on the table.

As she returned with the serving dishes, she placed them in the centre of the table and sat down as Paul appeared from the utility room carrying a bottle of red wine, and selected two glasses from the cabinet behind her.

'Paul that's your special...'

'I want to...' he said, easing out the cork. He poured a glass and handed it to her. 'To say thank you...'

'What for?'

'...For rescuing me,' he replied simply.

'Someone had to...' She almost whispered it, clinking his glass with her own in salute.

'I'm glad it was you though...' he said, taking a sip.

# Chapter thirty nine

It was now just two days before the wedding and Paul was up to something and Jules knew it. Twice she walked into the study to get something and he'd hung up his phone, smiling guiltily when she walked in. She of course feared the worst; that he was back in touch with Catherine.

Having him in the house again and so close to her was lovely, and just like old times; better in fact. He was being lovely to her; just like the old Paul, loving and attentive and eager to please... despite her continued guardedness; but he was definitely being secretive and it was very confusing.

In fact, Paul had been talking to the only person he knew of that could help him in his current predicament: Dizzy.

'I know you've apologised to her Paul but that's just the first step... you'll have to go a lot further than that to win her back,' she said quietly; Hector was in the same room and going through his daily ritual of attempting the Times crossword puzzle with a kitchen timer shaped like a tomato on the desk next to him. The unholy horrors were visible through the sitting room window, playing weddings in the garden, in preparation for their debut as bridesmaids on Friday.

'You have to show her that you have really seen and own what you've done to her and that you didn't just say sorry and hope that would do, like she thinks. And you need to realise that you have a very different Jules to deal with now. You're not the only one that went through a public divorce Paul...You have to show her that you love her... and only her, because being splashed all over the tabloids as the frumpy ex wife almost destroyed her you know, and so she isn't the same person anymore. She's had to pick herself up and *make* herself strong again. And she has. She's a lot stronger and more independent, but that doesn't mean she doesn't still love you with every cell in her body. We're talking about trust here Paul, which is a very different thing. She doesn't trust you. That's what you need to tackle. And in order to regain her trust in you, your life has to be an open book to her with no more secrets. No more long absences without phone calls. And remember she wants to be married to *you* Paul, not Hugo. Take her with you whenever you can... and be open with each other.... I know how hard that is, but if you're going to win back her trust you have to.

Discuss what went wrong in your marriage and how you can put it right and then above all, be willing to do it.'

'But what can I do?'

'That's your challenge, but mooning about and giving her the benefit of your big brown eyes won't do it. You need to do what I say and be completely open and honest… and then eventually the trust will come back.

As for the winning her back though; make a statement… but you have to make it unmistakably big and bold…. Like that awful painting that she sold from your dining room…' but he could hear she was smiling. 'Come on Paul think about it… it's obvious! She's a hopeless romantic! One look at her books and her DVD shelf should show you that…. So go on… sacrifice your pride and prejudice and do something brave!'

That was the first call that Jules walked in on, and the second one came very soon afterwards, after he saw something in the morning paper supplement and disappeared into the study with a smile of triumph on his face. Picking up his diary he flicked through the pages to find a telephone number. If he could pull this off he knew she was his.

✭

The morning of Marcus and Sam's wedding dawned clear and bright, and promised to be a gorgeous day. As the Bride and Groom they arrived on the Thursday afternoon in a car with its visibility severely limited by suit and dress bags on hangers for their rehearsal at the church at seven o'clock, after which they separated so that Sam could stick with the tradition that they should not see each other until she walked up the aisle.

And so it was that Marcus stayed in his old room at home and Tom and Martin, his two best men, and Sam's father, Brian, stayed too; so Jules had a house full of flappy men to keep calm. Sam stayed at Martin's cottage with Jemmie, so that she could help her to get ready in the morning.

Dizzy arrived at Clearwater House at 10am on the Big Day to collect the posies for the bridesmaids, to find Marcus in the kitchen looking slightly pale and trying to consume the huge fry up that Martin had provided to gird him for his nuptials.

Paul had just returned from walking Barney and Dipstick to get them out of everybody's way, looking far more like his usual self apart from looking decidedly nervy, and Jules was in the dining room, sitting at the table busy counting white rose button holes out of the bottom of the box they'd arrived in, and into its lid.

'Flowers in the church?' she said breathlessly, as Dizzy poked her head around the door.

'All under control Jules,' she said. 'Mother's Union in attendance at the crack of dawn with the biggest box of oasis I've ever seen in my life and at my guess, every wrought iron pedestal in the deanery... and if there's any greenery left in the Rectory garden I'll be very surprised!'

Jules smiled with relief at her relaxed, 'done all this before' attitude.

'I hope Sam knew what she was doing when she told them to go for it!'

'They do love a wedding...' Dizzy laughed. Then as she sat down she became quiet and picked up a rose, twirling it in her fingers, and the mood changed. 'They so wanted to help them do something happy in the church after having Henry's service there... we all did. Hector was so thrilled when they went to see him about getting married here because people so often label a church with the last sad thing that happened there and won't go back again... and really a church is there to record the whole story for posterity. ...A whole family tree of happy times as well as sad ones....' She paused and looked at Jules as she sat in a trance with a rose mid way between box lids. 'Anyway, enough of that now.' Dizzy put down the rose she was holding and Jules smiled at her slightly and went back to counting.

'Hector is in charge of damage limitation and making sure he can see them both through the vegetation to actually marry them, Sarah Palmer's got the girls and I'm keeping out of the way!' She looked at Jules and picked up a card of pins. 'I also came to see how you're doing...' she said quietly.

Knowing precisely what she meant in this instance Jules pulled a slight face. 'Absolutely no idea Dizz.... One minute he's being all attentive but the next he's... well... truthfully, Paul is acting very strangely. It's wonderful to have him back here but he... he's being very secretive and I think he's... well I'm not sure if he's...'

'He's not in touch with Catherine again if that's what you think...' she said gently. 'He's just treading carefully with you that's all...'

Jules looked unsure. 'I'm having trouble getting my head around all this. We're ok while we have plenty to do, that's for sure... he's been buzzing around out in the marquee since the sun came up... and a grand piano arrived in a Hickies van from Reading just now and I've got no idea what that's for.... As far as I knew Marcus and Sam had hired a DJ for later on...'

'For goodness sake breathe! You can't get your head around it because it's your head that's getting in the way! Everything's going to be fine.... Just relax and enjoy what is going to be a perfect day. Marcus and Sam are getting *married!*' She smiled, rubbing Jules' arm as if to rub away her doubtful mood. 'And what's a wedding without a secret or two after all?'

'I haven't had much luck with Paul and his secrets...' Jules sighed.

By 1.30pm Sam was ready, and she was an absolute vision in a beautiful wedding gown with a buttoned bodice that clung to her slim frame and a skirt that fell in delicate folds down to a short train at the back. Her father swallowed very hard as, veil down over her face, she came down the narrow staircase towards him. With tears of regret that his wife was not there to see her daughter on her special day, he told her the car was back outside, Jemmie having been duly delivered to the church in her lavender, now Sam's favourite colour, dress to meet up with Dizzy and the junior bridal contingent. Tess, Looby Loo and Batty all looked as if butter wouldn't melt in their mouths as they stood outside the west door in their little lavender dresses with cute white, butterfly buckled shoes. They were positively bursting with excitement, and the guests collectively smiled their approval as they each entered the church to the sound of the church bells.

Marcus and his best men were seated at the front by the time Jules arrived with Paul, and as they turned around to greet them she beamed her encouragement at Marcus as they took their place in the pew behind them, as parents of the Groom.

The organist, complete with spectacularly flowery hat, kept a regular eye on her rear view car mirror so that she could watch for the arrival of the bride, and busked her way through several pieces as people came in, without troubling the music, in her usual competent manner.

There was an increasing buzz of conversation in the church as the guests made their way in; catching up with friends and relatives already seated and mutually admiring dresses, hats and shoes; weight loss and pregnancies, haircuts and suntans. Marcus sat and nodded recognitions from time to time, and tapped his heels nervously. There was a brief respite from his nerves and a lovely smile appeared on his face when Tom's son Matthew spotted Marcus and bellowed 'Unca Marcuth!' at the top of his lungs, as Patsy came in the church with him on one hip and headed for a pew.

Once everyone was seated, there was a collective whisper of excitement as Hector walked from the west door to the chancel step carrying his service book and asked everyone to stand for the bride, and the organist took her cue and began the opening bars of Wagner's Bridal Chorus.

All eyes but two turned to watch Sam and her proud father come up the aisle. Jules' eyes though, were on her son, his gaze transfixed and shining with love as he watched Sam walk towards him on her father's right arm, and a stray tear made its way slowly down Jules' right cheek. A finger that wasn't her own wiped away her tear, and she turned her face to see Paul looking right into her eyes, and he winked at her and smiled. Flustered, she turned and reached into her bag for the tissue she knew she would undoubtedly need at some point today, and the spell was broken.

⋆

Hector performed magnificently, nobody objected to the union, the assembled guests sang heartily, once encouraged, the triplets ate the last of their keep-them-quiet- raisins wedged in the front pew on the bride's side by Jemmie, and Marcus and Sam became Man and Wife.

Once out in the churchyard the photographer battled with the triumphant peal of church bells to keep everyone in order and the unholy horrors, now outside, were chasing each other around the ancient headstones as Dizzy battled to round them up before they got completely filthy.

Photos at the church duly completed, Man and Wife gingerly clambered aboard Chris Palmer's ribbon bedecked open carriage as Whisper, Amy's skewbald pony, stood patiently with one back hoof tucked under, waiting to lead them off to the reception in the garden marquee at Clearwater House.

The bridesmaids and the best men piled into the waiting limousine that then purred elegantly away, and the rest of the guests took advantage of the beautiful day, and walked through the square and down the lane to the reception.

Jules set off from the churchyard with some of the guests too: secure in the knowledge that the photographer was going to keep Marcus and Sam busy down at the lake for ages before she would be needed in the meet and greet line. Paul, seeing that she had chosen to do that, rushed to catch up with her, but hung back when his phone began to ring. She turned to see if he was coming and saw him standing to the side of the lane; finger in the other ear to shield himself from the chatter going on all around, and talking urgently into his phone. Even on his son's wedding day, she thought irritably, and walked on briskly.

The wedding guests mingled in the garden and admired the fish pond, and Jules watched as Amy returned her pony to his paddock with a large red apple clamped firmly between his teeth as his wages.

Hearing her name called, she turned. Ben the vet was walking towards her with, unless she was much mistaken, his nurse on his arm, who was looking extremely pretty in a flimsy cotton dress that barely covered her thighs and high heels that were sinking into the lawn.

He kissed her lightly on the cheek and admired the wedding couple dutifully, but Jules' mind was drifting, so nodding amiably and making her excuses, she left them; glad if he had really found someone to love, and wanting to be away from him just in case he hadn't and gave her one of his meaningful looks.

Heading back towards the house, she needed a few minutes to draw breath before the festivities began, and slipped quietly in through the kitchen door.

Paul had beaten her to it and was sitting at the table with a bottle wine and two glasses, and she stopped abruptly.

'I guessed you'd sneak back in here if I waited long enough,' he said quietly, pouring the second glass. Then, as she turned to go back out; 'please Jules, I need to talk to you... now please.'

'We should be outside... we'll be missed...'

'Not for ten minutes, Jules, please.'

She sat down and took the glass he held out for her, and sipped at the cool white wine gratefully.

'Do you remember when you found out you were pregnant with Marcus?' he asked, swirling the wine in his glass.

Grateful for a different conversation to the one she was expecting, she smiled at him. 'Of course I do,' she began slowly. 'I was so scared to tell you. We were living in that tiny little flat above the shoe shop and we hadn't been married more than a couple of months...'

'Not quite three,' he said.

'Not quite three... and your mother was busy counting with her fingers to make sure tongues wouldn't be able to wag...'

He smiled at the memory. 'They've got all of it ahead of them just like we had now, haven't they?'

'Not all of it Paul, hopefully....' She looked down into her wineglass.

They sat quietly for a full minute, and the air was tight with tension.

'I'm sorry Jules,' he said finally, simply. 'I'm sorry for what I did to you; I was wrong. I've been such a blind fool.... I love you Jules... it's always been you.... Please... let me come home...?'

'You are home...'

'Not like this... you know what I mean.... It will be different Jules... I'll be so open and honest with you you'll get sick of listening to me!'

She looked at him; but her face to him was giving nothing away.

She shook her head slightly. 'We've both changed too much,' she said, 'that's the problem. I'm not the same woman I was before, and the Paul I fell in love with has long gone... and I saw it happening.'

He looked confused.

'To begin with, each time you went away you'd send me notes; just one or two lines... and I kept all of them. But after a while they stopped...'

'I carried on writing them...' he said, 'I just didn't post them... I didn't have time... and then after a while... well...'

'And then you'd come back and each time a bit more of the real you had gone, until eventually there was nothing left of my Paul, and in his place was a proud and arrogant man, used to everyone around him jumping to attention when he came anywhere near. Permanently cross, and so inevitably alienating his wife and his family. I couldn't do anything to please you anymore. None of us could do anything right.'

He shook his head but she stopped him.

'No, really: I'd look at you sometimes, once the children had left home and when you did occasionally honour me with your presence, and weren't just holed up in your studio all the hours God gave you in one day and then I didn't dare going anywhere near you. I'd watch you, sitting with a newspaper or sitting at your computer. And then you'd look back at me; and that look still haunts me Paul; resentment; pure resentment. I was at home here, told I didn't need to work but then belittled for being a housewife... with nothing of value to say that was worth your listening to. And meanwhile you were pursuing your work and, worse still, the celebrity lifestyle that came with it. Until eventually it got the better of you and you found you didn't want us anymore: didn't want me anymore anyway... and whatever you say to me now about it all having been a huge mistake, Catherine didn't force you to leave me... you made the decision to leave me with your eyes wide open Paul... and there was I soldiering bravely on, swallowing the fact I knew you were having an affair for *months* before you left... but I obviously meant so little to you by then you couldn't even be bothered to tell me you weren't coming back.'

'What do you mean... couldn't be bothered to tell you? I...'

'*Hugo* told me Paul. You never said a single word to explain yourself properly until you sat here at this table, with her to back you up, and humiliate me even further.'

'Humiliate *you?* What about that night I came back here and Martin was here and you said...'

'Don't remind me what I said. You have no idea what it feels like to find out you've been dumped for a younger model... I was deranged for a while there, and had the added humiliation of seeing my deranged self in print next to a glamorous photo of Catherine on the front pages of the morning papers.'

'And then I saw your car at his cottage that day I came back for my things and I thought...'

'I was hiding from you. I saw you down the hill on my way home from college. Even through the fog I saw your car parked there on the driveway; that great black thing sitting there like the angel of death.... Martin wasn't even home that day. It's Jemmie he loves Paul, not me. You must be able to see that... any fool can see that!' She paused to draw breath. 'So if you thought all that back then, why did you still divorce me?'

'I thought you wanted to.... You said...'

'You hurt me Paul... you told the newspapers you'd never been happier.... What did you expect?' she shook her head irritably. 'We've had this conversation already and this isn't the day for...'

'You have to forgive me Jules... I love you.'

'We'd better get back outside,' she said, standing up.

'I love you.'

'I know you do,' she said, heading for the door. 'I'm trying Paul, really I am. But I honestly think this is harder than when you left me!'

# Chapter forty

Out at the marquee Paul and Jules put on a united front as they greeted the guests in the receiving line, and finally took their places at the top table for the meal. Dizzy and Hector and their girls were sitting directly in front of them, and Paul caught Dizzy's eye as she gave him an encouraging smile.

Hugo arrived late, for just about the only time in his life, and sat at a table full of Mother's Union ladies, catching Paul's attention and inquisitive look, and answering it with a discreet thumbs up. Jules noticed, but said nothing, noting that Paul was smiling to himself.

He was definitely up to something.

Meal over and speeches underway, Jules dutifully laughed and sighed as appropriate, and at the first opportunity made an excuse and made her way outside, in need of a few minutes peace and quiet.

She made her way down the garden path and out of the gate, and then set off on the footpath around the lake until she came to Jemmie's bench from a few months before. Sitting down, she kicked off her killer shoes gratefully, closed her eyes and leaned back; drinking in the peace and quiet, but for the occasional dip and splash of passing waterfowl.

Minutes passed and, dozing blissfully, inside Jules' bag her phone began to ring. Waking abruptly, she reached in for it and pulled a face, expecting it to be Paul asking where she was. But her face broke into a smile when she heard; 'Hello my darling are you surviving? how is it all going?'

'Michel!' she exclaimed, as a huge smile spread across her face. 'Oh it's so good to hear your voice! It was wonderful: just as they'd planned it. They're in the marquee now…. The meal was fabulous… I just slipped out… I needed to be by myself for a few minutes…'

'Where are you?'

'Sitting by the lake.'

'And where is Paul?'

'Still in there. Michel, something's going on, I feel it…'

'What do you mean?'

'He's… well he's… Oh I don't know! He's acting as if he's sorry and loves me and wants to come back but then he… he…'

'Did he say he loves you?

'Yes he did…'

'Well isn't that what you wanted? And did you tell him you love him?'

'No... not exactly... I...'

'Do you love him Jules?'

'Of course I do! It's just...'

'He needs to hear it too you know.... Jules, you need to be a bit brave here my darling... love is a two way thing.'

'I...'

'Don't say you can't... you can... you can Jules...'

'I'm trying to... I'm not strong enough yet.... I still can't forget how he...'

'Now remember we worked on this.... He can see you've changed Jules.... He can see you won't get walked over anymore... he will have really thought this through so won't be letting you down again.... So don't you become that old pebble again and start on that 'I'm not strong enough' crap...'

She could hear the smile in his voice and she laughed a little. 'You're right...as usual.... They should bottle you and market you as a life saver!'

Back in the marquee the formalities were over and the atmosphere was alive with chatter and laughter. Marcus and Sam were working the room and music was playing discreetly in the background. Paul, she could see, was sitting with Hector and Dizzy, though Hector had his back to them and was discussing ride on lawn mowing techniques with a man on the table next to him. Paul and Dizzy, meanwhile, were in deep discussion with their heads close together, and she could just guess what about, so she gave them a wide berth. Jemmie was sitting on Martin's lap, laughing at something he'd said, and Sam's father was sitting at another table chatting to Hugo.

The unholy horrors had discovered that the dance floor was slippery and were demonstrating it to everyone's enjoyment as she made her way across the room to the bar and ordered herself a lime and soda, longing for a cool drink in the stifling tent. Sipping it gratefully she looked around the room and caught Hugo's eye as he smiled and winked at her. Brows knotting together into their original unibrow she made her way between the tables and sat down next to him. Sam's father had just moved away and was talking to them both over by the top table, and so Jules looked directly at him.

'What's going on Hugo?' she asked, directly.

'I don't know what you mean!' he smiled, camply.

'Yes you do! I've been watching you and Paul... and what was with that wink?'

'Just a little encouragement...'

'What are you up to? What is he up to?'

'I couldn't possibly say...'

'Hugo...?'

'Sorry Jules I'm sworn to secrecy, but all will be revealed...'

'When?'

'When the time is right...' he winked, and stood up. 'Sorry poppet, nature calls. I'm off to the ladies...' and he walked away leaving her still tied up in knots with curiosity. .

Their first dance was announced and Marcus and Sam took to the floor. Paul appeared from nowhere and sat down next to her as she watched them. 'They'll be next I reckon...' he said, and as she followed his gaze, her eyes fell on Jemmie and Martin.

'You think so? She murmured. 'They're just like us at the beginning. Never a cross word after a bit of a shaky start.... But marriage? I'd like to think so but these days? maybe they will, maybe they won't.'

They sat quietly and watched the dance, and then as other couples began to join them on the dance floor; 'Dance with me,' Paul said, standing up and offering her his hand across the table.

Standing up, she took it and he led her to the floor. Laying her hand on his shoulder as he slipped his arm around her waist she felt stiff and awkward, her heart pounding as she tried to relax, and conscious of the many eyes on them as they danced their 'look as us aren't we getting on fine?' united front way around the floor.

Then all too soon it was late and Marcus and Sam were saying goodbye and setting off to Guildford for the night before leaving for their honeymoon in the morning. No one had any idea where they were going and speculation had been rife in the room throughout. Nothing out of the ordinary had happened, even though Jules had been on tenterhooks all evening, and the piano still sat forlorn and un-played in the corner, adding to the air of mystery.

Hector and Dizzy had lasted out until just after nine and then taken their over tired triplets home to bed and, having waved goodbye to the only married Mr. and Mrs. Taylor at the wedding Jules stifled a yawn as she sank gratefully into a chair and kicked off her killer shoes again. The reception had reached that point where people were beginning to track down jackets and bags and hug and say their goodbyes, and the waitresses were beginning to clear the glasses, until the piercing sound of microphone feedback made everyone jump and turn to see what was happening. Paul was standing on the dance floor and looking straight at Jules with the microphone in one hand and rather shaky hand grasping a glass of champagne in the other.

'Oh my God… what now…' she said under her breath.

'Sorry everyone!' he smiled nervously. 'I just wanted to say, thank you all for coming. We've made all the speeches and proposed all the toasts… but we missed one. Jules, this one's for you…' and he sipped from his glass. 'I wanted to say… I… I need to say… something to you…Jules…'

All eyes turned to her as she sat rooted to her chair.

'Jules... I love you so much... I've always loved you... I...' he swallowed hard and she gasped as she realised he'd begun to cry. He hadn't cried in her presence since the day Marcus was born. Back when they were...

Before she knew what she was doing she leaped to her feet and, still minus her shoes, rushed over to him and hugged him; he pulling her to him as if his life depended on it.

Now oblivious to the watching eyes and able to feel his heart under his shirt, she said 'It's ok Paul... I love you too... I...'

'Dance with me then...' he said breathlessly, 'and dance with me like you really want to this time...'

'But Paul... I haven't got any shoes on!'

He kicked off his shoes, sending them both in different directions, and people around them began to smile at what was obviously happening in front of them.

'There. Now we can start a new trend.' He grinned at her; a great big grin that went all the way to his eyes.

Oh that smile, she thought. Welcome back Paul.

'And there's no music.... Paul... this is silly... come and sit down....'

'No Jules, this is romantic... there's a difference....' He lifted a stray wisp of hair from her eyes, and then he looked across to the piano, where a man in a very nice grey suit had appeared from somewhere and sat watching them, waiting for his cue. Paul nodded briefly, and the man turned to face the keyboard and began to play the opening notes of the song she recognised instantly.

She smiled and laid her face against Paul's chest, and he wrapped his arms around her, as the man at the piano began to sing. Then as his voice filled the air and the remaining people in the marquee began to mumble with increasing awareness and clap apprehensively, if disbelievingly, she looked across to the piano, and her eyes almost popped out of her head.

'Paul... that's... Michael... Bublé!'

He pulled her closer. 'Really...?' he said innocently, then he kissed the tip of her nose. 'I knew how much you'd love this...'

'But how...?'

'I met him a couple of years ago... on a plane...'

'You what..?'

He nodded. 'I drew him while he was asleep and he said if there was ever anything he could do for me... so.... He jumped at the chance to help me when I rang him... I know how much you love him Jules and this song... it really says it all for me. But then you walked in on me and I had to hang up... and then I thought I'd blown it because I couldn't get hold of him again.... You have absolutely *no* idea how hard it is to get hold of him! I tried and tried but... then he called *me* back just after we came out of the church today... and so I sent Hugo to pick him up... and he has to fly back to Canada straight after this. I was so relieved when he finally got here... he can say it so much better than I can...'

'Say it anyway...' she murmured. 'Let him help you...'

And so he joined in the words and whispered softly into her ear.

*I'm just too far*
*From where you are*
*I'm coming back home...*

Jemmie and Martin watched them as they danced.

'I think he's cracked it...' she said.

'He certainly has...' he replied with a little smile. 'I must say I never thought I'd see it...'

'See what? See them get back together?'

'No. See your dad being romantic...'

'He always was you know Martin. He just forgot who he was supposed to be romantic with for a while. That's all...'

'I haven't...' he smiled, shifting her slightly on his lap so he could reach his jacket pocket on the back of the chair.

'Oh Martin!' Jemmie gasped, looking at the open ring box in his hand, and at the solitaire diamond that was glinting in the light of the almost spent candle in the centre of the table.

'Told you...' said Paul to Jules, indicating Jules over to where they were sitting with a nod of his head.

'I'll never doubt anything you say ever again...' Jules smiled up into his eyes.

'You won't have to....' he said.


The End

# Home.

**by Amy Foster-Gillies and Michael Bublé**

Another summer day
Is come and gone away
In Paris or Rome
But I wanna go home
Mmmmmmmm

Maybe surrounded by
A million people I
Still feel all alone
I just wanna go home
Oh I miss you, you know

And I've been keeping all the letters
that I wrote to you
Each one a line or two
I'm fine baby, how are you?
Well I would send them but I know
that it's just not enough
My words were cold and flat
And you deserve more than that

Another aeroplane
Another sunny place
I'm lucky I know
But I wanna go home
Mmmm, I've got to go home

Let me go home
I'm just too far from where you are

I wanna come home

And I feel just like I'm living
someone else's life
It's like I just stepped outside
When everything was going right
And I know just why you could not
Come along with me
But this was not your dream
But you always believed in me

Another winter day has come
And gone away
And even Paris and Rome
And I wanna go home
Let me go home

And I'm surrounded by
A million people I
Still feel alone
Oh, let go home
Oh, I miss you, you know

Let me go home
I've had my run
Baby, I'm done
I gotta go home
Let me go home
It will all right
I'll be home tonight
I'm coming back home…

Lightning Source UK Ltd.
Milton Keynes UK
12 August 2010

158287UK00001B/3/P